THE QUARANTINED CITY

JAMES EVERINGTON

infinity plus

Copyright © 2015, 2016 James Everington

Parts of this novel were originally published individually by Spectral Press in 2015.

Cover image © ABCDK
Cover design © Keith Brooke

All rights reserved.

Published by infinity plus
www.infinityplus.co.uk
Follow @ipebooks on Twitter

No portion of this book may be reproduced by any means, mechanical, electronic, or otherwise, without first obtaining the permission of the copyright holder.

The moral right of James Everington to be identified as the author of this work has been asserted by him in accordance with the Copyright, Designs and Patents Act of 1988.

ISBN-13: 978-1533255662
ISBN-10: 1533255660

BY THE SAME AUTHOR

Falling Over
The Other Room
The Shelter
Trying to be so Quiet
The Hyde Hotel (editor, with Dan Howarth)

CONTENTS

PART ONE: THE SMELL OF PAPRIKA 9
PART TWO: INTO THE RAIN 43
PART THREE: SPOT THE DIFFERENCE 77
PART FOUR: A LACK OF DEMONS 115
PART FIVE: THE PANDA PRINCIPLE 149
PART SIX: THE QUARANTINE 187

PART ONE

THE SMELL OF PAPRIKA

Fellows tries to shut the door on the ghost behind him, but it sticks in the heat and refuses to close. Frustrated, he slams his body against it until the latch clicks, and he stands on the empty street as his breathing slows. The city is quiet; it is still early morning. He can't hear anything from inside his house, but then the ghost never makes a sound, anyway. He wouldn't even know if it was just the other side of his door. He imagines its crippled hand silently scratching at the wood.

George, his large shabby black cat, saunters through the makeshift cat-flap, mewing, and as he bends to pet it he feels a moment's irritation—weren't animals supposed to be sensitive to the presence of the supernatural? But George has never once reacted to the presence of the broken, ghostly child; only Fellows has seen it. And the child, in turn, only has eyes for him—white eyes without pupil or iris fixed on him as it tries to get near. He has seen it in his house almost every day since the quarantine has been in place.

But the ghost's body is insubstantial and its deformities mean it moves too slowly to ever take him by surprise; it is disquieting but does he really need to be afraid? It seems a stupid thing to worry about as the sun rises above his city, and the heat starts to build. Maybe every house in the city has its ghosts. He has his routines, and no translucent kid is going to put him off them. First, coffee. He strokes George one last time and heads down the tree-lined street to turn right into a small square, where his favourite café is.

The Carousel is at the far corner of the square; to one side of it the more cramped streets of the old town begin; on the other side a cobbled road leads down to the port. Fellows likes to sit outside The Carousel if the weather is clear enough, which during this hot summer it always is, listening to the cries of gulls and sometimes the alarms and sirens from the harbour. If it gets too hot he will sit inside the small, smoke-filled interior—The Carousel is known to be one of the few places still able to obtain filter cigarettes and expensive cigars since the quarantine, as well as real coffee and imported spirits and wine. But the smell of cigarettes always reminds Fellows of his youth when he had smoked; before Lana had persuaded him to give up. Just one of the many ways she had changed him, worked him into some shape more pleasing to herself and then, job all but done, moved on to a different project. He can no longer remember the precise trigger for her leaving, just the taste of Champagne on his tongue and the atmosphere of angry bitterness (and yes, maybe some guilt) she had left in her wake.

He goes inside to order his coffee and pastry, and to collect his daily paper which Gregor keeps behind the counter for him; he absently notices that the black-haired waitress is not working. He likes the look of the waitress and thinks that, ten years ago, she maybe would have liked the look of him. The fact that he is beyond such opportunities now he obscurely blames on Lana too, for taking those ten years from him. As if they wouldn't have passed anyway, and just as damned quick.

Ten years ago he wouldn't have been sat in a café like this reading the newspaper like anyone else; he would have been scribbling in his black bound notebook, trying to pull off the 'sensitive writer' look, bullshit as it was, and sometimes, in other cafés in other cities, customers or waitresses had fallen for his act. Lana for one, he thinks bitterly.

Fellows pays Gregor and puts the change in the tips jar, noticing with amusement the gruff owner's lack of reaction as he does so. The tip jar is nearly full and is neatly divided in two when you look at it—old silver and gold coins from before the quarantine up to about halfway, and then the thinner, duller looking coins that are the currency now. Fellows is always reminded of strata in the cliffs above the bay when he sees it. There are muttered complaints from the city's population that the new coins won't be worth anything when the quarantine is lifted, but such a distant issue is not one Fellows is going to worry about too much.

He sits at his usual table outside, from which you can see the harbour and deep water beyond—see, in theory, the outside world, although most days nothing is visible but a misty haze. He unfolds his paper, blows on his coffee to cool it, and then flinches as he hears in the clear morning air the sound of motorcar brakes screeching from a distant street. He tells himself it is just the rarity of the sound that made him jump; private cars have all but disappeared from the streets since the petrol rationing. And all for the better, Fellows thinks, as the quiet and calm returns. He closes his eyes and allows the silence to seep into him and settle his nerves, much as he had after the ghost's face had peered at him through the banisters in his hall this morning. But life in the quarantined city is slower, nowadays, and he can be confident there will be no further shocks to his system today.

So, he thinks, turning to his paper, let's see if there's any news about Boursier.

But he will not allow himself to turn to the back pages and see if there has been a reply to his classified ad; he steels himself for the disappointment by forcing himself to read from the front. The local newspaper is a smaller, slimmer thing since the quarantine, printed in black and white and on noticeably poorer quality paper. And of course there are no stories from the outside world, anymore. The ink comes off on Fellows's hands as he reads—the two local political parties are at each other's throats again, despite supposedly having formed a unity government for the duration of the quarantine. There are the usual stories about the effect the hot summer is having on food supplies, stories about the petty crimes of the protest movement, and the regular announcements of feel-good fêtes and other events to try to keep the people's spirits up. On the letters page there's a smattering of conspiracy theories that attract more and more people to their simple, black and white answers as the summer drags on and things still don't change. There is no mention of ghosts or supernatural activity; it seems only Fellows has been seeing such things. But then, he reflects, maybe other people just aren't reporting their ghosts and demons, just as he hasn't. Easier, quieter, to just keep it from his mind.

And then, at the back of the classifieds, he sees someone has finally placed an answer to his advert:

> To the cash buyer looking for works by Boursier—call
> The Echo Bookshop on 2795 if serious buyer.

Fellows blinks in surprise at the reply—it had been over a week since he placed the wanted ad, and he had expected it would be members of the public who might have books by the reclusive Boursier for sale, not a bookshop. He'd assumed he knew every bookshop in the city—his house is stuffed with second hand books—but this one is new to him and he will have to phone for directions.

This will be a good day, he thinks.

Trying to contain his feeling of excitement (after all, it may come to nothing) he goes back inside the café. The regulars are already smoking and he wafts it away from his face as he makes his way to the payphone at the back. He picks up the receiver and notices it is dusty; he tries to put a coin in the slot and realises: Gregor hasn't changed the mechanism. The phone is still set up to take pre-quarantine coins.

He goes to the counter and asks Gregor if he can change some of his cash for the old-style coins in the tip jar. The big man blinks at him slowly.

"You want to take my tips?"

"No, Gregor, I just want some money for the phone."

"Phone's over there." There is a wave of the man's big, tattooed hand.

"I know Gregor, but it only takes... Look, I'll make it worth your while." Fellows reaches for the jar, meaning to unscrew the lid with the slit in it and exchange at least three times the price of the phone call in new money for old. But Gregor bats his hand away.

He doesn't understand why the café owner won't let him—maybe he thinks the quarantine will be lifted and the old money will have value again soon?—but Fellows decides not to argue. He meets Gregor's gaze and smiles; the other man remains blank-faced. He puts another coin into the tip jar to show there are no hard feelings; it is his favourite café, and he supposes the black haired waitress will get some of the money. Then he heads back outside to his table, takes his time finishing his coffee and breakfast while he decides what to do. He doesn't have a phone at his house.

Georgia, he thinks, Georgia has a phone. After he has finished his second coffee he walks across the square, scattering pigeons and indignant gulls, and into the curved streets of the old town.

THE NARROW STREETS OF THE old town always make Fellows feel slightly claustrophobic; the buildings seem to lean towards each other and their shadows at street level always touch. Many a tourist, in the days when tourists were still allowed, has been fooled by the words 'old town' on the city map, expecting maybe medieval churches or town halls, something historic with grandeur, rather than the somewhat seedy streets of bars, street painters, and poorly disguised brothels that in fact comprise the old town. There *is* history here, but it is a history of pogroms, of unresolved murders, of children crushed between the wheels and hooves of rich gentry's coach and horses. It is not the kind of history that gets commemorated on plaques or in tourist guides.

The streets nowadays don't have sewage running down the sides nor the piles of rubbish home to families of cat-sized rats of yesteryear, but the feeling remains, as if the grime has never quite rubbed off, as if a faint memory of the stench still lingers. People sit on the steps of their apartment block or lean out the balconies of their flats calling across to each other, or just watching Fellows sullenly as he passes. There is still little employment for the inhabitants of the old town, at least of the kind that takes place in daylight and is known to the city's tax officials.

Fellows has no idea why Georgia chooses to live here.

As he walks he hears the sound of the motorcar again, somewhere in another part of the city (the streets of the old town are too narrow for automobiles, having never been modernised) but it still stirs Fellows from his thoughts and seems too loud. Too fast. He mentally braces himself for the sound of a collision that never comes, for there is just the noise of the motor fading away into the morning silence.

He arrives at Georgia's building, a tall apartment block which faces the street with boarded-up windows and broken guttering. Inside the floor is worn stone and he calls down the clattering old lift to take him to her floor. Its iron doors close like a slow, toothless mouth behind him and it jerks him erratically up the six storeys. It always takes longer than he expects, and each time Fellows can't help but wonder at the strangeness of his friendship with Georgia.

She had been the first woman he had made a pass at after Lana had left him. It had been just hours after the quarantine had been declared; rather than attempt to preserve the city's stocks of wine and liqueurs most of the inhabitants had made the seemingly spontaneous decision to go out and drink as much as they possibly could. There had been a decadent, uninhibited air, like it was the end of a millennium or start of a war. Fellows had been drunk on absinthe, despite the inflated prices it was already commanding. He had looked across the bar and when his eyes focused he noticed Georgia on the arm of another woman. He realises now that the angry, hostile part of him had wanted to be rejected, to have some excuse to vent all the bitter guilt the separation had left him with. Trying to chat up someone so obviously unavailable had just been his unconscious way of ensuring that rejection happened.

He had been so drunk that the seedy, smoke-filled, wood-panelled bar had, as he had staggered towards her, seemed bright and mirrored in his doubling vision. His head had pounded despite its apparent lightness, and whatever words he had said to Georgia had seemed to come from someone else. He could never remember his attempted chat-up line afterwards and she had refused to tell him; all he could recall was her look of amused incredulity and her partner's hostile disdain.

"Oh piss off you stinking drunk," the other woman had said, turning from him and trying to make Georgia do the same. The two of them had similar make up on, similar severe fringes and pale faces; when they faced each other it was like one person doubled. But for some reason Georgia was the only one of the pair he found attractive.

"We can't just leave him like *this*," Georgia had said, shouting over the hubbub and assuming Fellows was too drunk to understand. She turned to him. "Where do you live?" she said to him slowly, like he was a lost child. "Can you get a taxi from here? You need to sleep this off. Are the taxis still running?" she added, speaking to her girlfriend, who just shrugged.

He'd slurred something lecherous about Georgia coming with him, and she'd just laughed at him. "Even if I *were* that way inclined there's nothing you could do to help me, state you're in. How many have you had?" Her voice was almost admiring.

"Let's just leave," her girlfriend said. "He's just another drunken idiot who can't stand to see two women together." It was as if her sober scowl was the only way she had of distinguishing herself from Georgia's wry smile.

"I'd better help get the twat back home," Georgia said, and downed her drink.

"*What?*"

Georgia had pulled away from the other woman's arm, whose hands failed to hold her. Looking back, Fellows realises it was a big step, some shift in the balance of power in the relationship that broke it completely. He had never learnt the other woman's name; Georgia had forbidden him to ask. She had told him not to feel guilty, that he was just the catalyst and something similar would have happened anyway, but he still does.

He had got Georgia back to his house that night after all, but the only touching had been when she shoved him onto the sofa to sleep while she took his room; that and when she'd rushed to him the next morning when he'd cried out, convinced he'd seen the broken body of a child pull itself across the wooden floor towards him before it faded into nothingness...

That had been the first time.

"Hello, you twat," Georgia says with a grin when she opens the door to him—she never lets him forget what a fool he had been that night.

"Hi," he says after she has shut the door behind him. "Can I use your phone?"

"Yes, I'm just dandy, and how are you?" Georgia says.

"Sorry, but I'm just... I finally got a lead on this Boursier guy."

"How do you know it's a guy?" Georgia says, clearing a space on a flaccid sofa for him. "Just from a surname? You sexist twat. Or can only men write good stories in your world?"

"Georgia, all the newspaper columns say he's a man..."

"But no one's ever seen him, right? Or her. So it could be a her, and it could be all you sexist men are just assuming..."

"Georgia, can I just please use your phone?"

"Sure. But you have to have a glass of wine with me first."

He is about to protest but then he looks at his watch; it is later than he thinks, as if he has spent hours walking to Georgia's flat rather than the thirty minutes it should have taken. He isn't sure at all how it is already late morning. Had he been daydreaming? But sod it, he thinks, the most important point is that it isn't too early to have a glass of wine, which he suddenly finds himself wanting.

"So you've found out where in the city he is?" Georgia says. "Boursier? I'm just saying 'he' to avoid another argument with a sexist throwback, you understand."

"No," he says smiling. Georgia's turns of phrase constantly surprise him, like he is in a foreign country. "But I've found somewhere that says they have some of his stories for sale."

"I still don't get—god this wine is piss isn't it? Blame the quarantine... I still don't get why you're so interested in this guy?"

"Or girl."

"Or *woman*."

"You're right, it is piss."

"Oh fuck off." Georgia giggles, settles her legs under herself on the other side of the sofa. Because of the way it sags they are both leaning towards each other; she peers at him from beneath an unruly fringe. Georgia's flat is on the top floor and for a second neither speaks as they listen to the sound of a gull landing heavily on the roof, with its raucous, repetitive cries.

"*Because*," Fellows says, "it's incredible, don't you think it's incredible that there's this talented, reclusive writer who just happens to be in *this* city while it's in lockdown, who writes stories like the ones I used to write according to what everyone says..."

"I still want to read one of *your* stories," Georgia says.

"I told you, I don't write anymore. Boursier..."

"You must still have them, the ones you did write? Who knows, maybe reading this Boursier guy will kick-start your own writing again."

He just shakes his head and looks out the window of her flat, at the slanted roofs of old town, repeating like a mosaic; in the distance he can see the bigger houses of the Enclave on the hill overlooking the bay, and the spires of three churches; the Mariners' Church is the most distinctive, with its weather vane shaped like a fish. Whenever anyone is lost at sea, the service is held there.

"Georgia, *please* can I use your phone?"

"You haven't finished your wine."

He necks it in one gulp, puts down the glass on the unvarnished wooden table covered in circular marks from previous glasses, and looks at her in triumph despite the taste. She calls him a twat again, and pours him another glass, right to the brim this time.

"You haven't finished your wine. So, tell me again just why you're obsessed with this guy..."

THE TRUTH IS, FELLOWS DOESN'T really know.

From Georgia's house he takes the quickest route out of the old town, walking down towards the docks, intending to take the route round the harbour walls and back up to the marketplace, where he has been told the bookshop is. When Georgia had finally allowed him to use her phone, the switchboard operator had tried to put the call through three times without reply; the voice that had finally answered had been blunt, aggressive even, as if annoyed at the intrusion. Fellows had doubted for a moment that the newspaper had printed the right number. But yes—the deep, croaky voice had confirmed it was the owner of The Echo Bookshop.

"What times are you open?" Fellows asked, after saying he was interested in the Boursier works the bookseller had.

"Later."

So he has allowed himself the more scenic route, and as he walks he smells a hint of spice on the air and his stomach rumbles hungrily. A man is selling potatoes dusted with paprika from a small rotisserie stall; the potatoes are cooking in the dripping fat from the chickens turning above. Fellows buys a carton of the potatoes and sits eating them overlooking the sea as it reared up against the harbour walls. The way the walls stop the sea getting in makes him think of the quarantine, as if that were protecting the city from the outside world and not the other way round; the truth is the quarantine doesn't bother Fellows much. Some boats are pulling out to sea but they are small ones, fishing in the designated area around the city. The bigger boats and ships, which used to sail to other ports, to other countries, already have a neglected air; one of the biggest lies lopsided in the water as if it had just been abandoned; one flank of it is raised above the waterline, revealing rust and barnacles. Cormorants are drying their wings on its deck and rigging.

Fellows licks the grease and paprika from his fingers, tasting the faintest hint of newspaper ink underneath. He realises he is deliberately delaying setting off again, because something about the bookseller's tone, his implication that Fellows was a timewaster, has made him anxious. He has the ridiculous feeling that what should be a simple commercial transaction is going to be confrontational, and he shrinks from it. No wonder he has never come across The Echo Bookshop before, if this was the way it treated potential customers (and what kind of name was The Echo, anyway?). But then Fellows thinks that he might, finally, be about to get his hands on some Boursier stories, and some of his excitement returns. He throws his last potato to the shrieking gulls and then heads off at a pace towards the marketplace. The voice had informed him that the bookshop was to be found in a nameless alley behind the square. Of course, Fellows had thought, why make it easy for your customers to find you? It would serve the man right if he doesn't show up…

But yet here he is, hurrying up towards the square despite the relentless summer, moving twice as fast as anyone else in the lethargic afternoon streets. You twat, he thinks to himself, smiling as he thinks of Georgia. It's an odd word, and one he's never heard but from her. Is it foreign? He will have to ask her. Its meaning is clear enough regardless, he thinks, with another smile.

Stories about Boursier had begun appearing in the local paper not long after the quarantine had been imposed, but Fellows has the impression that those articles had been preceded by overheard conversations in the street, elusive snatches of gossip and innuendo. All about this mysterious writer called Boursier. No first name was ever mentioned, no personal details. Some said he was a spy come to see how the city coped with the quarantine, some said he was on the run from the law or paying some kind of penitence by his isolation. Regardless, as there were no new books coming into the city from outside anymore, the mere presence of Boursier in the quarantined city had been enough for the newspapers to latch onto. Fellows supposes the writer's talent may well have been exaggerated, but still he had been intrigued by what he had heard: short stories set in a fantasy world, but not one that differed too much from real life. People who had read Boursier's work, or claimed to have, said that they had a confusing, teasing quality, full of alien details but written in such a way it was as if the writer expected people to know what was meant. No explanation, no context. He might be imagining it, but to Fellows they sound like the kind of short stories he would have tried to write, back before...

But he isn't going to think of that.

The market square is full of people and stalls and birds squabbling for scraps; an illusion of normalcy. But most of the stalls have meagre offerings: whatever crops people have managed to grow in the derisory ring of agricultural land this side of the quarantine. The summer-long lack of rain has not helped. Only the fish stalls are still close to being as bountiful as before. But the market is still packed with people, as if they have nowhere else to be, going through the motions of haggling over a small bunch of radishes or a jar of dried herbs using currency they don't fully know the worth of. Others just hang around as if drawn here like the ghosts of their previous lives, standing around unable to progress, staring vacantly at the empty cheese stall and the sparse cuts of meat (about which rumours as to their origin swirl) and then walking away.

There is a commotion towards one end of the market; Fellows sees a small group of men and women with placards, trying to get a chant going with minimal success. He goes over; one of them presses a mimeographed leaflet into his hand without making eye-contact, then starts back as if surprised Fellows has taken it. He glances at it as he walks through the crowd: it is calling for more 'radical' solutions in order to get the quarantine lifted. Idiots, he thinks, crumpling the leaflet in his hand and dropping it to the floor without reading further. At the far end of the crowd he sees two Guardia approaching at speed, unbuttoning the holsters of their revolvers as they do so. They glance at him as they pass, and Fellows is glad he dropped the leaflet. The crowd parts for them as they stride into it, the most energetic action he has seen in this husk of a market. The protestors have already scattered.

He finds the alleyway that the voice on the phone must have been talking about, and steps inside; its shadows mean it is several degrees cooler than in the sunlight and he almost shivers. After the throng of people in the market square the alley's emptiness, its quietness seem the more unnerving. As if he hasn't just turned a corner but somehow ended up far from home. He resists the urge to look behind himself for reassurance. The alley is narrow and unevenly cobbled and an absolutely preposterous location for any kind of commercial endeavour. Can there really be a bookshop down here? Fellows thinks. He wonders if he is the victim of some elaborate, opaque prank. Or could it be something more sinister? Was some gang trying to lure him into the alleyway to mug him, to steal from him all the money they thought he would have withdrawn from the city bank to purchase Boursier's works? In reality he has little on him; although Boursier has gained some notoriety in the local press and among the literati, such as they are, in the quarantined city, he hadn't considered the possibility that his books would be changing hands for silly money. Surely he isn't actually *successful?* Because his stories sound in some ways similar to what he had used to write, Fellows has assumed Boursier's lifestyle to be similar to his own back then: periods of dull but dependable employment leaving the evenings to write in, punctuated by irregular, fruitless attempts to 'make a living' from fiction, eking out cheap coffee and a pack of cigarettes a week, dreaming of actually making enough money so that he won't have to return to the real world... Maybe this Boursier has actually achieved that?

Bastard, Fellows thinks, and heads down the alley wearily. There is faint, metallic odour to the air that he can't quite place, and the sound of dripping water from the guttering above. What the hell? he thinks. It hasn't rained for months. When he looks up he sees the gutters of the buildings are overflowing with lush vegetation, greener and brighter than anything he has seen for months, a miniature jungle out of place against the brown stone and grey slate around it.

At the bottom of the alleyway is a pile of garbage bags which an energetic seagull is tearing into, and an open wooden door with peeling white paint that leads into one of the buildings to the left. Fellows pauses. From this angle he can't see what it opens into; he thinks again he should just turn and leave, forget about this absurd Boursier character and the memories of his own failed literary ambitions he has stirred up...

But he walks up to the door, and goes inside. The gull clatters upwards on white wings.

The room he finds himself in has an uneven floor, an uneven ceiling, as if it has been hollowed out of rock rather than being made of brick and timber. It is large, or would feel so if it weren't for the aisles and aisles of bookshelves it is filled with, so tight together any prospective customers could only move between in single file. Not that there are any other customers; the only echoes in here seem to be his own. Despite himself Fellows is excited by the sight of so many books, of the old musty smell of them: the books overflow from the shelves and are piled at the ends of the aisles. He walks down one of the aisles; he stops when he sees a sign in felt-tip pen saying *Fictions B*, but he can't see any books by Boursier on the shelves. He hopes this means the proprietor, wherever he is, has kept the books safe for him rather than sold them already. Fellows doesn't recognise the names of any of the authors—Boddings, Bergeron, Belacqua—as he moves towards *Fictions A*. Am I so out of touch? he thinks.

At the end of the aisle he comes to a halt, for he sees what he presumes is the sales desk, which is little more than a table piled high with yet more books as well as an ancient looking cash register. There is an office chair, the kind with wheels, in front of the desk, turning slightly as if someone has just risen from it and dashed out of sight. And on the other side of the desk staring at him is a young man of about eighteen, Fellows guesses. The boy is pale and shiny to the point of looking unwell and his close cropped hair is suggestive of the gaol. He has one eye that doesn't look in the direction it should.

"Uh, hi," Fellows says. "Is your... is the owner around? I called earlier and..."

"You?" the boy says. "You're the person who called about these bloody Boursier stories?" Fellows is shocked to hear the same hoarse, vaguely aggressive voice he heard on the telephone.

"Yes, that was me," he says. The boy gives a low whistle and chuckles to himself; Fellows wonders again if the books really are expensive, and if his somewhat worn and crumpled linen suit marks him out as someone who surely won't be able to able to purchase them...

"Well, okay..." the boy says, and bends down to open a drawer of his desk. As he does so there is a noticeable disturbance of dust. He angrily clears some free space from the desk by knocking some of the books there to the floor, and puts the contents of the drawer in the vacated space. They are not what Fellows was expecting.

There are no actual books per se; there are some cheap looking literary journals and magazines, dog-eared at the corners. He opens one to its contents page and sees at least it isn't a trick—the third line says *Spot The Difference* by Boursier. There is no forename or initial. As well as the magazines there is a story in what appears to be a succession of newspaper clippings, and one that appears to have been hand-produced by a mimeograph. There are six stories in all, he sees. He doesn't try to hide his disappointment, but after all what does it matter where and how these stories were published if they are as good as the rumours suggest? And maybe the fact he looks a little nonplussed will help him bargain the bookseller's price down.

"Hmmmm," he says, "well I suppose they might be worth a read. How much?" he adds, pulling out the lowest denomination note from his wallet as some kind of starting point.

"Old money only," the boy says, and Fellows sees he is smiling, although because of the boy's rogue eye he isn't sure if it is at him or not.

"What?"

"Seller's instructions: pre-quarantine money only. Pounds and pence."

"What? But I... I don't have any on me," Fellows says in annoyance. "Why would I be carrying around money I can't bloody spend any more?" A thought strikes him. "And what do you mean, seller's instructions?"

The bookseller gives that little mocking whistle again, as though Fellows is a simpleton who has failed to grasp the obvious. "I'm just on commission," he says. "Do you think I *bought* this junk?" He gestures dismissively at the pile of Boursier stories between them. "Of course not. I only buy books that are properly published, properly bound..." He sniffs as if the dust of his shop has irritated him. "But how could I turn him down? The guy came in the other week and asked me to try and sell these, for fifty percent of the takings. It's not like they take up much room so I said yes, on the condition that if they didn't sell in a month he'd have to come back and take them away. Which I fully expected. But then here's you."

"That's when you saw my advert then?" Fellows says. "And put your reply in the paper today?"

"What? Why the hell would *I* pay for an advert in the paper for this junk? I didn't place any advert," the boy says. Is he crazy, Fellows wonders, some kind of compulsive liar?

"Anyway. He gave... other instructions too. One of which was old money only."

"Wait. Who did? Who's selling these?"

"The author, who else? Who else but a struggling no-talent author would offer me fifty percent?"

"Boursier?"

"So he said," the boy says in his croaky voice that doesn't match his face. He sniffs again. His smile annoys Fellows no end.

"Well, have *you* got any old money?" he says, "that I could buy from you?"

"A bit, but it won't get you all of the stories," the boy says. "Just the one. And I charge a bastard of a commission."

Fellows tells himself not to do it, to walk away, but finds himself agreeing. For some reason the boy insists on playing out the whole transaction, giving him the old orange note in exchange for about half the contents of Fellow's wallet in new money, writing out a receipt, then taking the note back from Fellows before allowing him one of the magazines, and writing out another receipt. Fellows snatches the magazine angrily from the boy, not bothering to hide his annoyance. He sees his fingers are still stained with newspaper ink and hopes he won't mark the pages he's paid so much for.

"I'll be back for the others tomorrow," he says flatly.

"Maybe not once you've *read* that one," the boy says grinning. "Drivel."

Fellows bites back on his reply and leaves the shop.

IT IS LATE AFTERNOON AND the day has retained all the heat that has been burnt into it by the sun; the city seems even more torpid than normal to Fellows. Most people have been working fewer hours since the quarantine because there is genuinely less to do, but it is more than the fact that people are taking longer siestas. There is a sense the quarantined city is holding its breath, waiting for what comes after.

It's a hiatus Fellows admits to enjoying, an escape from old tension, and he enjoys too the feeling of the sun on his face as he walks. He decides to go and read the Boursier story he has bought for such a ridiculous price in the nearby park; by the time he has read it and is ready to walk home the day might have cooled. He stops to buy some bottles of beer on the way, and as he comes out the shop Fellows hears the intrusive noise of the car engine that he has heard on and off all day. He shudders. But still he steps out into the road without thinking; the noise is an annoyance he has ceased to associate with actual traffic, for the streets of the quarantined city have been empty of that for so long.

The car swerves and shoots past him with a loud scream of its horn to chastise him. Fellows staggers backwards; all he can comprehend for a second is the sudden hostile black bulk of the thing, the swirl of air and dust it blasts into his face.

"Idiot!" he shouts at its retreating form, not caring if it *is* a government official's car (they being the only ones still allowed unlimited petrol) for the car had been going too fast and driving up the centre of the road like it owned it all, rather than on the right-hand side as it should.

Fellows swears again, under his breath this time—his breathing is coming in heavy, painful gulps and his heart is pounding. He is leaning against one of the street signs for support. Relax, nothing happened, he thinks, but it is a long time before he can do so.

The sun is finally lowering itself for the day when he gets to the park, and the first prostitutes and rent-boys are already lazily gathering down by the fountain. Fellows gives the women a quick glance, but knows that the vague ache he feels is loneliness dressed up as lust rather than lust itself. And besides, he barely has any money on him after buying the beer and being ripped off in The Echo Bookshop.

Sighing, he sits on a bench furthest from the fountain, near the statue of the man who apparently founded the city, so worn and splattered with gull shit whoever it was is almost unrecognisable. Fellows opens one of the beers, using the side of the wooden bench to lever the bottle-top off, and takes a swig. It is warm and flat and tasteless; when he looks at the bottle he sees the label on its side hasn't spelled the name of the brand correctly, and is already peeling off due to the cheap glue. Blame the quarantine, Georgia says in his mind, and he smiles.

He takes out the journal he has bought; it is called *Other Rooms, Other Cities*, and he supposes even if the Boursier story isn't any good there is at least an outside chance one of the others will be worth reading. But he will read the Boursier story first; time to finally see what all the fuss was about. Taking another swig of the beer, he begins.

The Smell Of Paprika by Boursier

Brent felt like he had been driving all day, the monotony of the motorway forming no memories in his mind and so not allowing him to gauge time's passing. It is only the near accident that caused him to come back to himself—a large, official-looking black car in the middle lane swerved across into his own and then slowed down, causing him to steer right around it, only just avoiding clipping it and sending himself spinning off the road. As he drove past he looked at the car but its windows were all tinted black and he couldn't see the driver. He held down his horn to chastise it.

"Twat!" he shouted.

He pulled back into the left hand lane and in the rear view mirror watched the black car get swallowed up in the grey fog as he accelerated. He was somewhat shaken up, feeling the tremors from his arm twitch the steering wheel, and it was then he saw the sign: *Next Services 6 Miles*. Brent was so tired he couldn't at that moment recall the length of his journey and if here (wherever here was) was a good place to make a stop, but he decided not to worry about that for the moment. When he reached the junction for the services, the sign almost illegible in the mist around it, he pulled in.

The car park was packed, everyone else seemingly having had the same idea as him—in the mist the different makes and colours of cars all looked the same. Some of the cars even had a neglected air, parked carelessly over two or more spaces, splattered with bird crap and brown leaves as if the owner had just abandoned them there. Brent looked up to where he could hear the calls of birds in the low grey sky, and maybe he saw a glimpse of ghostly white wings. Gulls? he thinks. They had sounded like seagulls too, although he hadn't thought himself anywhere near the coast.

He got out of his car and pressed the key to lock it, its clunk muffled in the fog, then he walked towards the pale glow of the services building, looking like an abandoned, listing ship. Halfway, he turned and wondered how the hell he was going to find his car again if the fog didn't clear, for behind him all he could see was row upon row of indistinct grey shapes.

The automatic doors slid open as he approached and he entered the building. It was as if some of the fog had leaked inside, for it still seemed an effort to see clearly. The interior walls might have been painted white but they looked a dull grey colour, in some places smudged with hand prints as if people with dirty palms had beaten against them like trapped flies, years ago.

There were the usual franchises selling fast food, coffee, maps and books around a central seating area. Some of the

company's logos he didn't recall seeing for years. As he
saw what was on offer at the various food stalls Brent
couldn't help but notice that their selection seemed paltry
compared to usual. Maybe for some reason the expected
deliveries hadn't got through? Although his stomach felt
empty none of the available food appealed to him; now the
adrenaline of the near collision had faded from his system
he just felt weary. It didn't help his mood that so many
people were just stood around in the central area, or
milling between empty spaces with a distracted air, as if
they had nowhere else to be; as if the motorway services
were a destination they had arrived at rather than a stop on
a journey, and now they were here they didn't know what
to do other than go through the motions...

Irritated, Brent decided to go to the Gents and relieve the
pressure on his bladder before he decided what to eat.
Obscurely, he thought of a holiday in Brittany with his
parents as a child, and how they had eaten paprika-
flavoured roast potatoes while looking at the expensive
boats and yachts on the marina. The potatoes had been
cooked in the dripping fat from a rotisserie, and the man
had been about to shut for the day and had given them all
he had left, in exchange for barely any money—Francs, he
remembered; old money. Brent shook his head. The bright
memory seemed to have more reality than anything around
him, but it was stupid tantalising himself with the idea of
food that wasn't available; that in all probability he would
never get the chance to eat again.

All the cubicles in the Gents were occupied, and only
the middle urinal was free—feeling uncomfortable Brent
went and stood at it, trying not to look at the men either
side of him. He couldn't help but notice how ashen they
looked though, how motionless their bent faces were. It
was silent in the toilets and Brent wondered if he'd ever be
able to piss; he sometimes couldn't go when there were
other men at the urinals. He waited for one of the others,
who had been standing there when he entered, to finish
and leave, but neither did and he felt a mounting

annoyance. He eventually managed to go, the sound very loud and obvious, and then zipped himself and made to leave. As he washed his hands he could see in the mirror the two men stood with their heads bowed behind him. They were completely motionless and silent, and Brent had the odd impression that they hadn't even unzipped themselves.

Brent left the Gents and went out into the main services again—opposite was a cubicle full of arcade machine consoles, but they were all switched off and dusty; where the glow of their graphics should have been was just grey.

There are no kids in here at all, Brent thought.

He stood and looked at the open plan space in front of him, and something about it seemed wrong to his tired, misty eyes—people were queuing, but were the queues actually moving? People were walking but were they just going in circles? Everyone's movements looked lethargic, aimless, as if they were on the verge of ceasing movement altogether. A woman took a few steps from the crowd in Brent's direction and stopped; her eyes were vacant and they didn't seem to register his presence, and if they blinked he couldn't see it. Her mouth fell open, but then snapped shut without utterance. The woman turned and walked slowly back into the crowd; Brent noticed how faded and torn her clothes were.

He no longer felt hungry.

He looked behind him and saw a sign saying *Emergency Exit*, with a bar across the door to press down and he *almost...* But he told himself he was being stupid, that the tiredness and fog and the near accident on the motorway earlier had affected his nerves. He decided he'd drive to the next services, which would no doubt seem more normal than this benighted place, and he would eat there.

Brent walked through the centre of the services, avoiding the lurching people—he felt a strong distaste at the idea of them touching him. It was only then, when he was in amongst them, that he realised how *silent* the place was—he could hear the shuffling sound of shoes against the floor, but nothing else. No one was speaking.

And then his arm brushed against the flesh of someone who drifted past with a stagger, and Brent swore he felt a deadening chill at the touch. He looked but the woman was already past him—he couldn't tell if it was the same woman who had stared at him before, and if it would have meant anything if it was... She was soon lost in the crowd, or maybe just the increasing blurriness of his vision.

The last few metres towards the doors felt like an effort, and for a moment they didn't slide open as he approached as if not registering his presence, and he felt a mounting panic... But then, almost reluctantly, they did so. Brent left the services; no one else left with him.

Outside it was still grey with fog and Brent had no idea where his car was. Some of the cars had been here a *long* time he realised, seeing the flecks of rust, the deflated tires. He was holding his cold arm with his other hand, but couldn't feel his touch.

He took out his car key from his pocket and pressed the button—the car that lit up and clicked open was not the one he had arrived in. Nevertheless, he moved towards it—he looked up as he did so and saw again the briefest glimpse of white wings, impossibly out of reach.

He got behind the wheel of his new car, barely registering its colour or make. It's steering wheel was dusty. The next services, he thought. He will drive to the next services, which will be the same as this one (which was the same as the last one) and maybe he will make it to the one after that. But he is getting slower, he is getting so *tired*, and sooner or later he will reach the services that is the one he will simply stay in... He pulled out into the slow lane of the motorway; looked to his right and saw the other cars, people vacant behind the wheel, on their journeys towards the services that were the only places to travel to or between... He wondered what would have happened if he had collided with that black car earlier, wondered if his visions of flame and blood were even realistic in this world. Maybe the black car had swerved deliberately into his path; maybe he should have swerved to meet it? But he knew, deep down, that he was too cowardly to do so.

Next Services 6 Miles he saw and he knew he would pull in there, park, and go inside the identical services building. But not eat or piss or talk or touch.

For the briefest of moments, there is the ghostly smell of hot fat and paprika, and then it is gone.

FELLOWS BLINKS IN SURPRISE A few times after finishing *The Smell Of Paprika*—when he looks up, the view of the statue of the city founder with the sunset behind it seems to have too many colours; when he forces himself to focus on the dates carved into its plinth they make no immediate sense. He can't recall having been so immersed in a work of fiction for years.

Nowadays, when he reads, the analytical part of his brain still takes over, nit-picking, deciding how *he* would write such a story even though he hasn't written a word of fiction for years. With Boursier's story it had been a different sensation, that of being engrossed, of losing himself entirely in something that wasn't real. And this despite all the odd detail—not just the futuristic, sci-fi feeling of it but the little, more telling things: the concept of the 'services' themselves, the idea of so many people owning cars, and driving on the other side of the road... all presented without contrast, as if the reader would just understand. Fellows wonders what nationality Boursier is; not everyone who's been trapped in the quarantined city had been a resident, it had happened that fast. But despite all the strangeness, all the surface-level confusion the story had *worked*, all the peculiarities and strange words all part of a spell Fellows had accepted totally upon reading it. And the strange coincidence of the paprika-flavoured potatoes—well, Fellows reflected, he *does* live in the same city as me, and there are only so many places to eat, so it's probably not that big a coincidence. He must have written the story only recently, he supposes—Fellows checks the back of *Other Rooms, Other Cities* but it is not the kind of journal to have a publication date.

I definitely want to read the others, Fellows thinks, although he is not sure how he will get hold of enough pre-quarantine money. Officially, there is not meant to be any left in circulation.

He stands from the park bench, puts his empty bottle of beer in the bin—the sun is falling more swiftly now and the old gas lights of the park have come on. God knows how the gas is still connected, he thinks. In their light the park seems darker, drabber, more old-fashioned than in the sunlight. He walks down towards the bottom entrance of the park, towards the sound of the fountain; he ignores the prostitutes asking if he has a light, if he has the time on him…

This exit from the park brings Fellows to one of the widest roads in the city, two lanes leading down to the city hall and old mercantile quarter. Fellows is still wrapped up in the story he has read, and without really thinking he looks to the right before crossing; he sees, as usual there is no traffic and he steps out…

He quickly steps back onto the pavement, wondering what the hell he was thinking—why was he looking for traffic driving on the *left*? If something had been coming the other way he would have walked straight out into it its path. Almost getting run over once today was surely enough, especially if this time it had been due to his own stupidity. Okay the roads are quiet but—yes, he *can* hear a car approaching. It sounds like the same one that almost ran him over earlier, the one whose noise, muffled by the odd acoustics of the quiet city seems to be coming from all directions at once.

But still some instinct makes him look right again, and he sees the same large black car coming up on his side of the road, driving on the left. He stares at it in confusion as it passes, as if hoping for someone to shout some explanation from its windows; but they are closed and tinted an opaque black.

He stares in equal confusion at the second, identical car that follows behind—it seems as strange, to Fellows, to see two cars together as it is to see them driving on the *wrong* side of...

Very slowly, like when he worries the ghost has sneaked behind him, Fellows turns to look at the road sign that he is standing next to. *Slow Children* (on the other side of the road from the park is the orphanage). To his left, facing him. Visible to traffic driving on the left-hand side of the road.

Like in the story, is his first thought, like in Boursier's story.

The two cars are going so fast he expects to hear the noise of a collision, but they disappear from view, round the corner that will lead them to whichever local government building they are headed. Now they are out of sight the reality of what he has just seen seems less pressing; it was an obscure prank, he thinks, or just two idiots driving on the wrong side of the road for the thrill of it, knowing they'll meet no one coming the other way. Or even, perhaps, this is another new, unintelligible policy imposed by the unity government—they changed the currency for no discernible reason, so why not the road laws? Ridiculous certainly, a pointless expense, but something new and that came into force *today*, and not something he can have been wrong about all of the time he has been living in the quarantined city.

He looks back up at the sign; the faded, rusted sign. He looks up the street and sees the others facing him; he looks down the street and sees the back of... No, no, no, he thinks.

He bends down, examines the pavement to see if it looked like the road sign had been recently fitted or tampered with, but he can see no evidence that it hasn't always been like this.

Another car is coming up the road, while Fellows is just standing there—Fellows can't remember when he last saw three cars almost simultaneously in the city. He hasn't seen *one* for weeks. It is the same long, sleek black model of the unity government, but going much slower. Again on the left. It pulls up and stops opposite the park. There is the honk of its horn, and one of the tinted windows is slowly wound down. Fellows can just see blackness in the interior. Behind him, Fellows hears the prostitutes start to move towards the sound of its still idling motor.

"Hey, hey," he calls out. He moves quickly to the driver's window. "Hey," he says, until the driver reluctantly winds down his window.

"Look, piss off mate," he says. "No offence to your sort, but *he* (the driver gestures towards the passenger seat behind him, which is behind a partition) isn't here for the men, if you get my drift. Some of them, but not him."

"No, I'm not..." Fellows gabbles, looking down at himself in his old suit. "I just... why are you driving on the wrong side of the road? It's not right, I know there's no traffic but..."

"Plenty enough tonight," the driver interrupts, a suggestion so stupid Fellows ignores it.

"... but just because there's no other traffic you should still drive on the right, the *right*, side of the road," Fellows says. "Why, I saw two cars earlier..."

"What are you on about? The right?" the driver says. He sniffs and Fellows supposes he can smell the alcohol on his breath. It was one beer, he wants to say. Behind him, he hears two of the prostitutes start talking to whoever is in the back.

"Good job *you* don't drive mate," the driver adds good-humouredly. "But now look, piss off like I said."

Some kind of agreement is made, and both prostitutes get into the back of the car. The driver winds his window up, still grinning at Fellows as he turns the handle, and then the car drives off. Fellows stares at it until it is out of sight.

Feeling a numbness in his limbs, he goes and sits back on the bench in the park. The prostitutes and rent boys, after seeing his exhibition at the car, are ignoring him completely now. He opens another beer and reads *The Smell Of Paprika* over and over, as if there could be some explanation there. The small text is hard to read in the gaslight, but by the time the sun has fully set he feels he knows most of the story off by heart anyway. *The ghostly smell of hot fat and paprika; the briefest glimpse of white wings.*

His thoughts loosen as he drinks, and he realises that sat in the small circle of light from the lamp above the bench, he is in danger of letting his doubts veer out of control, to overwhelm him. There will be an explanation, he thinks. Maybe he has got a touch of heat stroke today? It will be all right tomorrow, he thinks, somehow it will have... you'll be all right tomorrow.

He wants nothing more than to go and see Georgia, to speak to *someone* friendly, who can at least call him a twat when she tells him the obvious explanation for the cars driving on the left, but when he reaches her street the window of her flat is dark. Out drinking or asleep drunk, he thinks. The night is still warm and he looks up at the cloudless sky for a few moments, at the unceasing patterns of the stars. Then he heads back to his own house, feeling sober despite the beers, wide-eyed and staring at the quarantined city as if he is afraid other things familiar to him might have altered while he wasn't looking.

He shuts his front door on the strange streets behind him, and closes his eyes.

When he opens them it is to see the welcoming, disjointed arms of the ghostly child spread as if for an embrace, coming towards him in the dark of his house. He screams.

Outside, a car's brakes screech, but it doesn't stop.

JAMES EVERINGTON

PART TWO

INTO THE RAIN

FELLOWS STEPS FROM THE SHOWER, both the day's heat and the drink from the previous night making him feel sluggish. The events of yesterday don't seem to join up in his head to where he is now; what he remembers from the previous night doesn't seem like it could possibly have happened...

Still naked, Fellows goes to the window of his bedroom, through which he can feel an overbearing heat despite it only being mid-morning. He looks up and down the street but can't see any traffic; not unusual since the unity government introduced petrol rationing. So no way to see if people are still driving on the left, matching Boursier's story but not his own memories. Have I had it wrong, all these months in the quarantined city? he thinks. He doesn't actually drive anymore (the thought brings goosebumps despite the heat) so could he somehow have been mistaken, until Boursier made him see it?

He dresses slowly, his crumpled linen suit seeming an absurdity in the heat despite its thinness. The view from his window is as absent of clouds as automobiles, and he vaguely wonders when he last saw or felt rain. Although today is especially hot, the heat-wave had started with the quarantine, as if an invisible dome had been laid across the city, letting more heat in than out.

Right then, Fellows thinks, trying to shake the torpor from himself. He pats his pockets; the first task of the day is to find some of the pre-quarantine pounds and pence to pay the bookseller with. Maybe Gregor at The Carousel will be able to put him in touch with someone. Once he has bought the five remaining stories he'll get some of the piss that passes for beer in the city nowadays, and return to his house to read them in its comparative coolness. He'll not let things that don't concern him as a pedestrian worry him unduly.

Thinking so, he steps out onto the landing and the broken body of the ghost comes at him.

He jerks away before it can touch him, his body suddenly shivering. Despite its eagerness for him it is easy to avoid, for the ghost's twisted limbs didn't let it move quickly, barely let it stand unaided. Even as he watches it, the ghost totters and collapses soundlessly to the wooden floor, without disturbing any of the dust. It keeps its round, boyish face fixed on Fellows, although it is hard to tell from its pupil-less eyes whether it is looking at him or not. Fellows takes another step backwards, back into his bedroom so that the thing is out of sight. He shivers again as he realises his mistake: there is no other way out of the bedroom. There isn't even a door to shut. He thinks of dragging the bookcase across to block the doorway, but it is surely too laden with paperbacks to do so.

He stands, not knowing what to do, feeling the heat from the window on his back. The ghost or demon or entity is always completely silent, and out of sight it is hard to believe its broken form is just a few feet away, straining towards him. And why is he so afraid of it touching him, anyway; surely the one thing ghosts can't do is *touch*?

Maybe it has already faded—Fellows waits, watching the doorway. When something streaks into the bedroom towards him he cries out even as he realises it is too fast and low and black to be the crippled ghost.

"George!" Fellows says; the damn cat is slinking round his ankles wanting to be fed. He reaches down to pet him, still keeping a wary eye on the door. George has never reacted in the slightest to the presence of the ghost, so his being here now and hungry is no guarantee the thing isn't still soundlessly dragging itself across the dusty floorboards to reach him. Nevertheless, if the ghost had been outside George must have ran *through* it to reach Fellows, and the impossible picture this summons up in Fellows's mind gives him some confidence. He cautiously approaches the doorway, ignoring George's mews as he does so.

Just then he sees a small hand waver in the air before gripping the peeling white woodwork of the doorframe; one of its fingers is bent back and so can't grip, and Fellows sees how dirty the pad of it is, black as ink. The hand is about an inch from the floor, and as he watches appalled a second grips the doorframe a foot higher, as if the kid had sprawled onto its side and has grabbed for the doorframe to pull itself forward. The hands tighten, as if preparing to heave that sightless face into view...

When the hands fade, they do so suddenly, and leave no trace of their grime or blood on the peeling white paintwork.

Fellows remembers to breathe, then gags slightly, tasting stale alcohol rise in his throat. This is getting stupid, he thinks, this is getting *worse*. He tells himself he must do something about it, without having the slightest idea what. An exorcist—he doesn't know for sure if such people really exist, or if it is ghosts they cast out or demons. He supposes the boy could be either, if what it is even has a name. He can't comprehend how he could talk to someone about it without knowing what to call it. He hasn't spoken of the haunting to anyone, not even his best friend Georgia. *You twat,* she says in his head, and even that calms him somewhat.

His dread of the ghost often fades almost as quickly as its form does, and already the image of the hands gripping the doorway seems like something from a moment so far past it can't touch him here. Something not quite real, and certainly not as real as the increasingly agitated cat still pestering him for food, or as the ugly sound of the motorcar passing outside...

Fellows runs to the window, just in time to see the black car turn the corner at the top of his street. On the left, he thinks.

But that is another thing he can let George distract him from confronting for the moment.

OUTSIDE, THE HEAT MAKES HIM pause—surely this is not a day to be walking halfway across the city and back. The sky feels oppressive above him, its light changing the way his world looks, everything hazy and already beginning to shimmer. He heads towards The Carousel, hoping one of the inside tables will be free. He glances around the café twice as he enters, once to see if there is, and once looking to see if the waitress with the black, curly hair is working today. He sees her reflection in one of the mirrors on the wall before he sees her. Her reflected smile just makes him feel sad and old, for it is the lovely professional smile she would offer to any of the regulars who came in.

He places his order with Gregor at the counter, and takes the newspaper back to his table to read; he sees how its cheap quality has already stained his fingers before he has even finished the front page. All the stories are either about the heat-wave or the quarantine, or about the growing groups of protestors against the unity government and against the quarantine itself. *Idiots,* Fellows thinks. He doesn't actually mind the quarantine that much, other than the fact it has stopped his favourite drinks being available anywhere other than the black market. The quarantine has been in place all this hot summer, but given Fellows doesn't actually want to leave the city why should he care? They must have good reason for it, he supposes.

The waitress comes over with his coffee, looking flustered.

"This heat!" she says, and Fellows tries not to look as she flaps her blouse collar to air her neck.

"I know," he said, "there's something not quite right about it, isn't there?" He is aping something he has just read in the paper. She nods but doesn't say anything, doesn't move away either. "Almost too hot to walk in this weather," he continues clumsily. "But then you might drive here I guess..?"

"Drive?" She cocks her head. "No point learning to drive when no one can drive a car is there? Or afford one. Besides, I live close," she adds. "Just round the corner in the old town."

"I used to be able to drive," Fellows says. "Well, I'm sure I still could but I feel like I can hardly remember how to. Hardly remember we drive on the right..." He forces a laugh.

The waitress looks confused and is about to say something, when Gregor calls across the café at her.

"Leianna! Customers!"

With an apologetic smile and a glance that doesn't quite meet his, the waitress turns to deal with an impatient sailor at the table behind him; Leianna, Fellows thinks. He takes a sip of his coffee, clutching the cup in both hands as if it were winter. He shivers again despite the intense heat coming through the café windows.

After he finishes drinking he goes up to the counter to pay, putting an overly generous tip into the jar in the hope Leiana might be watching and forgive him for getting her in trouble. He sees Gregor is typically unmoved by his generosity. Fellows wonders about asking Gregor again if he could take some of the pre-quarantine money from the bottom strata of the tip jar, but that had not gone too well last time.

"Gregor," he says, "you know people who can… get things, right?" He gestures at the bottles of wines and spirits behind the man, who remains impassive. "I want to find someone who can get me some of the old money. The pre-quarantine money."

"Why?" Gregor says.

"Because… I need to buy something from someone who will only take…"

"What?"

"What? Some, well, some books," he says, feeling as stupid as Gregor's look obviously implies him to be; he imagines the waitress, Leianna, smiling mockingly behind him where he can't see her and he flushes.

Gregor stares at him for a long time.

"The only idiots who want the old money are those protestors. A group of them think if the old money is reintroduced it will help lift the quarantine."

"I don't think it quite works that way!" Fellows says, his laugh dying in the face of Gregor's silence. "So, do you know, uh, where…"

"The church," Gregor says, "with the fish. There's a square in front of it. They'll be handing out leaflets there at midday." The Mariners' Church, Fellows thinks. Something of a tourist attraction, until the quarantine.

"Thanks," he says, feeling compelled to add another coin to the jar, which Gregor doesn't acknowledge. He's just about to turn away when he remembers something.

"Can you drive, Gregor?" he says.

"Yes."

He opens his mouth to ask which side, but then just laughs. Pointless. He leaves Gregor looking even more nonplussed than before as he exits the café.

"CHRIST WHAT ARE YOU DOING here?" Georgia says, one eye peering above the chain on her door. "Even I know it's too early for a glass of wine."

"Can I come in?" Fellows says; it is too soon for him to head to The Mariners' Church. Georgia is, he supposes, the only friend he has in the city; he struggles to think of his friends the other side of the border, and what would be the point anyway?

"Come on then," Georgia says, taking the chain from the door and letting him in. "The corkscrew's over there."

"But I thought you said…"

"I know what I said. Twat." That word again, Fellows thinks.

"I read one of his stories," he says to Georgia when they are settled on her sagging sofa; he has to admit the cold wine is refreshing, despite the vinegary taste, and he fights the urge to gulp it. It is hot in Georgia's flat, even though her curtains are drawn over the view of the old town outside. "One of Boursier's."

"Really? He's actually real?" Georgia pauses to stare at him, her glass halfway to her lips.

"Well, this story is, at least. It's called *A Hint Of Paprika*. It's…" Fellows goes into a long rambling account of the story before Georgia stops him.

"Woah, woah there. So what *is* it? Like… science fiction? The future? That sort of boy's stuff doesn't interest me. Escapism doesn't interest me—I want stories about *here*."

"No, you'd like it," Fellows says, "it's not like science fiction…" But he can't explain what it *is* like, or the effect it had on him; he can see Georgia is losing interest.

"Not for me," she interrupts him again. "Still, *you're* obviously smitten. Has it inspired you? Made you want to write again?"

"No, that's behind me, I've told you that…"

"I think it would be good for you," Georgia says softly. "Would help."

"Help? What do I need help with?"

"Oh fuck off," Georgia said, laughing. He isn't sure what she is getting at, isn't sure he wants to know, so he changes the subject.

"Can you drive, Georgia?" She looks at him, raises her wine glass.

"I'm sitting drinking this piss before the sun's even finished rising; do I seem like the kind of person who ever learned to drive?" she says. "Twat. *She* was always hassling me to," she adds, referring to her ex he supposes; it had been Fellows who had inadvertently and drunkenly broken them up. "And I kept saying, what's the goddamn point? To drive from one end of this city to the other? There's nowhere to bloody drive to!" She takes a gulp of her wine. "It's fucking hot," she says, almost to herself.

"Wait, wait," Fellows says, "weren't you seeing *her* before the quarantine?"

"No, no don't think so," Georgia says, and Fellows is confused; he'd met the couple on the first night after the quarantine had been declared, so Georgia must have been with her for at least a few weeks prior.

"How long do you think the quarantine has been in force for?" he says, feeling a sudden yet obscure panic that somehow their timelines won't match.

"Six months," Georgia says, "almost to the day." Fellows is relieved, and he lets himself be distracted from his unease. Maybe the wine so early in the day is affecting him more than he realises.

"You're pretty weird today," Georgia says. "More than normal I mean. I swear, you even *smell* weird."

"Smell weird? That's a... weird thing to say," he says teasing.

"Piss off. So, stay and have another with me?"

"No I... I'm going to try and buy the rest of the stories. Boursier's."

"Well that won't take all day will it?"

"But I need to get some old money first," Fellows says. "The bookseller wants paying in pounds," he adds, almost defensively.

"Where the fuck are you going to get some of that pre-quarantine money from?" Georgia says. "They made people hand most of it in didn't they?"

"Apparently you can get some from the protestors; they think using the old money will help. Idiots," he says. "Idiots *anyway*," he says, suddenly feeling annoyed. "What's the point of trying to get the quarantine lifted?" Fellows doesn't know quite why the thought of people trying to get the quarantine lifted annoys him. There is just something about his life that feels settled, here and now, and the protestors, like the ghost or the motorcars on the wrong side of the road, feel like things trying to shake that feeling from him.

"It would mean we could stop drinking this vinegar," Georgia says, raising her nearly empty glass. But her gaze doesn't quite meet his, and her smile for once doesn't shine in her eyes. Fellows sees her glance towards the window and he wonders if she is apprehensive about something.

"Georgia?" he says.

"*God*," Georgia says, shaking her head and body as if throwing some troublesome notion from herself. She looks away from the window; grins. "Pour us both another then, if you're staying."

"But I'm not..." Fellows starts to say, then stops himself. Course you are, you twat, he thinks.

AS A CONSEQUENCE OF THE second glass of wine, it is sometime after midday when Fellows nears the Mariners' Church. Fortunately the sight of its fish-shaped weathervane had been all the guidance he needed through the city's streets, for there had been no one around to ask for directions. Most people are keeping inside as the heat of the day nears its peak. Fellows's shirt is damp and sticks to his skin like he has been caught in a rainstorm. Whenever he pauses in the shadow of the tall, white-stoned buildings in this part of the city he shivers, a sensation almost pleasant in this heat.

The movement of people in the square in front of the church seems almost unnatural after the still and deserted streets he has walked through. There is a man selling watermelons from the back of a cart, as well as iced tap-water for over-inflated prices. Fellows doesn't care at that point, and he shivers again as the cool water slides down his dry throat; he feels the urge to tip the water over his head. Feeling more refreshed he looks round the rest of the square—a huddle of people are standing in the shade of the church, somewhat forlornly clutching pamphlets.

They are a mixed group, some look like office workers or officials of some kind, some maybe sailors, some maybe servants for the rich folks of the Enclave, some farmers whose land is on the other side of the border. They all look slightly ragged, dejected in the heat that has defeated them. They have damp brows and are so wet with sweat they look almost bedraggled. They attempt to stand a little taller as Fellows approaches.

"Hi," Fellows says weakly; he feels compelled to take a leaflet when, as if in surprise the man nearest hands him one. The mimeographed pamphlet is limp; maybe it is the heat but it feels sticky as if the ink has not properly dried. It sags in his hand as he makes a pretence at reading it.

The contents surprise him—he had expected practical measures meant to apply pressure on the unity government to redouble their efforts to get the quarantine lifted. But no, the pamphlet contains tips about how people can make their life more like it was before the quarantine, as if that life could just be recreated; there's a quasi-mystical feel to the text, as if the quarantine being lifted depended on enlightenment and epiphany, and not the actions of a group of bureaucrats from outside the city.

Idiots, Fellows thinks, crazy bloody idiots, but he sees that one of the things the pamphlet suggests is for people to use the pre-quarantine money again, so he has an opening. But before he can speak, the man who had handed him the leaflet looks over his shoulder; his overly-prominent Adam's apple bobs as he gulps.

"Oh shit," he says.

"What?" Fellows looks round, and see two Guardia have just entered the square, heading first to the entrepreneur selling watermelons. The protestors begin hiding their leaflets and literature—although the various protest groups aren't illegal and the right to free assembly hasn't been curtailed (yet—the paper is constantly suggesting it will) it's well-known that the unity government takes a dim view of the protestors and the police have taken to moving them on or otherwise inconveniencing them for the most spurious of reasons. Although this has stirred up some resentment, most of the public (including Fellows himself) are not putting themselves out to defend the protestors, especially as their demands are so quixotic.

"Wait," says Fellows, "I need to ask you something." The man is stuffing all the leaflets in the inside pocket of a coat too thick and woollen to look anything other than suspicious in this heat.

"What?" the man whispers, as if the Guardia negotiating at the melon stall are close enough to overhear.

"I was told that you… I was told you had some of the pre-quarantine money?"

The man looks puzzled; his eyes dart around as if his very nodding were a crime. "Yeah. Of course. You need some? You?"

Fellows hasn't time to be confused, he just names an amount he hopes will cover the rest of the Boursier stories. But the man is already pulling out notes from his overcoat and stuffing them into Fellows's hand. After not seeing them for so long the notes look odd, almost futuristic with the shining metal stripe up one side; nevertheless they are also grubby and slightly damp, as if they have changed hands too many times. There are more than he asked for and Fellows struggles to pull out his wallet with his hands so full. He can hear the footsteps of the Guardia start to cross the square towards them, echoing in the still and quiet air.

"How much?" he whispers to the man, grabbing his arm so that he can't leave.

"Huh?"

"How much? How much *real* money do you want?" The man continued to look baffled, as if this whole transaction has a script and Fellows was suddenly changing his lines.

"Why would I take your money?" he says, so quietly Fellows can't tell which word he is stressing.

"Why would *I* take yours?" Fellows says. The footsteps are closer now, unmistakably heading their way (all the other protestors have fled). He glances guiltily over his shoulder although he has done nothing wrong; the shadows of the two Guardia are stretched out and distorted in the bright sunlight, their bodies looking as misshapen as that of the ghost in his house.

"Huh?" says the protestor again. "It's not *mine*." And with that he pulls away from Fellows and dashes off, head down. He looks ridiculous in his greatcoat, obviously suspicious, and Fellows is surprised when the Guardia still walk up to *him*.

"Everything all right sir?" one of them says; he turns and sees them looking at him, their lips still red from watermelon. Very casually, one of them shifts her stance so that he can see the holster at her hip.

"Yes, yes, fine, thank you," Fellows says quickly. He finishes stuffing his wallet in the pocket of his white linen jacket; he is aware his hands are stained with the ink from the mimeographed leaflet. "Just looking, uh, just looking for somewhere to get out of this heat. Phew!" He blows air into his face, feeling himself a fool. The two Guardia look at each other.

"I'd very much suggest," one says, "that you move along and do just that. Sir."

Relieved, Fellows heads off in the opposite direction to the one the protestor took. Bloody idiots, he thinks again.

HE TRIES TO REMEMBER HOW to get to The Echo Bookshop, his thoughts struggling in the heat to connect where he is to where he needs to be. The afternoon is so bright it plays tricks on his eyes, the old brick and wood of the city lit up like glass and metal. As he squints the roads seem wider, the buildings taller but casting no shadows. When he turns up the alley towards the bookshop it is like reality has reasserted itself, for there is shade again, and in the dim light the cracks and faded past of the city are visible once more.

The Echo is as deserted as it had been the day before; it would be a relaxing, quiet place if not for the hostile frown of the boy behind the counter. I've got your damn money, what's the problem? Fellows thinks but doesn't say.

"It's me," he says instead.

"Yes?" the boys says, in his parched voice that doesn't suit his face. "And who are we today?" What a... what a *twat*, Fellows thinks.

"I'm here to buy the rest of the Boursier stories," he says briskly. "I've jumped through your little hoops, got your pre-quarantine money..."

The boy sniffs at him. "Seller's instructions," he says.

"Okay, fine," Fellows says, irritated and hot. "How much for the rest of them?"

The boy names a price just greater than the amount Fellows has.

"You're kidding me?" he says. "How can each of these stories be worth so much more than the one yesterday?"

"*Seller's* instructions," the boy says again. "It's more expensive if you buy them altogether."

"Surely that should get me a discount?" Fellows says. "I know, I know," he adds hurriedly, to avoid the bookseller's anger. "Seller's instructions. Look, I'm a bit short, can't you..."

"Oh for God's sake!" the boy shouts, his dry dusty voice cracking in his throat. He turns and digs a note from his pocket—old money—and hands it to Fellows. "Here, here!"

"Why are you giving me money?"

"From yesterday!" the boy yells. "I'm sick of it all!"

Yesterday? Fellows closes his eyes, feels the heat and pressure threatening to bloom into a headache in the darkness.

Does it matter? The bookseller is obviously another lunatic, but he has enough money for the remaining Boursier stories now, so after today he never has to step foot in the place again.

"Right," he says, "fine, fine. Here's the cash then." He hands all the pre-quarantine money, including the orange note the boy has just handed him, over. Silently the boy takes the cash, and hands over the further five stories. The one on the top of the pile is called *Into The Rain*. It appears to have been published as a series of newspaper columns, which someone has cut out and stuck to a flimsy cardboard backing, although it is not from any newspaper Fellows recognises; certainly not the city's local.

Fellows is about to turn away without further response when the boy speaks to him; he sounds genuinely intrigued. "Did you read the story you bought yesterday. Did you *like* it?"

Fellows is at a loss how to reply, both because of the boy's sudden change in tone and because he isn't quite sure; *did* he like it?

"It... It made me look at things differently," he says.

The boy gives a mirthless, hollow laugh that makes Fellows dislike him all over again. Wordlessly he turns to go; even through the dusty glass of the bookshop door he can see the oppressive white light outside, the sun obviously having risen to a zenith that lets it scorch the alleyway too. The thought of going out into that heat and walking home fills Fellows with a sudden weariness.

In one corner of the bookshop he sees the chair on wheels he noticed yesterday, although not in front of the desk anymore, as if the boy had kicked it in pique and sent it rolling away into the corner.

"Any objection," Fellows says, "if I sit here and read until it cools down? *Buyer's* instructions," he adds sourly.

The boy laughs, this time seemingly genuinely amused although Fellows can't see why. "Sure, why the hell not?" he says. "What's one more bit of craziness going to matter?"

Ignoring him, Fellows sits on the chair; it has an adjustable height and angle, but it is already at the correct settings for him. Taking the top most story from the pile, he starts to read.

Into The Rain by Boursier

There was a noise outside, or rather a further noise, one not the pouring rain or howling wind. Laura was on her feet almost instantly.

"Was that him? Was that Mogwai?"

"No I don't think so," Trent said quietly, his voice almost lost because of the storm outside.

"Go and look? Please?"

Reluctantly, Trent got up from his seat—his hair was still wet from the shower he'd taken when he got back from work, and Laura noticed a mark on the sofa. His shirt clung oddly to him, as if he hadn't dried himself properly. Maybe he hadn't—he had said that he didn't feel himself.

She heard him walk slowly downstairs to the front door, which he flung open to the sounds of the storm outside— there was so much rain that it made a constant, muffling sound, broken only by the shriek of the wind and the shaking of the trees. What had happened to the weather, she wondered. What had they done?

"Mogwai? Mooooooogwai!" she heard Trent calling, his voice thrown out into the storm and swallowed by it. She knew it was stupid—the damn cat was probably hiding under a bush or parked car somewhere, and would come back when the rain abated. He had never not come home. But something about the weather unnerved Laura—the sheer unnatural ferocity of it made it hard to imagine it ever ending.

"Shake his treats!" she shouted down to Trent.

"What?"

"His cat treats—shake the box. He might come then. The box with the fish on top," she added. She heard Trent grumbling—he always did what she asked when he knew it was important to her, even if he thought it to be pointless. But the sound of him shaking the treats was lost to the storm even more than his voice had been.

He came back upstairs. They lived in a three-story townhouse and their lounge was on the middle-floor— something she was glad of when she saw news footage of people being flooded out of their homes in another city just further north. When Trent entered the room his hair was if anything even wetter, his face seemed to drip. Had he actually stepped out into the rain looking for the cat? He was good to her.

"Sorry," she said. "Glass of wine? We've got that nice dry one in the fridge."

He seemed to flinch at her words, to be distracted from himself—"Huh?"

"Wine? Not too early?"

"Oh. Okay. Yes please."

Laura went into the kitchen and took the bottle out of the fridge, poured two large glasses despite it being only early evening. Each night she swore they wouldn't open more than one bottle, because if one was opened they usually drank it all. But what did it matter if they did? she thought sourly. She knew, if she turned the bottle to look at the back she'd see the silhouette of a heavily pregnant woman drinking from a wine glass with a cross over the top. What did it matter at all, Laura thought, and took a big gulp.

The kitchen was also on the middle floor, and from where she stood all she could see out of the window was a dark sky shot through with rain, like the sky itself was something that would inevitably be eroded away by the incessant water. She thought of Mogwai out in the storm and something in her heart fluttered; she felt a heaviness in her stomach that wasn't just the wine. Although he was an unfussy male cat who was out all hours, she still couldn't help but think of Mogwai as being something fragile that needed her protection. She opened the kitchen window; the storm seemed to deliberately whip warm, heavy raindrops into her face. She wiped them away frantically, as if they were something less pure than rainwater.

"Mogwai!" she called from the window; he could be right in front of her but given he was completely black she'd never realise. "Mog..."

She almost shouted as she felt arms encircle her—she could normally tell Trent just by his smell but ever since he'd come out of the shower earlier she'd had the impression he smelt different to normal. He must have got a new brand of shower gel or something. She started to pull away from his embrace, knowing he thought her worry for the cat an overreaction, but then she relented and let him hold her. He was her man, after all, and things weren't his fault. Weren't *necessarily* his fault, anyway—the doctors didn't seem to know what was wrong. The annoyance and intimacy of their attempts to find out would have been worth it, would have been something she'd have undergone a thousand times over, if it had turned out as she wanted in the end... But no. Laura took another gulp of her wine.

"I'm sure he's okay," Trent said to her; he kissed the side of her neck from behind and she felt like his clammy skin must be leaving a mark on her... But this close, this connected, she could smell the old hints of him, detect the faint scent of what she unconsciously thought of as 'Trent's smell', and this reassured her.

"I know, I'm just... You know how I worry about him," Laura said.

They'd bought Mogwai when all hope had seemed gone, although because the clinic had never found anything conclusively wrong she'd never fully given up. Still hadn't, even now Mogwai was five. She knew Trent hadn't really wanted a cat, but he'd agreed because he knew how much she did. She thought he had grown to love Mogwai, just like he had grown to love the rest of her stupid failures and anxieties.

"I really am lucky to have you," she said to him, turning to him and giving him a kiss; the sound of the storm provided a backdrop she tried to ignore. She could hear the pattering of raindrops on the sill, coming in from the open window.

"Yes, yes you are," Trent said with a grin.

"Cheeky sod. Here, drink your wine." But then she didn't hand it to him but kissed him again, suddenly deciding she wanted something else. Her hands cupped his face as they kissed and she tried not to care about how damp he still felt to her touch. A forelock of his hair had dropped down with the weight of water, and she felt it against her brow. But still, she kissed him and felt his arms tighten around her and, maybe more tentatively than normal, move down to squeeze her behind. She was pressed against him; he wasn't hard yet but she knew he'd had a tiring day, and she could *smell* him, underneath the odour of whatever new product he'd used (and which she'd tell him to throw away, and which he would), smell her man and at that moment it didn't matter if it were just the two of them and the cat, didn't matter if that was all there was ever likely to be...

From the open window came a high, piecing sound, cutting through the wind and rain, shockingly loud. They sprang apart from each other and even though the noise had been nothing like she'd ever heard before, Laura's first thought was:

"Mogwai!"

"I don't think that was him..." Trent started to say.

The sound came again and there was something dreadful about it, something alien but also, Laura was convinced, something hurting.

"What else can it be?" she said frantically. "It's, it's a *yowling* sound isn't it? You know how he makes weird noises when he fights other cats. Or what if he's been hit by a car?"

"It didn't sound like a cat to me."

"Oh please, what if he's been hit by a car, please go and check he's okay?"

"Out? Into that?" Trent turned his head towards the open window. For a moment she thought that, for once, he wasn't going to do what she asked—he thought it silly and no doubt it *was* silly, but if he could see she was upset was he really going to refuse her?

But Trent sighed and went downstairs, she heard him struggle into his coat and get the torch from the drawer. She looked out the window again, into the seething dark sky, and her thoughts were an echo of his words: you're sending him out into that? Out from what she had made into a good, ordered home for them, despite how empty it felt in any bedroom but their own. The storm didn't seem to be abating; when she peered downward she could see water swirling around the drains which were unable to cope with the sheer volume of rainfall. She knew the chances of Trent finding Mogwai, who was probably sheltering somewhere sensible, were slim and she almost called him back, but then she heard the front door slam and saw his figure stalk out into the storm. Within a few metres she could barely make him out, his slim shape erased by the sheets of falling rain. She could see the light of his torch moving backwards and forwards, but it seemed dimmer than it should be. If he was calling Mogwai's name then she couldn't hear him.

She wanted to shut the window, to shut out the rain and gale, but somehow it didn't seem fair when she had sent him out into it all. Why hadn't she gone herself? She was not normally one to act like a helpless damsel in distress. But something about that storm though... She watched the drops of rain as they seeped into the house, wetting the worktops. And then she thought fuck it, downed her glass of wine, poured herself another, and went back into the lounge.

She sat waiting for Trent to come back with increasing agitation not soothed by each sip of wine. She had only expected him to go out and look for a few minutes, and as time passed and as the storm outside grew if anything more ferocious, she started to get worried. It's only rain, she told herself, only *water*. She wondered why she always worried about those she loved, wondered what unfocused emotion was making her feel sicker each minute Trent, and Mogwai, weren't back in from the rain. The wind outside seemed full of fury; she kidded herself she could feel the house shake. The attack of raindrops against the window stopped her thinking anything sensible, as did the second glass of wine. But still the worry remained, and after a few more minutes Laura got up suddenly from the sofa, and stood perplexed for a second wondering if she was imagining the feeling of dampness from her clothes.

She nervously went back into the kitchen—she looked out the window but couldn't even see the light of Trent's torch anymore. What was he doing, how far had he gone? She wondered how angry he would be when he returned. I don't care, she thought, I just want him back. She was shaking and it was as if she was being buffeted by the storm despite being safe from it inside.

The sound of the rain increased and for a paranoid second she imagined the unnatural storm had torn the roof from the house leaving the third floor, with its three hopeful bedrooms, exposed. But she realised it was just Trent coming back inside. She hadn't seen him from the window because the batteries in the torch must have gone—something else to make him angry with her. She turned to refill his wine glass where he had left it on the kitchen worktop, and saw it was untouched.

She didn't hear him come up the stairs but suddenly he was in the kitchen with her, rain dripping from him, sodden clothes making him look dishevelled. His head hung down, his hair dark with water, hiding his face. She distantly noted that he didn't have Mogwai with him.

"God, don't stand there like that you'll catch your death," she said, "let me get you a towel." She made to walk past him to the bathroom upstairs. She hoped he wasn't mad with her but couldn't tell.

He grabbed her waist as she walked past. "Let me get out of these clothes," he said lasciviously in her ear. He pulled her towards him—she felt water from his clothes start to soak through hers, and again she couldn't help but think it more than water, or less, something she shouldn't be letting touch her. His wet tongue licked her ear, then her neck; his sodden hair brushed against her face. Something about the heaviness of his wet clothes made his touch more clumsy and rough than normal, and his fingers were crinkled like he'd been in the bath too long.

Laura opened her mouth to speak, unsure what she was going to say—should she really refuse him when he'd been out into the storm for her?—and then she heard the sound of rain and wind seeming to rush in from downstairs. Had he left the front door open? Why on earth would he have done that? The shock of it made her breathe in deeply and she realised...

Realised Trent smelt of nothing. Absolutely nothing; washed clean.

She pushed him away, wondering if she were going mad—when she looked at him it was manifestly Trent, her man, despite the way his wet clothes clung to him, despite the patch of water he was standing in. But his smell, or lack of it—it didn't seem like him. Didn't seem like this person could possibly be her husband.

"C'mon sugar," Trent said, looking at her from beneath the weight of his fringe. From the way his wet jeans clung to him she could see he had an erection. "Let's make babies."

She gasped at him, wondering how he could say such a hurtful thing. Was he drunk? But he hadn't touched his wine...

It's not him, it's not him, she said in her head. How can it be, when he smells of such nothingness?

He took a step towards her.

There was a yowling noise from the foot of the stairs.

"Mogwai!" Laura cried. She ran to the top of the stairs, called his name again, and felt a deep pressure in her chest as she heard the patter of his feet against the wooden stairs, even over the sound of the rain. (Trent had left the door open for some reason, and she could already see the hall carpet was soaked.) Mogwai ran into her arms and he was soft and warm and somehow dry, having kept himself safe in that way cats have. She buried her face in his fur and breathed in deeply.

Trent came out of the kitchen behind her. She told herself it had just been stress, he surely couldn't have meant what he said to her in the way it had sounded—maybe he just held out hope too? And how could she expect him to smell the same when he had been out in that downpour? She was an idiot.

She turned to him, Mogwai gathered up in her arms.

Why had he left the front door open though, she thought, and what *were* those sounds? Was is starting to flood down there?

She tried to smile, and felt the cat tense in her arms. And then Mogwai screeched at Trent, a yowl of utter hatred and fear as though he'd never seen the man before.

As though he smelt funny, Laura thought.

Trent, staring at the cat, opened his mouth seemingly too wide, and shrieked back.

THERE IS NO AUTHOR BIOGRAPHY underneath the story; of course, Fellows thinks. He realises he is struggling to read; the interior of the bookshop has grown dim. Why is it so dark at this time? There is a sound at the window, a sound he realises has been in the background for some time...

"Hope it was worth it," the bookseller interrupts his thoughts. "No refunds if you already know the ending."

Fellows ignores him, stands from the chair and feels the muscles in his hands cramp; he remembers the feeling from when he used to write. He looks to the window and sees that the sound he can hear is heavy rain against the glass. The small patch of sky visible is the grey of a winter sea.

"Christ, that rolled in quick," he says to the bookseller, and immediately regrets it. Is there anything he could say that wouldn't cause the man or boy or whatever the fuck he is to sneer at him, to look at him like he was speaking drivel? Fellows is glad he won't ever have to come to The Echo Bookshop again.

He gathers together his things—the magazines and anthologies and torn mimeographed sheets containing Boursier's stories, and the newspaper he has been carrying round since reading it in the café. As he does so he glances at the headline. It is not what he read this morning.

Storm Fury Continues To Batter City. How Much Longer? it says.

Fellows stares. This morning, he had read the paper through and the front page headline had been: *Drought Continues To Scorch City. How Much Longer?* The story below had been about how the small allocation of land the quarantined city still had available for agriculture was parched and how crop yields were low, but fortunately catch from the city's fishing fleet was still plentiful. He reads the story in front of him now in the dim light, sees it claims exactly the reverse: the fishing boats of the quarantined city have been unable to sail for weeks due to the storms, but the rain has at least made the harvest more bountiful than expected...

Fellows feels the same dislocated feeling as before, the same feeling of waking from a dream to a reality that doesn't match up. Is someone playing a trick on him somehow? Could the bookseller have somehow swapped the paper while he had been so engrossed in Boursier's story (and he had been engrossed)? But then he looks to the grey sky, smeared into something broken and spiral-shaped by the rain drops sliding down the window. What has happened to the weather? he wonders.

"How long has it been raining?" he says to the bookseller, who laughs as if he has been asked something rhetorical. He shrugs.

"Months? Years? Bloody quarantine," he adds, apropos of nothing Fellows can tell.

Fellows goes to the bookshop door, opens it—water is cascading down from the sky and from the gutters of the alleyway. To his left he can just see the marketplace at the end of the alley. Everyone dashing past has an umbrella or a large coat on, prepared as if they knew when they stepped out this morning how the weather would turn... Fellows considers how soaked he is going to get stepping out there in just his linen suit. It will blow over surely, he thinks, as the wind whips litter around the alley. Somewhere in the distance he can hear a cat yowling; he hopes George is safe inside.

"Shut the bloody door!" the boy yells behind him; when he looks down he sees rainwater has started to seep over the threshold and inside the shop. No time like the present, Fellows thinks, and darts out into the storm. Immediately the buffeting wind and rain make him hunch into himself; as he walks it feels like they are fighting against him. When he exits the alley he sees that the market square is packed with people, and the sound of the rain is magnified as it falls and drips from the canvas roofs of stalls that weren't there when he came this way. Wasn't it market day yesterday? Fellows thinks, but that is the least of his worries. He is shivering; he can feel the cold touch of water against his skin from his already wet clothes. Or something less pure than water, he thinks... As he dashes through the market, he vaguely notices the rows and rows of onions and aubergines and potatoes, and the seafood stalls conspicuous by their absence. He stands indecisively at the far end of the marketplace, wondering which street will lead him to his house by the quickest route. His wet hair falls into his face as he tries to think and he has to wipe it away.

Georgia, he thinks, Georgia's flat is nearer than your place. It is an easy route there, and a glass of something warming seems very tempting...

Forgetting about going home, he heads towards the old town.

HE IS SOAKED WHEN HE arrives at the lobby to Georgia's apartment block. It is empty and all he can hear is the rain outside and the drip from his clothes onto the cracked and faded tiles. The inside of the building is warm and humid; it reminds Fellows of the changing rooms of the local baths. As does the faint smell of piss.

Before calling the lift he goes over to a small bench next to a hulking wrought-iron radiator, and checks the bag with the new Boursier stories in it to make sure they haven't got wet. They are mainly dry; the only damp one is the one produced on a mimeograph, which has started to run slightly. He glances at the title as he pats it dry: *The Quarantine*. So Boursier does write some straight realism then, he thinks, at least that one won't be set in some strange other world. At least that one won't change things.

He considers this as he calls the lift for Georgia's floor—is that what he really believes? Surely the storm had blown in suddenly, and everything else was just the bookseller playing some stupid joke? He tries to keep things straight in his head, picturing the places he knows well: Georgia's flat, The Carousel, the streets between, his house... But the last only calls to mind piles of second-hand paperbacks, and fading, sightless eyes set in a boyish face. He is glad he hasn't gone straight back.

"Christ look what the cat dragged in," Georgia says when she opens the door to her apartment. "You're *soaking*. And what the fuck are you *wearing* Fellows?"

"What I was wearing this morning," Fellows says irritably. Georgia rushes to get something to dry him with, makes him take off his jacket and shirt and wraps him in an old towel. She makes him sit in front of a two-bar fire which smells of smoke when she turns it on. Fellows can tell she is concerned because she has yet to call him a twat. When he surely has been one, although in what exact way he couldn't say.

"This morning?" she says finally. "But you were wearing..." She looks momentarily at a loss, her eyes leave his and return. "But you at least had a coat this morning. And an umbrella, didn't you? What have you done with them? Oh I know," she adds, still fussing with the towel around him, tucking it in.

"Huh? What?"

"You traded them, didn't you?" She glances at the plastic bag full of stories. "You couldn't get any of the old money so you traded your coat and umbrella for more stories by that Boursier guy. Girl. Woman."

"No, Georgia," he says, smiling in spite of himself. "I got the money. I got the stories..."

"I mean, why would you even go *out* in that?" Georgia says, looking at the storm beyond the window and shivering. He can't help but look too and the roofs and spires of the city look completely different to how he remembers yesterday, greyer and more blurred and the sea invisible. Maybe something about the view disturbs Georgia too, for she gets up suddenly and turns away. As if to hide her reaction, she goes and fills the kettle, lights the gas with a match, and puts the kettle on the hob.

"But I didn't," he says, "when I went out this morning it was scorching, remember?" His voice speeds up; surely she will remember? "The damn heat-wave which the newspaper is obsessed with, almost as much as the quarantine..."

"What?" Georgia says; the concern in her eyes when she turns unnerves him more than any mockery would. "Are you... Have you got a fever?"

Fellows sits back, closes his eyes wearily. "Go on then," he says. "Tell me."

"It's been raining almost every day since the quarantine," Georgia says. *"That's* what the paper won't shut up about. This damn storm." She waves her hand at the window without looking at it. "You know this, you tw... *You* moan about it to me, how it ruins your precious walks around the stupid city! Jesus, and I mean really Fellows, *are* you okay?"

"You're saying it's rained since the quarantine?" Fellows says. "All through the summer?"

"The summer...?" Georgia says. "Look at it out there, Fellows, does it look like summertime to you?" The city is even less visible out of her window than before, as if there were nothing in the world but Georgia's flat and a smudge of ill-defined shapes crowding round it.

Fellows feels a sick, tight feeling in his stomach; his face blanches and he suddenly feels shivery despite the warmth from the fire. He reaches for his bag, wanting not Boursier's stories this time but the newspaper he has been carrying round all day. There was one thing he didn't check back at the bookshop... The wet paper almost falls apart in his hands which become black with its ink, but he can still make out the date at the top of some of the pages. It is not the date it said this morning; it is a midwinter date which ties in with Georgia's chronology and not that in his head. Fellows suddenly feels very weary; he closes his eyes and sighs.

"What side of the road do we drive on Georgia?" he says quietly.

"What? Weirdo. The left."

"Always?"

"Christ," Georgia says, "*yes*. I thought you could drive? It would have kept you dry if nothing else," she adds.

"I don't drive anymore," Fellows says. Georgia doesn't speak, and for a few seconds he listens to the rain battering against the windows; it is hard not to imagine it getting inside. Then that noise is drowned out by the increased agitation of the kettle on the hob.

"Are you putting something more interesting in that coffee than milk?" he says. He still has his eyes closed but he can tell Georgia grins in response.

"Of course. Medicinal. You twat."

Fellows smiles.

"GEORGE? GEORGE!" FELLOWS CALLS OUT into the evening street from his front-door, where he is sheltering from the continued downpour. When he reluctantly left Georgia's and walked home, wrapped up in Georgia's hooded raincoat ("*I'm not going out there*," she'd said), the streets had seemed almost washed clean of other people, and it was not hard to imagine that the storm *had* lasted for months. The sewers of the old town had not been up to the downpour, and unclean water had been flowing down the sides of the streets.

"George!" he calls again. He has never really noticed before how close the name of his cat is to that of his only friend in the city; he struggles to remember whether he or Lana had named the animal but he can't. Every time he thinks of Lana feelings of bitterness and guilt overwhelm any concrete memories of their time together. Surely Lana would have named George if it was she who wanted a cat in the first place? But he can't even remember that.

Regardless, when he arrived home George had shot out the door as soon as he opened it, and now he is concerned whether the pesky animal is sheltered somewhere from the rain. *Shake his treats*, he thinks, then: what kind of utopian world was Boursier imagining where normal people can afford to give their cat treats? And why is he even worried about the stupid cat anyway?

Nevertheless Fellows can't help but feel relieved when he sees George appear from behind one of the gas street-lamps and run towards him; somehow he doesn't look too wet. The cat comes inside and winds round his legs, purring. But there is something wrong, something odd. Fellows scoops up the cat into his arms, sees that it now has a tag on its collar where there was none before. He turns it round so he can read it.

Mogwai.

He lets the cat fall from his arms, watches the familiar way it goes into the pantry and stands next to the cupboard where he keeps its food, turns to look at Fellows and makes an expectant, impatient noise.

In a daze Fellows feeds the cat—George? Mogwai?—and then sits halfway up the staircase so he can watch it eat. He pulls out *Into The Rain* from the bag and reads it again, just to be sure. The cat comes and nuzzles him affectionately as he does so, causing the papers to shake in his hand. He absently scratches it behind its ears as he reads.

There's no way he can sense it, because it isn't physically real, but something makes Fellows certain that the ghost is behind him on the staircase. He turns and sees a crippled hand that was only inches away from touching the back of his head; he cries out and practically falls down the bottom steps of the staircase in an effort to get away. His head hits a banister with a crack and his vision blurs; there is a moment close to his face but it is just the cat moving away in annoyance at his ceasing to pet it. Twat, he thinks vaguely, and realises he is close to passing out. The thought that this will leave him unable to stop the ghost reaching him jolts him awake; he scrambles to his feet just in time and the ghost tumbles down the steps in a failed attempt to reach him. Despite the demonic, blank-eyed nature of the thing Fellows can't help but wince as its already damaged and buckled body bounces down the stairs without any sound. It lands on its back and waves its twisted limbs in the air as if it can't right itself. Then, mercifully, it fades.

Fellows is as soaked with sweat as the rain had made him earlier; his heart is pounding in time to the noise of the gale outside. This can't go on, he thinks. This is unbearable and I can't have it touch me. Can't. But how…

Fellows looks at the spot where the ghost had faded from his vision, which is surrounded by the scattered pages of *Into The Rain*, which he had let go of in his fright. He looks at the cat sniffing at the pages before turning away in indifference, the new yet rusty name-tag around its neck glinting in the lamplight. He looks back at the pages and hears the incessant sound of the rain outside.

And suddenly he knows how.

Boursier.

He will get Boursier to write *him* a story. A ghost story, he thinks, before realising that is not right. What he needs is almost entirely the opposite of a ghost story.

He needs Boursier to write him an exorcism.

PART THREE

SPOT THE DIFFERENCE

FELLOWS KNOCKS AGAIN ON THE wooden door to The Echo Bookshop; he is huddled in the doorway trying to keep out of the rain. The rain that's been falling for six months—or that's what the quarantined city thinks anyway. It's not what Fellows remembers. He remembers a summer so hot that when he sat on the quay looking at the still sea, he'd felt the heat of the stone through his clothes. And the season wasn't the only change that had seemed to be caused by Boursier's stories. Fellows feels a new unease in the city; when he walks the streets he is not sure everything is as he remembers, but he can't put his finger on anything different. And so he feels more on edge than normal (the quarantine itself having hardly affected him), more paranoid that there are things happening that he doesn't understand.

But the solution is surely simple—he won't read any more of Boursier's stories. Then nothing else can change. The bad weather will pass, he doesn't care what side of the road people drive on (Fellows doesn't drive, anymore), he can learn to call his cat Mogwai.

Or it would be simple, if it wasn't for the fact that Fellows plans to read one more Boursier story; to get Boursier to write one for him, no less. For if stories really can alter the quarantined city there is one thing Fellows surely wants altered. He wants the blank-eyed and silent ghost of a young boy who haunts his house *gone*. Written out of reality as if it never was. Not that he is scared of the ghost as such, although its silent and crippled body is unnerving, as is the way that its one goal seems to be to reach out and *touch* Fellows…

"Open up!" Fellows shouts at the unyielding wooden door. The Echo Bookshop is the only lead he has on Boursier. The shop is situated at the end of a grubby alley hidden to one side of the market square; the alley's uneven cobbles are splattered with gull shit and water drips from its clogged gutters. The gutters had been dripping a few days ago when he had first come here, in the intense heat of a summer only he remembers; despite the drought the gutters had been leaking water and had been overflowing with bright green moss and mould. Like a small piece of the city, out of reach and unnoticed, had already changed to match Boursier's story before he'd even read it.

Fellows bangs on the door again; his wrist aches, and he smiles, thinking of the crude jokes Georgia will no doubt make when he sees her later. In his other hand he is clutching a waterproof bag, in which he has the journals and magazines featuring the other Boursier stories. Although he won't be reading them himself, he is loathe to leave them unattended. What if someone *else* read them? Read them all through and changed *everything*? He has no idea if such a thing is possible but why take that risk?

Of course I could just leave them here, no one would read them *here*, he thinks; he has never seen a single customer in The Echo Bookshop.

"Open up! Hello? Open…"

The door finally opens, shoving Fellows backwards and out into the rain. Annoyed he darts into the gloomy interior of the shop; the boy with the old man's voice and misaligned eyes takes a step back and curses.

"Oh Christ," he says, "what do *you* want? I told you no refunds. It's not my fault if you bought such drivel." His smile is as unfriendly as ever, conveying the idea that he knows something Fellows doesn't despite the fact that he talks such obvious shit.

"I don't want a refund," Fellows says, "I want to find the author."

"You...huh?" The boy's one straight eye bulges, as if Fellows has said something preposterous.

"Seller's instructions," Fellows says.

"What..?"

"Seller's instructions! That's what you took such joy saying yesterday!" Fellows tries to control his annoyance; he normally shrinks from confrontation but something about the bookseller riles him so. "You already told me you're just selling his works on commission, so I *know* you know how to contact Boursier."

The boy pauses, he is visibly weighing up his next words. He has shrunk back against one of the tall, dusty bookshelves (*Fictions F*) and he cautiously emerges from its shadow.

"He didn't give me an address," he says slowly, "and he said he's not on the telephone. He'll come here to get his commission but..."

"Then I'll just wait shall I?" Fellows says, but he has missed his chance; the boy has already regained some composure.

"Be my guest. He's coming the day after tomorrow."

"C'mon, something!" Fellows slams his palm against the bookshelf in frustration; it is so rickety it moves to his touch despite the weight of paperbacks it carries.

"God you're as annoying as *he* is," the boy says, looking at Fellows as if for some kind of reaction. Then he turns, saying, "He did leave me something, trying to convert me. Idiot." The boy walks with jerky movements to his desk and searches through the pile of books atop it, sniffling at the dust thrown up, until he finds one with a makeshift bookmark lolling out of its pages. He pulls out the piece of paper and, returning to Fellows, hands it to him.

Fellows unfolds it. *End The Quarantine Now!* he reads; the ink of the words has run as if it were once caught in the rain. *More Holistic Measures Needed!* he reads below, whatever *that* means. He doesn't read any more of the crudely printed leaflet.

"He's one of them?" he says. "You think Boursier is one of the protestors? But he might just have taken this rubbish in the street, out of politeness. Or for a bookmark, like you…"

"No," the bookseller says, his hauteur back. "Don't you listen? He tried to convert me. He isn't just a protestor. He's in charge; he's their leader."

THE STREETS OF THE CITY look a different colour in the rain, the stone of the buildings duller and the shadows cropped under the lid of clouds. Maybe the differences are why Fellows keeps getting lost as he walks towards the Mariners' Church; it is only the fact that every so often a gap in the buildings allows him to see its fish-topped spire that keeps him on the right path. There are fewer people around than usual at this time of the morning, because of the rain he supposes, but more motorcars than he has ever seen in the city before. The vehicles look faintly unreal in the spray they throw up from the wet roads. He feels they are disappearing from his vision too early, and the noise they make is muffled in the misty air. Where are they getting the petrol from? he thinks, looking at the rainbow patterns of oil in the water, trails that peter out too soon.

It is still early when he arrives at the small square in front of the church, and none of the protesters are there. Idiots, he thinks automatically, rushing to shelter in the church vestibule. He seems to have lost all sense of time since the clouds appeared overhead, blocking his view of the sun. Christ, you're not a sailor, he thinks to himself, annoyed by his own obscure thoughts. Surely you have... But when he raises his arm to look at his wrist there is no watch there, just the white mark of its absence against skin tanned by a summer heat-wave equally absent. At least it is some external evidence of what he remembers, proof that he isn't delusional.

But to his left, as if mocking that assertion, he sees a plaque on the vestibule wall; it shows the names and dates of fisherman and sailors from the city who have died at sea; this city reveres it sailors. What has caught his attention is that one of the dates is new, the lettering a brighter colour. Some other poor sod lost in the storms no doubt, the storms he can't remember. Nor can he remember any such story in the local newspaper, although it would have devoted pages to a sailor's death. There is only so much real news inside the city borders after all.

He tries to think if one of the characters in Boursier's stories had lost a watch, but can't remember.

Sod it, he thinks. You can't blame *everything* on Boursier. You're just tired; you've broken your routine and this is the consequence. He had not slept well. After his encounter with the ghost the previous evening he had lain as if paralysed, while in his dreams the blank-eyed boy had run his broken hands across Fellows's skin, a faint touch from hands too sensitive to their own pain. As if ghosts could touch, could feel! He still shudders to remember, but as always it isn't just the ghost which has faded, but the urgency and intensity of his revulsion towards it too, as if both routed by daylight.

Such daylight as there is—Fellows decides to go and get a coffee and then come back to the church to find the protestors later. He turns up his collar and heads back out into the rain. But it is as if the quarantined city is under curfew as well, for he sees few people out in the streets and nearly all of the shops and public buildings are shut. There are certainly no cafés open nearby, and after much walking and cursing Fellows resolves to just go to the Carousel, which he can't conceive would be shut, despite the walk.

Its door is open and its windows lit up as he approaches, a soft warm light seemingly from a different palette to the grey world around. He feels a certain relief, not just to be out of the rain but that at least this bit of the world tallies with his thoughts. At the counter he gives his usual order; as he fishes in his wallet for the fiddly, post-quarantine coins, he notices his fingers are smudged black again. For a moment he wonders if he is confused and he has already read the newspaper somewhere this morning, but no—when he sees the headline it is nothing he remembers. *Quarantine Decision Not Ours To Make Say Unity Government.*

"You're, uh, on your own today?" he says as casually as he can to Gregor when the man brings him his coffee; Gregor doesn't normally wait tables.

"Yes," Gregor says flatly.

"No, what's her name, Leianna, to help you?"

Gregor pauses, and Fellows sees something he has never seen before from the man: the briefest of smiles. He feels his face redden, bends to take a sip of his coffee and scolds his tongue.

"No, she said something had come up and she couldn't work today. Maybe to do with her son, you know?"

"She has a son?" Fellows says. "She doesn't look... I mean, how old?"

"Older than she looks," Gregor says. "The boy is seven now. Some bastard left her alone with him; the boy is a cripple."

"A cripple? So that's why her... husband..?"

"Just boyfriend. Just a boy," Gregor says with the same smile.

"... left her when he was born. God." Fellows blinks and is lost in his own thoughts; he doesn't hear what Gregor says next to him.

"No, no, the boy was okay when he was *born*."

"Uh, um..." Fellows comes back to himself, becomes aware Gregor is lingering. "Here, for the tip jar," he says, giving Gregor two of the thin coins; the new money is of such poor quality that the face of the city's founder is almost rubbed into anonymity.

"You weren't going to try and *take* the tips again?" Gregor says and slaps Fellows heavily on the shoulder with one broad, tattooed hand to show he is joking. Gregor joking! Fellows wonders if his daily patronage of the Carousel has paid off and he can be considered a regular, or if Gregor's new smile is just something else in this city different to how he remembers it being.

WHEN HE EVENTUALLY FINDS HIS way back to the Mariners' Church, the protestors from the previous day are there, looking as wretched in the rain as the sun. They stiffen as Fellows approaches as if suspecting him of being an undercover Guardia—not such a paranoid assumption, maybe, given the rumours.

Fellows endures the same stop-start, awkward conversation with the protestor who had given him the pre-quarantine money yesterday; the man gives no sign of remembering him or the sunlight they'd both sweated in. Fellows quickly realises that the protestor isn't going to confirm Boursier is their leader, much less tell him where the writer lives. Taking a different approach, he asks how he can help lift the quarantine, despite how ridiculous and unpalatable the idea is to him.

"But, uh, no offence," he says, "but I'm not standing round in the rain handing out leaflets. Help you write them maybe—there were some shockingly misplaced semi-colons in that one you gave me yesterday!" He smiles to show he is joking, but the protestor just stares at him blankly. Then the man turns and confers with one of his fellows, the words hidden under the sound of rain on their coats.

"You're a writer?" the protestor says eventually.

"Yeah," says Fellows reluctantly; he feels more guilty about this small lie than the big one about wanting to join the protestors. Or maybe it isn't guilt, but unease. But why could it possibly matter now, after all these years? Lana would laugh to see him now, after all those times he'd crowed about it in the presence of other women.

"You can go to the house then," the protestor says, in a voice loaded with more import than the words seem to deserve.

IT INVOLVES ANOTHER WALK THROUGH the lessening rain to what Fellows thinks of as the 'posh' part of the city—tall houses sat on the higher ground above the cliffs and West Bay, looking down on the rest of the city, from which they are partially separated by a large civic park with a lake and bandstand in the centre.

"Boursier lives in the Enclave?" he had asked when the protestor had given him the address.

"No, no," the man had said, his eyes scanning Fellows's face for a reaction. "It's just somewhere we meet."

Mockingly, the people of the city have always called this quarter the 'Enclave', an inaccurate name that has nevertheless stuck. There are rumours that the inhabitants of the Enclave are manoeuvring to be excluded from the quarantine, leaving the rest of the city to its fate; how that would even be possible when they are all as sealed off as everyone else Fellows doesn't know. But he has no doubt their wealth and family connections will give them a greater chance of success than whatever ragtag methods the protestors are using. There must remain *some* connections to the outside world, and aside from the unity government itself the old-money clans of the Enclave are the most likely to know of and exploit them. But then how come the protestors have connections here; have they got patronage? Or are they being used in some way?

At least walking these streets Fellows is not much discomforted by the real or imagined differences with how he remembers them, for he very rarely comes to the Enclave. The avenues and boulevards seem strange to him all by themselves, spacious and tree-lined, a world apart from the part of the city he lives in, never mind somewhere like the old town. The houses are tall and classically proportioned, set back from the streets by large lawns and high walls. A few still have private cars displayed on their drives, more than Fellows was expecting. Bastards, he thinks vaguely.

The Enclave seems almost deserted, the only sound the storm wearing itself out in the trees. There's none of the cat-calling of the old town or hustle of the market or harbour. The only people Fellows sees—gardeners, delivery boys, dog-walkers, what he assumes is a wet nurse—are obviously not inhabitants either, and they give him a look of comradeship as if he were a servant here too. None of them speak other than a muttered greeting as they pass. Only the loud gulls are rebellious, cawing revolution from the crap-stained roofs.

When he finds the address he has been given he sees the house is hidden behind a tall white wall; from the entrance he can see a pebbled drive with tyre ruts down the middle curving through a large garden, but the house itself isn't visible. A squat standing stone marks the boundary, with holes in the top that Fellows can't fathom the purpose of. He is about to start the walk up to the house when he feels a presence behind him; he turns and sees two Guardia behind him. Private guards for the rich, he thinks sourly.

"Everything alright sir?" one says; he has the confused feeling they are the same two he saw yesterday, although surely their beat wouldn't encompass both the church square and the Enclave. Nevertheless, the way one of them shifts her stance so that the holster of her gun becomes visible gives him a feeling of déjà-vu.

"Yes, uh, fine," he says.

"This is private property you know," the male Guardia says casually; Fellows does not think it will do any good to say that in fact the street is a public space and he hasn't actually stepped onto the driveway.

"Sure, I was just, well..." His powers of invention desert him.

"It's okay he's with me!" someone calls out behind the two Guardia; fortunately the fact they both turn round to look means he doesn't have to keep the look of surprise off his face.

"New boy," Leianna says to the Guardia, nodding at Fellows. "I meant to get here before him but you know, late night." She grins at the male Guardia; a fake grin Fellows recognises from her interactions with over-friendly customers in the Carousel.

"I'll bet," the Guardia says, trying to leer; his colleague looks away in disgust.

"C'mon you," Leianna says, taking Fellows by the arm and leading him up the drive; the male Guardia says something else to her as a parting shot which in his confusion Fellows doesn't catch.

"Twat," Leianna says under her breath.

For a few moments, conscious of the Guardia at their back they walk in silence through the dying rain; the crunch of the gravel underfoot seems loud and accusatory. When they have walked far enough to be out of sight they stop.

"What are *you* doing here?" Fellows says.

"I should be asking the same of you, hanging around outside," Leianna says. "I assume you were sent. Or have you been stalking me?" Her voice is self-deprecating, albeit with the hint of something more steely beneath. She is dressed in a large raincoat with a hood that hides her thick curly hair and rustles as she speaks.

"No, I... Of course not," Fellows says. "I'm looking for Boursier. I was told by the people handing out leaflets to come here."

"Boursier?" Leianna says. "Here?"

"Yes, I'm trying to find him," Fellows says. "I'm a writer too," he adds, partly because he knows telling her the real reason would sound crazy, but also because he realises he wants to impress her. He tries to change the subject before she can react: "But what are you... Do you work here?"

"What? No!"

"Don't worry, I won't tell Gregor if you're moonlighting," he says nervously. "After all, I know you must need the extra money, I guess, with your son and..."

"How do you know about my son? If you know so much about it you should know it's not money I need." Leianna looks away from him, up to the birds in the sky. "But no, I don't work here. Don't tell Gregor you saw me, but I don't work here. Look, let's get inside out of this weather. But I'll tell you now, there's no Boursier in there."

They continue up the drive which is so deep with pebbles that walking is an effort, like a beach of shifting sands. When the house comes into view Fellows sees it is tall and made of cream-coloured stone; it has all its shutters closed but he notices smoke coming from the chimneys. The drive continues round the back of the building; the small discreet sign that points the way says *Tradesmen* and this is the route Leianna leads him. There is an equally spacious lawn and garden at the back of the house, lined with winter roses and tall conifers screening out the sounds from outside.

Leianna opens a black varnished wooden door at the back of the house and leads Fellows into a small, ill-lit corridor. She takes her coat off and shakes loose her hair; Fellows notices with surprise she is wearing her waitress uniform. In the dim light of the house it makes her look like a servant.

"It's me!" she shouts into the gloom but there's no response.

"Won't the... won't the owners hear?" Fellows says cautiously.

Leianna looks at him for a few seconds, then steps back across the threshold and into the drizzle outside. She beckons Fellows to do the same.

"They're not around," she says. "I thought you would have been told otherwise I'd have said already. The family who lived here, some posh buggers, they were on vacation when the quarantine was enforced. Just the two of them; couldn't have children I guess. But anyway, they weren't allowed back in. And with no one to pay their wages the servants soon stopped coming here too. And one of those servants joined us…"

"So they just gave you the keys? Isn't that illegal?"

"You saw... The Guardia haven't twigged. They thought *you* were a servant." Leianna giggles slightly.

"But you've still got *your* job," Fellows says. "Why do you need to join the protestors?"

"I have my reasons. I don't want to have to explain it all to you if you can't work it out." Before Fellows can say anything else she quickly steps back across the threshold of the house.

"It's me!" she shouts in exactly the same way as before. Again there is no reply. She looks at Fellows expectantly, the look of annoyance from her face gone. He steps inside.

Leianna leads him down the dark corridor, not speaking. In the silence he is aware of the bag he is carrying rustling as they walk. "Books," he says apologetically, although she hadn't asked. He is surprised when she gives a brief laugh at this.

She opens a door for him and leads him into a kitchen dominated by a large wooden table and two unlit stoves; it is a kitchen for people whose idea of entertaining is to feed upwards of twenty people. But it is quiet and spotless today, although Fellows sees there are two people present. One old man with sailors' tattoos on his arms is sitting at the oak table reading a newspaper; Fellows sees it is an old one, from before the quarantine. The headline is about the threat of war in some far off place; Fellows had been passionately opposed to the war at the time, but now he finds he can barely remember the name of the country threatened. It's probably all over now, he thinks, out there. His memories of the outside world are there but weakened, like atrophied muscles.

The other person in the room is a teenage girl who is methodically taking down canned goods from the shelves and reading the labels intently. Fellows looks to Leianna and is about to say something but she puts one finger to her lips to stop him.

She leads him from the kitchen and out into a large dining room lit by candles which drip wax onto the dark gleaming wooden sideboard, atop which a stuffed gull is frozen in a silent shriek. Each place at the central table is laid as if for a four-course meal. Every seat but one is occupied but no one is eating, there is no food. Each seated figure is reading something: books, magazines, catalogues. The one man who has risen from his seat is looking intently at framed maps on the walls; Fellows can't quite comprehend their outlines in the flickering light but none of them seem to be of the quarantined city itself.

None of the people present even look up at Fellows and Leianna.

"Look, what is going on?" Fellows says, too loudly—the man perusing the maps on the walls looks up at them in disapproval. Fellows has spent too much of his life in libraries and quiet bookshops not to feel chastised. He drops his voice to a whisper. "Are they protestors? But what are they doing?" Despite the absurdity something about the room full of people reading makes him uneasy; he thinks of the pamphlet he took from the protestor in the heat and the quasi-mystical ways to end the quarantine it contained.

Leianna stands on tiptoes to whisper into his ear, and despite his confusion he can't help but notice the intimacy of that, of her hand touching his waist to steady herself.

"I can't explain. I don't fully understand it myself. Jaques will explain. C'mon."

Outside the dining room is the front door and the grand front entrance of the house, rather than the servants' door they had used. There are plush carpets, paintings on the wall, and an imposing staircase leading up to a set of balconies circling the first floor. On every step of the staircase, two abreast, people are sat reading. Somewhat needlessly, because he hadn't been about to speak, Leianna looks at him and puts her finger to her lips again. Then she takes his hand and leads him up the staircase past the people who are reading, who ignore them completely. Their frozen postures remind Fellows of the cormorants drying their wings on the abandoned ships in the harbour. He can't help but glance at the book titles as he passes—*The Famished Market*; *A Drop Of Ink*; *The Circle Sea*—but none are any he recognises. At the top of the staircase they turn left and Leianna lets go of his hand, and gestures for him to go through into one of the first-floor rooms.

The sudden sound of voices is confusing, especially as they are talking over each other and Fellows cannot immediately identify a source. In front of him a man with expansive white hair sits at a bureau; the large window behind him gives a clear view of the Enclave houses and mansions and gardens, and the blue sky and sea in the background. The man's eyes are closed and he appears to be trying to concentrate on what the voices are saying.

A man stands on each side of the room, both reciting from what appears to be a script in their hands. Both have the stocky build and uneven features of professional fighters. Their eyes are closed, as if trying to show they have memorised their lines.

"Am I being lifted up?" the man on Fellows's left says.

"They'll never be a perfect fit," the man opposite says; Fellows can't tell if it is meant to be in reply or not.

Leianna quietly shuts the door behind her and walks up to the man at the desk, who doesn't open his eyes.

"Jaques?" she says quietly, and then again when he doesn't stir.

The man looks at her like someone awakening from a dream; a particularly pleasant one perhaps for he does not look happy at the interruption.

"Jaques, this is Fellows," Leianna says quickly. The man raises a languid eyebrow; "Fellows?" he says as if doubting it.

"The expected deliveries hadn't got through," one of the men says.

"Five petals," the other says. Fellows has the crazy notion that if he snatches the pieces of paper from their hands they would be blank.

"Okay Fellows," Jaques says. "And what can we do for you?"

"I want to find Boursier."

Jaques stares at him for a few seconds, then claps his hands once. The men stop mid-sentence. "We're in danger of going off script here," he mutters, glancing at Leianna as he does so, who looks away. The room seems very quiet with the cessation of the voices and Fellows tells himself not to buckle and speak first.

"So, is he here or not?" he says eventually.

"No. He isn't. But I can tell you where he is," Jaques says.

"Okay, where?"

"Why do you want to find him? Do you even *know* this person?" Jaques adds, looking at Leianna. "How do we know he isn't a spy?"

"Oh for heaven's sake..." Fellows says. "I want him to write me a story, okay?" He's pleased that Jaques looks confused at this, even if what he has said is just the truth. He reminds himself that all this craziness will be worth it to rid himself of the damned ghost.

"And you'll read this story when he's written it?" Jaques says, slowly as if thinking something through.

"What? Of course I will, that's the whole point! To change..." Fellows stops himself from speaking; his idea seems nonsense if he were to speak it aloud. The idea that stories can change reality.

"To change something. Yes." Jaques says.

"Wait, what? You know..?"

Jaques waves a hand towards the door, back out to the house full of people reading.

"What do you think *we're* trying to do?" he says.

FELLOWS ALLOWS THE TWO MEN to pull him away from the door, his energy spent. His fist aches from hammering on the door which he hadn't realised Leianna had locked behind him. His throat is raw from shouting. You crazy bastards, *stop*, you crazy crazy bastards...

The two men fling him down onto a sofa to the side of the bureau, from which Jaques hasn't moved despite the commotion. Something about Jaques annoys him; to the manor born, he thinks. Most of the protestors in this house no doubt feel as out of place as he does, but he gets the impression Jaques feels right at home. I bet the Guardia didn't challenge you coming up the drive, he thinks sourly, and I bet you didn't scuttle round the back to servants' door.

With a glance at Jaques as if for approval, Leianna sits next to Fellows. He turns to smile at her, wincing at the pain where he had been dragged away from the doorway as he does so.

"It's okay," she says softly.

He shakes his head, unsure if it is. He remembers the sick feeling of panic at Jaques's words, at the idea that everyone reading in this crazed house was trying to twist what was real as much as he had by reading Boursier's stories. He'd felt like if that were true then he could just be swept away, everything he'd thought a solid foundation shifting. But maybe he had overreacted. After all, the implication is they have been following this crazy path for some time. Maybe the idiots are doing nothing more than giving themselves eyestrain.

"Why?" he says without looking at Jaques. "Why?"

"My theory," Jaques says, "*our* theory, is that the quarantine is as much mental as physical or political; that those of us inside the city are as responsible as those on the outside."

"What nonsense!" Fellows says laughing. "The reports in the paper said it was enforced by agencies outside of..."

"Have they ever said *why* the quarantine was imposed on us?"

"Well, no."

"Is there any disease? Any plague?"

"Depends if you believe the conspiracy theories," Fellows shrugs. "The bodies dumped at night out at sea." He doesn't believe it himself; no one he knows has got sick or mysteriously vanished. But then who does he see with anything like regularity? Just Gregor and Georgia, really.

"We don't believe in conspiracy theories," Jaques says solemnly.

Fellows can't help but laugh again. "But what, you believe that reading stories will help lift the quarantine? That stories can change things?" Saying it out loud, he ceases to believe it himself. The city must always have driven on the left, he must have been confused about there having been a heat-wave...

"We believe that reading of life *outside* the quarantine, of life before and after the quarantine, will help break the mental bonds that form the quarantine."

"What crap," Fellows says. "And besides, what's so *bad* about the quarantine anyway?"

Leianna breathes out an exasperated sigh next to him; he feels her body stiffen before it slowly loosens again, as if she were forcing herself to relax. It's only now he realises how close she has sat next to him on the sofa.

"Think it crap all you want," Jaques says smoothly, "but I'm not giving you one hint of Boursier's location unless you read something for us. Here, now."

"What?"

"After all, you've come prepared," Jaques says, having lost all pretence of being friendly. His tone of voice is that of a member of the gentry asking someone to do something that he could just order them to do anyway. He takes one of Boursier's stories from the bag Fellows had brought with him. Jaques looks at the title and gives a snorting laugh. "Of course..." he says. He hands it to Fellows.

Spot The Diff...

"I'm not reading this," Fellows says, looking away. But then if the whole thing is nonsense, if he is mistaken and reading is just reading why should he care? But then, if that is the case he doesn't need to find Boursier anyway...

He is so confused by what he believes, feeling both afraid and sheepish at his fear, that he doesn't know what to do. And in his indecision, when Leianna leans into him, lets her leg press against his, and says "please?" into his ear, it's a tipping point that, while small, is enough.

He begins to read.

Spot The Difference by Boursier

"But they look *the same* Daddy!" Alicia said in frustration.
Stefan gestured towards the two pictures.
"Look closer."
He was sat with the younger (by three minutes) of his two daughters at the dining table; two of the four seats were empty. Alexia could be heard on the swings outside. Stefan was trying to get Alicia to look at two black and white drawings that did at first glance seem identical; they showed a clown getting out of a clown-car even as it was

still moving; one of the clown's large shoes was about to step on the tail of a startled looked cat.

"They're the *same*," Alicia said, squirming in her seat.

He'd tried to get Alexia interested in the book too, but she'd just asked why *they* couldn't have a cat, and he'd had to explain yet again that they didn't actually own the bungalow in which they lived. That the Mackenzies had built on the grounds, hidden from the main house by a row of conifers that Stefan had had to plant himself. Of course when they'd built the new servants' quarters (as Stefan couldn't help but think of the bungalow) the Mackenzies hadn't known what would happen to Alana. They'd been very good letting him and the girls stay on, despite the reduced hours Stefan could do in the garden. Very good; everyone said so. Stefan gritted his teeth.

"Look at the flower on his jacket..." he said.

"It's squirting water!"

"Yes, but look how many petals it has. One, two, three, four, five, six. But over here..." He pointed to the left-hand picture.

"There's... " Alicia counted. "Five petals!"

"That's right, so draw a ring around them on each side. That's one difference we've found. There are nine others, can you see any?"

"No."

The book was called *Spot The Difference! Fifty Fun Puzzles!* although already Stefan was doubting it had been a wise purchase. Alexia hadn't even entertained the notion of looking at a book (he could hear a rusty squeak outside, every time she reached the height of a swing) and Alicia didn't seem to be giving it her full attention.

"Just try darling, have another look."

"Maybe Echo will be able to see some," Alicia said.

"Maybe. Ask him."

Before the accident, he and Alana had quarrelled over how harmful to her development Alicia's imaginary friend might be. Stefan had thought 'Echo' nothing more than a half-conscious way for Alicia to distinguish herself from her twin sister now they were growing up, but Alana had not liked the idea of her daughter believing the products of her imagination to be real. Stefan had been an aspiring writer when he'd met Alana, but partly due to her indifferent attitude to anything fictional he'd let it slip.

"Echo says the cat's collar," Alicia said, breaking into his thoughts. She didn't have any special way of talking to Echo, no waggling Redrum finger or rolled back eyes. She just paused for a few seconds, as if she really were listening to someone. "He says it's got different letters."

Stefan blinked; quite right he saw—on the left picture the collar was marked GF and on the right MW. That had been the one difference he'd not yet spotted himself.

"Well done, Alicia," he said.

"Well done, *Echo*," Alicia said primly. "Also, Echo says in this one you can see the car's back wheel but in this one you can't. *Look*, Daddy."

"That's right," he said, "seven more to go..."

He didn't have to help Alicia as much as he'd thought he might; once she'd grasped the concept she (via Echo) quickly spotted the remaining differences. On the next page, as a reward for completing the puzzle, was a story about the clown: the driverless car crashed into the jelly factory so everyone got to eat jelly, including the cat whose tail remained mercifully untrodden on.

"Stories are good, aren't they Daddy?" Alicia said.

"Yes," he told her, "stories are very special, don't forget that."

"Stories are rubbish," Alexia said from behind them, making him jump. "They don't *do* anything." He could only tell her apart from Alicia by the leaf in her hair and the scabs on her knees.

The next day it poured, which was good because it meant the Mackenzies were less likely to come across to 'see how he was', but bad because it meant Alexia was trapped inside the bungalow. She would have gone tramping out in the rain and mud if Stefan hadn't forbidden it; a few weeks ago she'd disobeyed him and he'd had to call her name from the door like she was a cat he wanted to come home, just as the Mackenzies had walked by. They had given him a look, half sympathetic half condescending; a look of pity from one end of the social spectrum to the other. He'd been sterner than normal when Alexia had finally tramped in out of the drizzle.

The twins didn't ever seem to play together, meaning Stefan had to direct his attention to two parts of the lounge simultaneously. At least it kept his mind from the disturbing news reports on TV that morning. But his heart sank when he looked away from Alexia to see Alicia, sat in front of a window framing a grey sky falling in on itself, playing with a toy carousel. Alexia's favourite toy.

Alexia had taken to the model carousel, with its cheap plastic horses and metallic tune, more than anything else he or Alana had ever bought her. The one and only time Alicia had played with it there had been a total meltdown, screaming from both girls as Alexia had tried to take it back. He'd felt like screaming himself, by the end.

Hurriedly, before Alexia could see, Stefan went over. "Now Alicia," he'd whispered, "you know you can play with other toys belonging to your sister, but not that one."

"But it's not *hers* Daddy."

"Alicia..."

"It's not hers. Echo made it for me."

"Now look..."

"He did!"

Stefan closed his eyes briefly. Had Alana been right and 'Echo' was symptomatic of some deeper issue? He took the carousel from Alicia's hands ready to take it back to her sister and then blinked in surprise.

It wasn't the same.

For a start it didn't move, the model was made all of a single piece. And it didn't look right: the horses, which should have had bright eyes and flaring nostrils, were more lumpen things, their mouths toothless slits. They had stumps not hooves, and the poles of the carousel looked fused into their bodies... Stefan didn't know what to make of it. Had the model somehow fallen into the fire and the plastic melted? There was a certain slick congealed texture to it that might suggest so, but that hardly explained the clammy feeling he had holding it...

"It's a bit wrong but he says he'll get better," Alicia said; he realised she had been 'listening' again.

Behind him he heard a familiar, tinny music; Stefan turned to see Alexia playing with her carousel, which looked exactly as it should as its white horses turned. He looked again at the model in his hand.

"Alicia," he said, "where did you get this?"

"I told you, Echo made it," she said.

He couldn't get any other answer from her that day.

The Mackenzies had invited him round for dinner; they'd arranged for a 'babysitter', which actually meant one of their staff on overtime: a dark, curly-haired girl who ten years before Stefan would have been attracted to. Or maybe the years themselves weren't the issue, but the numbing loss and grief with which they'd ended. If it could all end so suddenly—one old man's lack of attention for a single second—Stefan didn't want to be close to anyone again. The thought of his girls grown up made him nervous, as did the stories on the news of what kind of world they might be growing up into. He knew that with today's weapons, a moment of confusion as brief as that of the old man behind the wheel from someone in charge could damn them all.

The meal at the Mackenzies was as he expected: delicious, expensive, strained. He knew he shouldn't dislike them so, they were kind people in their own way, the gap between their lives and his one they no doubt genuinely regretted (especially by the third glass of wine). Stefan didn't know if he'd said too much or too little, or just the wrong things either way. He brooded over it walking back to the bungalow, the silence broken by what was either a thunderstorm or a jet overhead.

"Any problems?" he said to the babysitter; he'd told her to let the girls stay up until he returned. Since the accident they'd taken a long time to settle at night.

"Oh no, good as gold," she said brightly—too much so, all the staff knew about Alana. "They were playing with their toys all night. God, the music from those carousels is enough to drive you mad isn't it? Especially Alicia's; I think the batteries are going."

Confused, Stefan gave her an extra tenner over and above what the Mackenzies had paid her, and went into the lounge. Alexia was playing Twister by herself, still full of energy at this late hour. Alicia was sitting in front of the TV despite the fact it was switched off, playing with her carousel. Stefan could see the unformed, misshapen horses, so it definitely was the weird toy Alicia had obtained from somewhere. But the horses were *turning* and to an alien version of a familiar tune, the notes as ill-formed as the horses themselves. It couldn't be the same toy as the one she'd had the previous day, surely?

"Honey where did you get that?" Stefan said.

"Why'd you get her such a cheap one?" Alexia shouted from a contorted pose on the Twister mat.

"It's not cheap, Echo made it!" Alicia shouted. "It's better this one Daddy, look. He said he didn't realise it was allowed there could be two of things as long as they're different slightly."

Stefan felt his tiredness stifle any coherent response to this, and after all it was just childhood nonsense.

"It's not as good as *mine!*" Alexia shouted, her head hanging between her knees and her hands planted on two ink-blue circles.

"Yes it is!" Alicia shouted. "*Echo* gave me it!" The twins could go from friendly to argumentative (and back again) quicker than Stefan could react. Especially if he had an evening's worth of drink inside of him.

"Well *Mummy* gave me mine!" Alexia said, springing up onto her feet like a jack in the box, and the carousel's distorted tune was lost beneath the resulting sound of tears. It was gone midnight by the time Stefan got to bed.

The next day Stefan had to spend working; a group of protestors had breached the walls of the Mackenzies' estate and planted food and crop seeds in the flowerbeds and lawns. The protestors believed that at times like this all available land should be used for food. Stefan couldn't say he disagreed with them in abstract, but protected by Mackenzies' walls and further protected by the sea and closed borders, it was hard to believe what he saw on the news could affect him. He tried to stop the girls from watching it, they'd had enough to cope with since the accident, but he couldn't supervise them twenty-four hours and he wondered how much of it they'd absorbed.

He replanted the roses and orchids and forsythia, and wondered if he was a hypocrite.

"Alicia, we need to talk," he said when he went back inside.

"I'm *not* Alicia," Alexia said, pouting.

When he found her, he saw Alicia was playing with more of the strange, melted looking toys, all again made of a single piece of plastic (if plastic it was), all warped and inaccurate. First drafts, he thought, not quite sure where the thought came from. As he watched, Alicia picked up what was presumably meant to be a doll—he'd always hated dolls, with their smooth featureless faces, their blank orbs that he still felt the urge to make eye contact with. And *this* one...

Alicia held the 'doll' out to him; the way its limbs hung was as if it were crippled.

"Spot the difference!" she said.

He shuddered as he took it and put it into the toy basket. How could Alicia calmly tend to something so, so horribly *inaccurate?* And just where were these new toys coming from? Could it somehow be linked to the protestors? The idea seemed ridiculous, and he decided the main thing was to focus on Alicia's mental wellbeing.

"We need to talk about Echo," he said.

"Okay." Alicia picked up a book—a book in which all the pages were fused together like candle wax—and avoided Stefan's eye.

"Now you know he's not real don't you? Not really real?"

"He is real, he's making all these things." Alicia gestured at her new collection of toys.

"Now I know sometimes when we're lonely it's nice to pretend a person..."

"Oh I know Echo's not a person," Alicia said airily. "Echo says calling him a boy isn't really right too. I don't understand all he says," she added in a quieter voice.

"Can he... Can Echo hear me?" Stefan said. He wondered if pretending to talk directly to Echo rather than Alicia would help. Like an exorcism.

"Of course he can Daddy."

"Okay. Hello Echo."

A pause. "He says Echo's not his real name. But you can call him it too."

"Thank you, Echo. Where do you live, Echo?"

A longer pause. "He says across the border."

"The border? You mean abroad?"

"No he says... I don't understand all the words, Daddy. But not that kind of border."

"Okay. So, why is he... Sorry, why are *you*, Echo, making these strange toys?"

"He says to take back."

"Take back? Across the border?"

"They're not *ours* Daddy, I'm just borrowing. That's okay isn't it, borrowing?"

"Yes honey, of course. But why toys?"

"He says it doesn't matter what they are, he wants to take one of *everything*. To... I don't understand Daddy. He says they'll be in his head, like dreams, but real too."

"But why?"

"So when it's all gone he'll be able to remember. That's his *job*. To tell people. Like, like stories in his head."

"When what's all gone?"

"The *world*, silly," Alicia said with a grin. "Bang!"

Later that night, drinking wine and trying to find a channel not showing the Special Broadcasts, Stefan pulled out the *Spot the Difference!* book. Every one of the fifty puzzles was completed, in a hand that looked steadier than Alicia's.

The next morning he found it hard to concentrate on his work; he felt like there was a faint noise constantly on the edge of hearing. It wasn't the constant squeak squeak of Alexia on the swings, although he pretended that it was. Have to oil them, he thought.

There were other noises too: a disturbance at the gates to the Mackenzies house curtailed by the police, a military helicopter overhead. But none were the noise that tormented him.

About noon, he heard the servants' door at the back of the house open; he straightened from his gardening half-hoping it would be the curly haired girl, but he saw it was Mister Mackenzie, clutching the daily newspaper in his hand. (Stefan didn't read the papers but he was aware that they'd recently become more like he remembered in his youth: slimmer, black and white, sombre headlines with all hysteria edited out.)

"Eh, no need to work today Stefan," Mister Mackenzie said; Stefan felt his heckles rise. Was he never to be allowed to forget the accident?

"I'm fine," he said tightly. "If I don't get these pruned back they'll be no growth next year..."

Mister Mackenzie gave a short, hollow laugh that caught in his throat; when he coughed Stefan could smell alcohol.

"No need to work today," he said. "Go and spend time with your family." Stefan could hear a new sound: the paper in Mister Mackenzie's ink-stained hand was rustling, because the man was trembling.

Another helicopter as grey as the sky roared overhead. Stefan went back to the bungalow.

Later, he refused to put the TV on; what would be the point in knowing? And besides, Alexia was asleep on the couch in front of the TV and he didn't want to wake her.

She must have finally worn herself out on that swing, he thought.

"Hello Daddy," Alicia said coming into the room.

"Hello sweetheart. Shhh, don't wake your sister."

Alicia looked at him for a second as if he'd said something stupid, then shrugged.

"Echo says he's got to go soon. He says goodbye."

"Over the border?" Stefan said.

"Yes."

"Can he take us with him?" Stefan said, with a sad smile.

A pause. "No, he says there's too many differences. He says sorry, he says he *tried*."

"He tried?" Stefan said, but he wasn't really listening. He'd become aware of a sound outside—the rusty squeak of the swing. He turned and looked at Alexia on the sofa...

Outside, it darkened perceptibly, like time-lapsed photograph of the night falling.

And maybe it was just the new shadows, but Stefan wasn't sure he could see Alexia's chest rise and fall as she slept on the sofa; wasn't sure if she *was* asleep because couldn't he see two eyes staring at him? Eyes staring at him in a face that was oddly still, and whose flesh hung oddly, as if its raw material was wrong...

He heard Alexia come bursting into the house, fleeing from the newly fallen dark outside.

The eyes of the thing continued to stare at him as everything darkened, unblinking as if they couldn't move.

In the hallway, Alexia was shrieking.

Stefan couldn't look away from the thing on the sofa.

"Spot the difference Daddy!" Alicia said excitedly.

FELLOWS FINISHES THE STORY AND hands it back to Jaques with a shrug to hide his unease, not wanting to give the man the satisfaction of seeing it. He feels like a kid who has done something wrong but has yet to know if he's been found out; will there be consequences?

"Well, a deal's a deal," Jaques says. "Boursier lives in the old town, above a liquor shop." He scribbles down the address for Fellows, who takes it along with his bag of Boursier stories. The last thing he wants is these crazy bastards reading them.

"You're mad you know," he says, wanting a parting shot. "Stories can't lift the quarantine."

"Then nor can they change whatever you wish," Jaques says as Fellows opens the door. "Nonetheless I wish you luck; I think you'll find we're actually on the same side." The man's smugness would annoy Fellows, apart from the fact that Leianna leaves with him. Without looking at him, and with an air he can't quite decipher, she takes his hand to lead him out the house, as if he didn't know the way himself. The excitement he feels is nostalgic, for he hasn't felt it in years.

"He's a posh idiot," she says, and Fellows knows she wouldn't have said that thirty minutes ago; she is saying it just to agree with him.

Leianna leads him down the stairs, still thronged with silent readers, and back towards the servants' door at the back of the house. She pauses before she opens it, turns to him blocking his exit.

"Maybe I could come with you when you go to find Boursier?" she says.

"Sure," Fellows says off-balance. "I mean... you're interested in him too?"

"No," Leianna says, smiling at him.

The words Fellows knows he should say next seem to come from far away, for they are words he has only ever said in other years, in other cities.

"We could go for a drink afterwards, maybe, or food...?"

Leianna closes her eyes and gives a brief nod; she steps aside from the door and opens it. As Fellows steps through and turns round to face her, he sees her arch her back and close her eyes as if she has just finished doing something unpleasant or tedious.

"So when…?"

Leianna sighs and steps outside the house with him. "Oh you poor sod," she says, her voice different.

"What?"

"Look, don't you understand what goes on in here?" She gestures to the gloom of the corridor behind her. "Reading stories, it's *all* stories when you're inside, those are Jaques's rules, or whatever he's calling himself today."

"I don't understand," Fellows says. "What does this have to do with us going to see…"

"It was a, a *script*. I tried to memorise it but Jaques can't write for shit." Leianna holds up her hand; it is covered in short-hand symbols and prompts, somewhat smudged. When he glances down at this own hand that she had held, it is smudged with a mirror-version of the same story.

"A script?"

"Well semi-improvised. A *story*, you silly sod. It's *all* a story in there. A first draft. I mean did you *really* think…" She stops herself.

"Go on," Fellows says.

"Oh Christ, look. You seem nice, okay, you tip well at the Carousel, I get that. But I'm twenty-five and you're… however old. I have a son, a *cripple* as you've no doubt been told…"

"I…"

"And he needs medicine and care," Leianna says, suddenly angry, "and this fucking quarantine is stopping me getting them for him. And *you*… you treat this whole thing as a joke. And maybe it is but nobody *else* is trying to lift it, are they? So fuck you; we haven't all got the luxury of swanning around looking for stupid books, Fellows. Maybe if things had been different… but no, the answer to that pathetic question in your eyes is no. This story isn't coming true." She spits on her palm to rub the ink from it, before slamming the door in his face.

Face flaming, Fellows turns away and walks down the drive, the crunch of the pebbles loud in his ears. He almost slips they are that deep, and the gulls holler their amusement from the roof of the house. He resists the urge to pick up the stones to throw at them, or at the windows of the house. Bloody lunatics! he thinks. But what if they're not, what if they're capable of changing things, of warping things, as much as he?

Sod them, he thinks, sod them.

Sod *her*.

He steps into the street, past the strange boundary stone, and is immediately stopped by the same two Guardia, who appear to have been lurking just round the corner. In his frustration it is an effort not to say something to them he would no doubt be made to regret.

"You didn't last long," the male Guardia says. "Sacked by the toffs already?"

"There's no toffs in there," Fellows says. "Well maybe one," he adds, thinking of Jaques.

"What do you mean? Now look, move along..."

"The *owners* aren't there, you idiots!" Fellows shouts at them. "They're somewhere on the other side of the quarantine! You're patrolling out here and all the while letting people past who aren't real servants! They're protestors."

"What?" The female Guardia steps forward.

"This is where they *meet*. Who knows what they're plotting in there?" Fellows says. "That's why I left, to tell you."

The Guardia aren't listening to him anymore but looking at each other, they don't react as he turns away so he puts his hands in his pocket and starts walking. When he reaches the corner of the street he hears the sound of footsteps sprinting up the pebble driveway.

Sod them, he thinks, sod...

A short time later he hears shouting, but as he keeps walking away from the Enclave, the angry cries are lost to the sound of the sea.

Now, he thinks, pulling out the slip of paper Jaques had given him, let's see if *this* was made up.

He heads towards the address where Boursier apparently lives.

"COME IN THEN," GEORGIA SAYS. "I would say I'll open a bottle but hey, way ahead of you. Where have you *been*? Fellows?"

Fellows doesn't reply as he walks into Georgia's flat; he's still feeling a sense of both anti-climax and unreal excitement. Has he really just met Boursier, after all these months of rumour?

"Are you okay?" Georgia says. "Here, take this." She hands him a glass of wine. "Fellows, hello? You know that quiet sensitive schtick isn't going to work on me, right?"

"I met him today," Fellows says. "Met Boursier."

"Woah," says Georgia. "Well c'mon then, drink up and tell me about it. It can't be that bad. Was he a twat? I bet he was a twat. You should never meet your idols you know..."

Fellows sits down, takes a big gulp of the wine, which is warm as if Georgia hasn't bothered chilling it before she opened it. His hands leave a black smudge on the glass like evidence. He stares at it blankly.

"C'mon," Georgia says, "tell me. Was he some weird pretentious type? Or someone famous from the unity government in disguise or... *shit*." Her face falls. "He isn't real is he?" she says in a flatter voice.

This finally rouses Fellows.

"What?"

"Boursier, he's not really real. When you saw him he was your spit wasn't he? Your doppelgänger. And you realised those stories…"

"Georgia what are you talking about? He didn't look anything like me."

"What? Oh." She laughs, takes a big gulp from her glass. "Then *tell me*, you twat! Fuck's sake."

"And I told you I don't write anymore."

"Okay, okay. So what *did* he look like then?"

"Average, really… nondescript."

"You sure you're not writing again, with that descriptive flair?"

"Piss off," he says, finally laughing. Georgia is almost exactly what he needed; *she* doesn't change. "But seriously, it was like there was nothing about him *to* describe. No distinguishing features. He just seemed to shrink into the background. He'd make a great spy." He's making light of how unnerving the encounter seems in retrospect, how it feels like after a few days he might not remember Boursier at all. Already it is slipping from him.

"Can't you ever just give a straight answer? Did he have black hair and a curly moustache? Bald as a coot and bad teeth?"

Fellows laughs and shakes his head.

"Okay, well what did you two talk about? Can you remember that?"

Fellows empties his glass and puts it down on the table.

"There are a few things I need to tell you first Georgia," he says, somewhat nervously. "Fill me up will you?" He pauses, then plunges in: "First, there's something in my house…"

THEY'VE NEARLY EMPTIED THE SECOND bottle by the time he finishes. He has told her all of it—the ghost, the way he is sure Boursier's stories are changing the quarantined city in ways only he notices, even his humiliation at the hands of Leianna. Georgia didn't interrupt once and when he falls silent her face is different to how he has ever seen it before.

"Well?" he says anxiously when she doesn't speak. "Going to call me a twat?"

"Why do you think I spend all day in my flat?" Georgia says, not meeting his eye. "I never used to be like this, when I was with *her*. Not until I met you."

"What? I don't…"

"I even get the wine delivered you know. Food and booze, brought by some crippled kid who has to struggle up all these flights of stairs—he's scared of the lift—and I give him double what it's worth."

"Why?" Fellows says quietly. Georgia gets up from the bowed sofa and looks out at the night falling over the city, isolating it further. The moon is the other side of the low clouds and it is like a dome of darkness is gradually contracting with them in its centre.

"Last time I went outside," Georgia says, "it was *different*. The city, the streets. Too wide, too big. I went to try and find *her* place, you know, to get some of my things back, and I couldn't find it. I'd walked there a thousand times, but I couldn't find it. And the people I asked for directions were dressed oddly, and looked at me like I was speaking a different language. I gave up and just wanted to get back home—it took me *hours*, Fellows, I couldn't even retrace my route. I thought I'd never get back."

Fellows knows better than to say out loud that his friend has no doubt staggered drunkenly about for hours before. For what else could it be? He's never seen the city change as much as Georgia describes and something in him shrinks from thinking that it could be altered to such a degree.

"Is it different each time?" he says. "Or is it... *set* in its new..."

"I don't know, do I? I've not gone out *again*." Georgia laughs with no humour. "When I look out from *here* it all looks as I remember. But if I went out... who knows? Too scared to find out I suppose. And what's so special out there anyway? So yeah I believe you."

"Good, I..."

"You still might be going crazy about the ghost though," Georgia says with something like her normal smile. "Even I'm not crazy enough to have seen ghosts."

"Just the one," Fellows says. "But that's the reason you see. Why I wanted to find Boursier."

"What? I don't get it."

"I went to his place; it's not far from here, an apartment above a liquor shop..."

"Good man."

"He invited me up and it was completely lacking in personality, like he'd just moved in, despite all the dust. Just a bed, a desk, some books..."

"And your place is much different, Fellows?"

"I said I'd read his stories, trying to get a reaction, but he didn't seem bothered. A writer who doesn't want validation? Now *that's* odd. So I told him what I thought, that reading his stories was changing things and he... he shrugged."

"He *shrugged?* Like he already knew?"

"Or like it was unimportant," Fellows says. He is aware he isn't really describing the encounter very well, but his memories of it are hazy, the particulars blurred. "I didn't know how to react, so I just blurted it out. How I wanted him to write me a story, to get rid of the ghost in my house..."

"Wait, what?"

"That's why I wanted to find him."

"That sounds like a *bad* idea Fellows. Even by your standards." Georgia sighs. "But what do I know about ghosts? So what did he say? Will he do it?"

"He said... he said he already *had*."

Fellows pulls out one of the manuscripts he bought from The Echo Bookshop and has been carrying around all day.

"This is one of the stories I bought yesterday."

"But how could he...?"

Fellows shrugs hopelessly.

"I'm scared Georgia. Not that it won't work, but that it's a trick and it changes..." He gestures towards the black veil of the window. What if it is hiding a different city to that they know should be there? "But," he says, "I don't think it works if someone *else* reads the story. Or at least it's not nearly as strong."

"Oh *no*, Fellows..." Georgia begins.

"Can *you* read it for me Georgia?" Fellows says. "First?"

He holds out the story to her, and looking like it might stain her hand, Georgia takes it.

It is entitled *A Lack Of Demons*.

PART FOUR

A LACK OF DEMONS

"I DON'T THINK YOU SHOULD read this," Georgia says.

Fellows is barely through the door to Georgia's apartment before she is waving the manuscript in his face.

"Christ, what's got into you?" he says, his tiredness making him irritable. He has waited as long as he could before coming, knowing Georgia is not an early riser, and indeed she has answered the door in her dressing gown. Maybe that is why she is so abrupt with him but given the morning he has had—kicked out of the Carousel!—Fellows doesn't too much care.

"You've read it? When?" Fellows says, trying to take the sheafs of paper from Georgia's hand—she moves them out of his reach.

"Last night after you left. But look, Fellows…"

"Then it didn't work when *you* read it."

"Huh?" Georgia sits on the familiar, sagging sofa and gestures for Fellows to do the same.

"The ghost was there this morning," he says as he does so, not looking at her.

"Look," Georgia says, taking his hand—he knows she must be serious by the gesture; she is normally so careful not to risk false signals after the way he'd come onto her the night the quarantine had been declared.

"Why read it?" she continues. "It's not a spell; Boursier isn't a magician. Why do you want to change things out there?" She gestures towards the window, the effect of which is lessened by the fact that the curtain is still tightly drawn. But Fellows knows what she means—why risk changing any more of the city which is, despite the quarantine, still a decent place to live? Georgia moans about not being able to get decent wine except for silly money from the blackmarket, but she is not one of the protesters.

"But Georgia," he says, "*you* won't notice any changes. *You* think we've always driven on the left; *you* think my cat's always been called Mogwai."

"But that's worse, don't you see? That's like it's changing *me*." Despite her evident hangover Georgia's eyes are intense on his under the disheveled line of her fringe. "Of course it could be you're just fucking crazy. Twat." She looks away from him and he can see she is struggling with a feeling of unease.

He has told her about the ghost but wasn't able to explain why it affected him so much. Why the thought of it wanting to touch him scares the hell out of him; it seems to him such a touch will lead to a rupture as fundamental as that caused by Boursier's stories. Why he thinks such a thing, when the damned ghost is barely even there he doesn't know; the ghostly child has so little effect on the world around it even George—Mogwai—can't sense it.

"I'm going to read the story, Georgia," he says quietly.

"Fine," she says tightly, giving it to him. "But you're not reading it here."

"Fair enough."

There's a silence such as there never normally is between them, broken only by the sound of accordion music and shouting from the streets and alleys of the old town below.

"Something to drink?" Fellows says eventually.

"Bit early," Georgia says, "even for me." Her voice is without its usual sparkle and she is refusing to meet his eye.

"Did you like it?" Fellows says. "The story?"

"No," Georgia says. "No. It didn't make any… It was like déjà vu, you know? But of stuff that wasn't real."

"Ghosts?"

"No, I mean… There might have been ghosts or spirits in it, but that's not what I mean. It's not *set* anywhere real…"

"I know, I know, you don't like escapism," Fellows says.

"No, I like my fiction to be set right here." She waves her hand towards the window, but doesn't look at it. "But don't worry, it *has* got some exorcist chap in it, so it will no doubt do the trick for you. Not that I believe in it all, mind. But if I did."

"Sure, if you did," Fellows says, relieved that the weird tension between them seems to be lifting. He yawns; without his usual coffee he feels lethargic, feels the threat of a headache hanging over him like storm clouds in the sky.

"Christ," Georgia says, "you'll set me off. Look, piss off out of here will you, I'm not even awake. I'm not even dressed." The fact that he doesn't know where he can go must show on Fellows' face, for Georgia giggles at him. "You'll be fine, it's not even raining anymore. At least the fishing boats will be able to get out again… Hey, it wasn't raining in Boursier's story either—*spooky*."

"Piss off," Fellows laughs.

"No, seriously though, come back later, Fellows. I've got something special being delivered. By my best friend the lame kid. So do piss off, but come back this afternoon, okay?"

"You could always come with me," Fellows says, "we could sit by the docks, have those spicy potatoes and watch…"

"I… I can't Fellows. No. I'm not… No." When she looks down, when her voice goes so quiet, he wonders how much he actually knows Georgia and how much just her act. He thinks of her lost on the dark streets of the city, convinced they had changed around her, and he thinks of taking her hand and leading her home.

"So what is this special something?" he says aloud.

"A surprise. You'll see. Now seriously Fellows, *piss* off."

HIS DAY HAD NOT started well.

In the shuddering lift with nothing to distract himself Fellows tries to fight back the nausea he feels; he remembers seeing the ghost when he woke that morning, its eyes of solid white almost level with his. Its straining body had been held upright by dirty hands gripping his bed frame. Just centimetres away. When it had let go with one hand to reach towards Fellows, its other arm had not been able to support its weight and it had collapsed to the dusty wooden floorboards. Fellows assumes he had run from the room at that point, fled from the house, although he can't remember doing so, or dressing or grabbing the Boursier stories on the way out. His next memory is of walking the streets of the old town, the winter sky above him as clear as the boy's eyes, blankly watching. He'd felt like he was seeing himself from without—hurrying head down and clutching his bag under his arm—like a story in the wrong tense. He was deeper into the old town's narrow streets than he normally went, well beyond Georgia's apartment, and drawing looks from its inhabitants both suspicious and appraising. Nevertheless he had not turned round, as if eager to get somewhere—but beyond the old town was just the crumbling cliffs of the west bay and the high wall that separated the civic park and the Enclave from the rest of the city. Anyone who lived in the old town but worked in the Enclave had to take the long way round.

Fellows must have turned round himself, for the next thing he remembers he was crossing the square towards the Carousel. Still facing the same direction, as if the quarantined city was a sphere or Möbius strip, and you could arrive back where you started from just by walking in a straight line.

He glances up at Georgia's apartment as he walks away from her building, but the curtain is still closed. He thinks of her, disorientated and wandering the streets of her own city for hours until she finally found her way back. Was that what he had been like this morning? But Georgia is an alcoholic (he supposes he should face up to that) whereas he had been in shock from seeing the ghost so close. He had been lost in his fears and got turned round and ended up back near the Carousel. That was all.

Fellows had stared at the Carousel uncertainly; its windows opaque in the dull morning light. It will be fine, he thought, you'll just have your usual coffee and pastry, read whatever nonsense the protestors have got up to in the paper, then you can go and see if Georgia has read the story or not. *A Lack Of Demons*—his life, after today. He crossed the small, deserted square and went inside the café.

He was immediately aware that Leianna was back at work, and he saw by the way her posture stiffened that she had noticed him in one of the unpolished mirrors on the café's walls. She didn't turn to face him, and after a second Fellows headed past her towards the counter. It can't have been too bad then, he thought, the Guardia can't have given them too much trouble if she's here and working. And he hadn't wanted to create trouble for them (except maybe that stuck up prick Jaques), just to stop the idiots reading, memorising scripts, and who knew what other craziness in their efforts to lift the quarantine. Idiots, he thought, placing his usual order with Gregor behind the counter.

He took his paper and found somewhere to sit, pretending to read but really waiting nervously for Leianna to bring his coffee. It will be fine, he thought again, they probably just asked her a few questions and that was it, we'll probably have a laugh about it and…

She brushed close to him as she placed the pastry in front of him, but only so she could whisper "you're a fucking bastard," in his ear as she did so. He remembered the things she had whispered to him in the grand house in the Enclave yesterday, and her later claims that it was all just scripted. He looked up to study the angry scowl of her face for further evidence of acting, that she liked him underneath. Her face was pale except for the dark smudges beneath her eyes; her gaze seemed held together only by contempt for him. He looked guiltily away and he remembered how he had looked away from the ghost's eyes too, and that he had the same feeling of guilt, as absurd as that was.

"I'll just get your coffee, *sir*," she said as she moved away, too loudly and satirically for people not to notice. She walked back to the counter and the interior of the café was hushed apart from the rustling of the newspaper in Fellows's hands. A pause in the script, the audience waiting to see what she would say when she returned.

The sudden noise of a car backfiring somewhere in the city, and the angry heckling of the gulls in response, seemed very loud.

Leianna returned with his coffee, placing it in front of him without a word. Almost involuntarily, driven to it by the continuing silence, Fellows murmured her name as she was turning away.

"What?" she said, and it was so quiet her voice was audible even to those in the back seats of the café.

"About yesterday…" Fellows said, barely more than a mumble.

"Yesterday, what happened yesterday?" Leianna said, her voice becoming louder and more brittle. "Oh yes, I was stuck in some windowless room for hours. They didn't call it a cell, but it was. I was *questioned*, when I'd not broken the law! It was dark when I got home, my son was *frantic*, he'd tried to take his medication himself but couldn't get the cap off. And all because some fucking idiot who wanted to get inside my single-parent knickers…"

"Leianna…" he said imploringly, but his weak voice was drowned out by Gregor shouting the same thing across the café.

"*What?*" Leianna snapped at Gregor. "I told you, didn't I, what this *twat* did?"

How does she know that word, that's Georgia's word, Fellows thought absently. The other customers have given up even the pretence of not watching what is going on.

"I think you'd better leave," Gregor said and at first Fellows felt dreadful because he thought he'd got Leianna sacked on top of everything else. But then he realised Gregor was talking to him.

AS HE WALKS, FELLOWS PERIODICALLY stops to check that *A Lack Of Demons* is still in the bag of Boursier stories he is carrying, paranoid it will somehow have vanished. The streets of the quarantined city seem still and quiet, as if everything were frozen in place by the blank stare of the sky. The sun seems as pale as the sky around it, but without any wind it is still passably warm, and Fellows decides to sit outside to read.

The thought of going home before the story has had a chance to work its magic-trick is intolerable.

He enters the park by the entrance near the fountain; fortunately it is still too early for any prostitutes to be out. He walks up past the flower beds, and notices that they have been dug up, their fresh brown soil exposed to the sky. Bamboo canes are stood in the soil, atop of which are crudely written signs; evidently the protestors have been here and replaced the civic flowerbeds with seeds for foodstuffs. The scrawled slogans serve to annoy Fellows; they are chastising the unity government for acquiescing with the quarantine but what do they actually expect it to *do*?

As he walks through the park he marvels that it is just three days since he was here last, on a summer day that according to the rest of the quarantined city never existed. It is as if he can still feel the warmth of it on his face as he sits down on the same bench, in front of the statue of the city's founder. He pulls out the story from his bag.

A Lack Of Demons he thinks; well maybe it is a demon in his home and not a ghost. After all, why would his house be haunted? Whatever the bloody thing is it will be gone soon. Will he even remember it having existed?

Thinking of its cloudless eyes, he hopes not.

A Lack Of Demons by Boursier

"I can help you," the man in the white suit said.

Erica turned to look at him, almost doubting the figure in her peripheral vision would prove real, for his words so nearly echoed her own thoughts: *help me.*

Help me. *Stop* him.

On stage, a beaming young woman was blinking into the flashlights, accepting an over-sized cheque from a representative of the Taschen Foundation. The Foundation's logo, a stylised wave and seabird, was bright behind them; to one side sat Erica's husband, Charles Taschen, faintly smiling, beatific. He didn't rise for the applause that broke out from the crowd, nor the clink of champagne glasses in the toast that followed. Erica didn't hear what was toasted, but she heard what people said *soto voce* afterwards. The fashionably wealthy crowd only gave to charity for tax or publicity purposes, and they all thought her husband mad.

They didn't know the half to if, Erica thought.

"I can help you," the man said again. "Help your husband." She looked at him more closely: he was all straight lines, dressed in an angular white suit which hadn't crumpled despite the heat of the room. His tie was a black bar below a square knot; the bones of his gaunt face turned at right angles beneath the skin. When she took his proffered hand Erica expected it to be cold, but it felt hot like brick in the sun.

"That's very kind of you," she said, "but Charles has seen specialists, seen doctors and psychiatrists and behavioural-therapists and god knows who else." All at her insistence of course; Charles hadn't believe there was anything wrong with him but he had acceded to her wishes. Meekly, of course. Her voice rose in pitch: "So I'm not sure that you *can* help." You're not getting any of our money, she thought, I might not be able to stop him bloody giving it away but I'll be damned if another quack is going to take any more before it's gone.

"I'm not a doctor," he said.

"Oh," Erica said. She had misunderstood. "Well, if you'd like to make a donation to…"

"I'm an exorcist," the man said.

She almost laughed. Maybe she did laugh, that harsh bitter laugh she'd lately confronted the world with, for several people turned from looking at the stage to glare at her sanctimoniously. *It's my fucking money he's giving away!* she wanted to yell at them but she restrained herself.

"An exorcist," she said. "Really. Been to too many movies lately, have we? Well at least it's original, I'll give you that." She paused for control, and then wondered why. "But all the same you're just *another* fucking quack, who's come to take our money while there's still some left..."

Before the man could respond, one of the maids they'd persuaded to be a waitress for the night came up to them with the champagne tray. The young one, Erica noticed, who despite her unruly black hair and telltale tan was undeniably pretty. Not that Erica had to worry about that, anymore. She took a glass from the tray; the man in the white suit refused.

"I don't want your money," he said gravely. "And I apologise for using the word 'exorcist' but there is no other you'd understand. What I do is not based on religion; I don't believe in ghosts or demons..."

"Then what," Erica said, "do you believe?"

"I believe there are... entities," he said, "or maybe not even that. *Forces*. Generated by the laws of physics like the rest of creation, but *other*. Attracted to our otherness, maybe. I believe they can enter us, influence us once inside, use us for their own ends without us even being aware..."

"What shit."

"And I believe such a force is in your husband." The man's voice was still level, but his eyes were ablaze, she realised, as if in some other reality he was hollering the words from a pulpit.

"You're crazy," Erica said. "Forces? Just make a donation and piss off. It's such a worthy cause," she added, her voice a bitter parody of her husband's. "Do you know how many children suffer disfiguring injuries on our roads?"

When his hand gripped hers to stop her turning from him it was if anything even hotter than before, although still bone dry.

"Do you really believe," he said, "that your husband is himself?" And he looked (so she looked) towards the man on stage, expensive tailored suit hanging like a cloak from his slim body (Charles had been fasting for weeks), not even stepping up to take the applause as he gave another chunk of his fortune away. "What have you got to lose?" the man in the white suit added.

At this rate not much, Erica thought, as the reporters from the local newspaper rose yet again to take a picture of a cheque being handed over.

Charles Taschen was a man made by both old money and new, able to trace his inherited wealth back generations but also a canny investor who had made his own fortune on top of that bequeathed to him. Or so he liked to tell people. He lived in the same city he had grown up in, but on a new estate he'd built himself, isolated from the rest by high walls, private security, and CCTV. Erica was his second wife and only ten years younger than him. She'd hardly been destitute when she married him—the same newspaper which had insinuated she was a gold-digger was the one so desperate for pictures of her husband's largesse now. How she hated them, how she disliked the way the cheap ink came off on her hands when she read them. But still, they had a point, for whatever words might have realistically been used to describe Charles Taschen when she married him, 'charitable' wouldn't have been one of them. 'Lavish' or 'opulent', maybe, 'decadent' certainly. Like some kind of latter day Gatsby his parties had been renowned but, Erica had soon learnt, they hadn't been thrown to lure just one woman to him. Lure several in reality, lure *scores* of women over the years, sometimes in pairs or threes. And lure the people with drugs, with the champagne, with the imported absinthe from some unknown source. Lure the judges to get him off his traffic offences, lure the police commissioners to make sure he didn't get caught again. Worse than traffic offences maybe; Erica had never known.

Lure Erica. She hadn't much minded, the first few years, and in the more recent ones, well, at least the champagne had kept flowing.

Had.

There had been no gradual change. Looking at the man in the uncrumpled white suit, with his angular features but fiery eyes she had to admit to the thought that Charles had been acting like a man possessed. She'd meant metaphorically, but still—there was no physical sign of disease, no infection or brain tumour pressing against some vital nerve. No obvious psychological issues or drug flashbacks had distorted Taschen's view of reality as far as anyone could tell. He just seemed to have decided, one day, to fast, to meditate and lock himself away for hours, and to give away all of his fortune bit by bit. To renounce drink and drugs and fast cars and, well, renounce Erica too. The fact that he seemed to have renounced all other women as well was surprisingly little comfort.

And didn't she have to admit that since it had started she'd often spoken to him like he was a different person? "Give me back my marriage!" she'd yelled at him one day, as if he were a stranger who had taken something physical from her.

Fuck it, she thought. "Okay, what are you proposing?" she said to the man in the white suit.

The quick flash of a smile as quickly repressed was not something she expected from him, nor the eager, hungry aspect it so briefly leant him.

"Charles, this is Mr. Staedtler ," Erica said, introducing him as most of the other guests were leaving. Her husband's smile, sincere and solicitous to someone he'd never met before, made her sick. That smile, that goddamn smile—how many times had she wanted to slap it from his face?

"He's an exorcist," she said; Staedtler had been right, there was no other word. Perhaps that was why none of this seemed real.

"An exorcist?" Charles said. "Do we still have those? I thought the demons had given up on us, or us on them." Despite the way his personality had changed his voice was still the same; he still had that Taschen lilt that had got him so much in life. Mr. Staedtler didn't interrupt and so

Charles continued. "Still, I suppose those unfortunates in the city hospice or the asylum might still believe in it all. Devils and angels. Some placebo effect. So yes, yes—how much do you want?" His smile broadened, intolerably.

"Charles, he doesn't want your money!" Erica said in dismay. "*Our* money, remember?" But it wasn't, according to the terms of the prenup. Her lawyer had double- and triple-checked the exemption clauses—Erica knew them by heart. And as no one could say Charles Taschen was mad or being coerced by others, he was free to piss away his money as he wished... Erica fiddled with the weight of the wedding ring on her finger; that at least was unambiguously hers.

"I don't want your money, Mr. Taschen," Staedtler said. He had refused to disclose his first name to her; looking at his humourless, excessively grave face Erica wondered if she had imagined his fervent smile earlier. Maybe if you spend all your time thinking you're saving souls you become like that, she thought. But then, Staedtler didn't believe in souls; he'd said so.

"That's good," Charles said, "not to want. Wanting is the source of so much pain..."

Erica wanted to scream.

"I don't believe in demons," Mr. Staedtler continued, "or poltergeists or... I don't believe. But I know there are forces that can corrupt people, infect them from outside. Your current actions might seem like your own choices to you, but to Mrs. Taschen and me they look like those of someone, something else."

"You think I'm possessed? By some kind of spirit?"

"If we must talk in those terms, then yes. One that is antithetical to your own position."

"But I'm doing *good*," Taschen said, in the voice of one announcing the first mate in an inevitable victory.

"Escapism," Staedtler said flatly. "You are retreating from the real world, from the full range of emotional experience. Not feeling anger, not feeling avarice, not feeling jealousy or hurt or lust—these are all still not feeling."

Charles paused before he replied, and it was in that pause that Erica started to think that maybe, just maybe there was something in what Staedtler claimed. For her husband's face seemed to flutter with confusion, his expression briefly more complicated than that of the serene, pacific person he had become. Could there really be something alien in him, something this man in his white suit could cast out?

"He can *help*," Erica said to Charles. "Help you feel like you did again."

"And what would this process involve?" Charles said.

"Isolation in the first instance. Quarantine."

"Quarantine? Am I infectious?" Charles said, smiling.

"Maybe," Staedtler said. "But then we talk. Just talk. It may take some days."

"Talk? You can talk a demon out of me?"

"I don't believe in demons. But yes."

It was agreed that Staedtler would stay in the Taschen house for the duration of the 'cure' and so Erica called the pretty maid to take him to one of the guest rooms. She noticed Staedtler didn't meet the girl's gaze as she smiled at him; he avoided looking at her behind as she led him from the room. Charles hadn't looked, either—she'd checked. She turned her wedding ring around her finger again. All the various frustrations she felt due to the changes in her husband focused into one within her; she sat next to Charles, not bothering to pull her dress down when it hitched up. She was on stage but no one was left to watch. She leant into him, let him feel the curves of her, the heat of her. He'd have been on her in a second in the old days, she remembered, even if he had just fucked one of his interns at work hours before. He would have *tried* at least.

But she saw he had retreated inside himself, as he'd been doing ever since the changes; he called it meditation but it was more like a trance, like he was somewhere else.

Quarantine, she thought bitterly, he's already fucking quarantined himself. He normally came out of one of these trances with some new idea about how he could help the poor, the dispossessed, the powerless. And tell Erica how he was going to finance it in a rapturous voice, tears of joy in his eyes. They were still tears of joy even when she shrieked at him, once scratched his face. How could he just give it all away!

"Charles! Charles!" she said, shaking him. "Come back to me." The desperate actions of her hands across his chest, then lower, made her despise herself. But she had to try one more time. His eyes flickered open at the touch, his mouth framed a smile as he looked at her and for a moment she thought...

But the love in his expression was the same serene love he had for all the world now, not particular to her. And she knew no other part of his body was reacting to her touch, as if she weren't there at all, but just a ghost.

Fine then, she thought as she stood up. So be it.

He had already closed his eyes and gone back into himself by the time she reached the door.

Erica went to the smoking room, opened the liquor cabinet and poured herself a glass of Charles' most expensive port (he'd already auctioned off the unopened bottles in his spirit collection) and called for the maid.

"Tell Mr. Staedtler he can join me for a drink if he wishes," she said. "I don't want to drink alone," she surprised herself by adding. Volunteering such secrets to the hired staff! But she felt a strange kinship with the curly haired girl—Charles wasn't trying to sleep with either of them.

While she waited for Staedtler she made a phone call, the result of which was ... satisfactory. No one could blame her. She'd tried.

She was still smiling when he came in, looking awkward in his white suit.

"You've not changed for dinner?" she said, enjoying how uncomfortable he looked. Despite his protests she poured him a drink, sat and gestured for him to sit next to her. When he gracelessly did so, she saw that one of his cuff buttons was hanging from white thread, saw worn patches at his elbows. You might not have asked for money, she thought, but you *do* need it.

"Your organisation," she said, "is it just you?"

He didn't look at her. "Others help," he said. "When they can. But I can't pay them. Most think what we do is scripted, a confidence trick."

"So, you didn't ask for money up front to cure my husband but when you do—if you do—a 'donation would be much appreciated', yes?"

"No."

"Why?"

He snorted, a repressed bitter laugh. It was the first real emotion she had seen from him. "Maybe I've got one of them inside of me too, stopping me. A demon."

"You just want to help people?" Erica said. Her hands touched his, bone dry and brick hot. "Maybe you can help me."

Whether he did so out of lust or whether it was just to help her she didn't mind, nor did she mind the brief, shocked glimpse of the maid's face at the door.

"This had better work," she said the next day, "for Charles' sake."

"You shouldn't be coming in with me," Mr. Staedtler said. "When it's out of him it might be... unpredictable."

"Do you think I trust you in there alone?" Erica said. "What if I find out when you've finished you've fleeced him of the rest of our fortune?"

Without another word Staedtler went into Charles' room.

"The exorcist! Well this will be interesting..." Charles said, as Erica entered and shut the door behind her.

After that she struggled to remember much, the whole process blurred in her memory, like something that had occurred only in the corner of her vision. She remembered Mr. Staedtler reading from a book, and then making

Charles read aloud from the same book, and her husband's confused words: "What is this, *stories?* Fairy tales?" Staedtler hadn't replied, but remained as unsmiling as he had the previous night. And the words he made Charles read aloud had seemed at once both crystal clear and unintelligible; each had seemed to ring inside of Erica like the chime of a just-tuned bell. It was like all the incidentals in her life were shown for what they were, stripping her thoughts and feelings back to the actual reality of her being: this, *this,* is who I am. And her husband, her husband...

Her husband had collapsed, sprawled onto the bed his face slick with sweat like one just released from a fever, a look of bafflement on his face. He seemed about a stone lighter. His arms were thrown wide like he'd cast something from himself into the room...

Out the window Erica saw a flock of birds rise up, circle on white wings, and fly towards her. She blinked and when she opened her eyes they were gone, already overhead.

Staedtler had pronounced it a success, and Erica wondered how she already knew.

The whole thing had taken about twenty-four hours.

When she awoke late the following day, Erica could have believed it all a dream, save for the ache in her body and the sound of Charles shouting at someone on his mobile phone two storeys down.

"I don't care how you do it, just do it! Cancel it. All of it! Cancelled or revoked or... I don't know, I pay *you* to know..."

Erica smiled.

Later, she saw Mr. Staedtler as he was leaving.

"Thank you," she said. "You did it. It's out of him, he's back to his old self." Charles had already ordered replacement bottles for the liquor cabinet and wine cellar, and cancelled all of the oversized charity cheques that hadn't yet been cashed.

Mr. Staedtler just nodded gravely; if he was thinking about their time together in the smoking room he didn't show it. Didn't show anything.

"And you still don't believe in demons?"

He shook his head, once.

Erica smiled. "Maybe I do, now. What else could it be?"

Charles was shouting at someone else on the phone and it could be heard across the whole house. He doesn't know, yet, Erica thought.

"And what about you?" Erica said. "*Is* there a demon in you? Or will you take some money as a thank you?"

Eventually, just as stony-faced and seemingly reluctant as the previous night, he capitulated to her. The heat of his hands as she pressed a cheque into them surprised her all over again.

"But this... this is too much!" he said, when he looked at the amount.

"It wasn't too much for Charles, so why should it be too much for me?" Erica said. "Thank you again, you don't know how much you've done."

Which is true, she thought, as she ushered him out of the door, Staedtler didn't know. She hoped the innocent man would never know. When she had spoken to her lawyer on the phone the evening of his arrival, he had been very clear: her husband calling in an exorcist, of all people, could be the answer. She could have him declared of 'unsound mind', which the prenup, so watertight in other respects, made allowances for. Control of the estate and all of his fortune bar a small allowance had passed to her, until he could be pronounced cured.

She'd already cancelled the champagne he'd ordered.

As she headed towards Charles' room to tell him, she saw the pretty maid was scurrying down towards his door as well. Erica called her over, and she couldn't tell if the girl's youthful face already looked guilty, or if she was innocent of what was to come.

But Erica was beyond all that now.

With a beaming smile, she took the priceless wedding ring from her finger and pressed it into the amazed hands of the maid. She raised one finger to her lips—ssssh—and told the girl to make sure Charles didn't see it.

Maybe she should have listened to Staedtler and not gone into the room when he had cast out whatever had been in Charles.

But Erica couldn't shake the idea that if felt so good, so *right*, to help people!

Especially as she now had so much more opportunity to do so.

FELLOWS TURNS THE PAGE AS if expecting more, but there is none. He blinks a few times, re-entering the real world. Was that it? Has he been had, conned? There was no actual haunting in the story, and any exorcism was ambiguous at best. Charles Taschen and Staedtler were only haunted by things in their own head, surely?

But why expect it to make sense? Fellows rises from the park bench, stretching his limbs that have become stiff in the cold still air. Does he really believe that fiction is so transparent in its workings, that allegory is nothing more than $X=Y$? And if not, why expect what Boursier had written to so neatly dovetail with his own life? For while he knows there have been some obvious changes in the quarantined city that he can see directly reflected in Boursier's stories, he believes there have been other, more subtle shifts in his surroundings. Like a change in pressure, invisible but altering everyone's inner weather. Why, even the statue of the city founder looks different today, less covered in gull shit for a start, and what can he have read to change that?

Or maybe it has just been cleaned, for he sees down near the fountain someone is pulling up the bamboo canes and signs of the protestors. The man is gamely ignoring both the calls of the birds waiting to get to the exposed soil and of the first prostitutes abroad, their faces twice as aged in the winter daylight as they will be under the gaslight tonight.

Fellows walks over to the gardener—an employee of the unity government no doubt.

"Bloody protestors," he says cheerfully, for something to say. "Idiots, eh?"

The gardener mutters something Fellows can't catch.

"What?" he says.

"Spare any change?" the gardener says, quietly and angrily; embarrassed and angry at his embarrassment, Fellows realises.

"What, but... You're not a beggar, you've got a *job*," Fellows says. "Why do you need to ask for money?"

"They only pay us in this new money, plague money I call it," the man says. "Will be worthless when this infection is over..."

"There is no infection," Fellows says, his voice sending the park pigeons and gulls clattering up into the sky. "That's just a rumour, gossip."

"Maybe, but still, they're paying us with kiddie money," the gardener says. "Look, the coins don't even look the same!" Aggrieved, he stands, and pulls two of the thin coins from his overalls, turns them both face upwards in his soil-stained palms. "Spot the difference," he says bitterly, and Fellows has to admit that the two profiles of the city founder do look slightly different, and neither resemble the statue behind him.

He shrugs. "What do you expect? What do you want the unity government to *do?*" The gardener stares at him from his weather-beaten face. "But anyway no, I haven't got any of the old money. What makes you think I would have?"

The man turns angrily from him, throws the bamboo canes into his wheelbarrow and goes to fill up his watering can at the fountain, to yet more catcalls from the prostitutes. Stony-faced, he comes back and waters the bare ground.

"Hey, aren't you supposed to be digging up what the protestors planted?" Fellows says.

The man angrily flicks the two coins at Fellows' face, causing him to flinch. They barely make a sound as they hit the path they are so thin.

"You're an idiot," the gardener says, not looking at him.

FELLOWS LEAVES THE PARK AND heads towards the sounds of the harbour, faint because the newly persistent noise of the city's motorcars is drowning out the dockers' cries and thud of machinery. The wind is coming from the sea—from beyond the quarantine he thinks as he buttons his jacket against its chill. He should surely get out of the cold, but he shrinks from the thought of returning home and seeing whether the story has worked. For what if it hasn't and the ghost is still present, then what options does he have? Despite its crippled body the fact that it is utterly silent makes him afraid that one day the boy will catch him unawares; he imagines its touch as cold and foreign as the wind assailing him.

Unacknowledged, there is another reason Fellows isn't simply going back home: he can't remember the way. That is, he can picture the route from where he is to Georgia's flat, and from there back to his house—the route he took this morning—but he can't think how to get directly home from the street outside the park. Every time he thinks he has it a car rushes past and drives the thoughts from his mind as he watches its blurred and hazy progress. He is not expert, but the models look newer as if the unity government, unable to get fresh peaches or salted butter through the quarantine, can somehow get the latest automobiles.

Fellows shakes his head to drive this fruitless speculation from it; home, he thinks, but again all he can picture are the streets leading to Georgia's apartment, and from there doubling back on himself to get home. Imagining stepping off these streets there is nothing, a black space in his internal map of the city. Here be dragons. It is the same when he tries to imagine how to get to other places too—he can remember the route from the Carousel to the harbour say, or from there to The Echo Bookshop, but his thoughts crumble if he tries to make the V into a triangle and go from the Carousel to the Echo.

Fuck it, he thinks, you're all worked up with worry about the ghost and whether Boursier's story will have got rid of it. So what if you go to Georgia's flat first? She *invited* you. Let's go and see what this surprise of hers is.

So thinking, he heads back up the road he took this morning, the shops and signs reassuringly familiar. See, nothing's *changed* he thinks. Even the faces of people walking towards him seem familiar, as if they are retracing their route too.

GEORGIA'S SURPRISE COMES WITH A sound like a car backfiring, causing Fellows to jump up from the sagging sofa in alarm. Georgia stares at him in surprise, and then realises frothing liquid is bubbling from the bottle she has just popped open.

"Shit, shit, shit," she says, quickly pouring some into two flute glasses. "Don't want to waste a drop of *this*. You wouldn't believe how much this is going for on the black market." Triumphant, she holds a glass out to Fellows, who is still frozen in shock. "Champagne!"

"What the fuck?" Fellows says. "Champagne?

"Yes, champagne. *Real* champagne from, you know, actual Champagne..." Georgia trails off when he doesn't react, doesn't step forward to take the proffered glass.

"But that's... It's just something from Boursier's stories," he says, "one of his, his *things* he's made up and expects you to understand like 'motorways' or 'mobile phones' or..."

"Hello? Fellows?" Georgia says. "It's champagne. It's alcohol. *Expensive* alcohol. So stop being weird and sit down and have a glass with me."

Fellows does as she says, but warily, taking the glass but not sipping from it. Even without tasting it the smell is familiar; the faint noise of the bubbles rising and bursting is familiar. The word, champagne, is familiar and not just from *A Lack Of Demons* despite what he said. But when he tries to think of it, of 'champagne', it is like when he tried to envisage the way home earlier—he can't get there directly. Instead, his thoughts have to go via an indirect route...

Via the night that Lana left him.

"Champagne?" Lana said in disgust; he'd popped the cork when she'd come up into the kitchen after work. The sound had been almost lost amidst the noise of rain against the windows outside.

"Sure," he said. "Why waste the bottle? And we might have something to celebrate after all. Some good luck."

"*Good luck?*" Lana said; she hadn't taken the glass he held out to her, frozen in the act of unbuttoning her coat.

"Sure, I called the lawyer and he thinks he sees a way out of it. A way to..."

Lana stepped forward and dashed the glass from his hand; it smashed against the side of the kitchen cabinet before it even hit the floor; the room will stink of stale champagne in the days after Lana leaves him, no matter how hard he scrubs. She turned from the room and went upstairs without a sound, not bothering to finish taking off her coat. Fellows listened to the noise of her packing but didn't leave the kitchen. *I hate this life*, he thought, downing his champagne and pouring another glass. *I hate this...*

Fellows comes back to the present; his memory can't be fully accurate if details from Boursier's stories are infecting it. 'Champagne'! The night Lana left him, and the memories that preceded it, are things he needs to keep sealed off. And he has been successful for the most part; today is just a temporary blip caused by...

He sips at the glass Georgia has given him, and the aroma makes him think of bleach and cleaning products, the taste is as if diluted by his own salty tears. He gags, feel as though he will be sick with a tremendous feeling of regret and guilt that bubbles through him, bursts inside him. With a cry he stands, dashes the glass to the floor. On Georgia's faded woven rug, it doesn't even shatter; but as its contents foam on the floor the sickly smell of it is almost overpowering.

"Why are you giving me this piss?" Fellows shouts. "Why are you calling this piss 'champagne' when there's no such thing?"

Georgia gives him a look half concern, half annoyance.

"Fellows, you can still get some genuine stuff from the blackmarket, how do you think all the toffs in the Enclave get by? Stuff gets lifted all the time. The lame boy who brings me stuff told me about this house all empty because the people who lived there were on the other side when the quarantine..."

Fellows gives a hollow laugh, as if his throat were parched.

"Oh so this was from those idiots was it? Did they read the label to you?"

"What?"

"Never mind. But that's not what I meant anyway, I meant there's *no such thing* as 'champagne', it doesn't exist..."

"Doesn't exist? You've just spilt it all over my bloody floor!" Georgia says, exasperated.

"And that's the worst crime imaginable isn't it, to an alcoholic like you? Spilt booze?"

He isn't looking at her when he says this, but in the resulting silence he does so and sees she has gone very still and pale. Something about the way her anger has hardened reminds him of that last night with Lana, and he hears *I hate this life* faintly in his own thoughts, as if it has never gone away and he has been hearing it ever since. And maybe something in his own body-language changes in response and serves to annoy Georgia further, for she suddenly throws her glass into his face. He manages to duck slightly but still he tastes the nauseating fizzy champagne and his own salty blood.

"Alcoholic am I?" Georgia says. "Get out."

"Georgia, I didn't mean…"

"Get out, get out," Georgia says very quietly. One look at her face and he knows there is no way to change her mind, the equations applied to his actions making the outcome inevitable from the start, like a man stamping on the brakes when all hope of stopping in time has passed…

"I didn't mean… Hey, I'm probably an alcoholic as much as you are," he says.

"Get the fuck out of here Fellows!" Georgia yells.

OUTSIDE GEORGIA'S BUILDING, HE TAKES a deep breath and shudders with the after-effects of his anger and nausea. And he is assailed by the same terrible gaps in his memory—where does he go from here? His mental map of the quarantined city seems to be shrinking; he pictures the city at night from above, each light a place he knows how to get to. And gradually they wink out—the Carousel, Georgia's flat, the house in the

Enclave. And as they do so the lines between them fade, and the possible routes he can envisage across the city diminish.

Home, he will have to go home, ghost or no. He has been putting it off too long. Let's see the results of Boursier's damn exorcism, he thinks.

But as he starts to walk the dark and watchful streets of the old town, he remembers there is somewhere else he knows how to get to, after all. Somewhere close by.

"I READ YOUR STORY," HE says to Boursier.

The other man blinks at him, the movement a brief ripple across his smooth and wrinkle-free features. Fellows was expecting some of the nervous expectation he used to feel when someone read his work (similar to how he now feels about going back to his house and checking for the ghost) but Boursier merely smiles in polite enquiry, waiting for Fellows to continue. He gives no sense of having been interrupted doing anything when Fellows knocked on his door, as if he had just been sitting in his small and empty room above the liquor shop waiting. His lodgings seem as empty of character as Boursier himself, as if he has just moved in without any baggage to unpack. Fellows is aware he has thought all these things before, but his first meeting with the man has faded from his memory like something imperfectly imagined, despite it being only yesterday. Another light blinking out.

"My friend read it too," he says in the face of Boursier's continuing silence.

"Did she like it?"

"No," Fellows says curtly, hoping to illicit a response. "She doesn't like fantasy; she likes her stories set in the here and now."

Boursier's only reaction is to smile so mildly it barely creases his face; Fellows imagines yelling at the man, slapping him and still receiving only the same maddeningly placid smile as the print of his hand faded from Boursier's face.

"I think your friend misunderstands how fiction works," Boursier says. When he hears the word 'friend', Fellows feels a sharp stab of regret and guilt.

"Yeah, well. I didn't come here for a literary criticism class," he says.

"Indeed."

"Look, you know why I'm here," Fellows says. "Will it have worked? Your story—can you assure me it will have *worked*, before I go back home?"

"Like a guarantee you mean?" Even the man's sarcasm feels bland, an arrow fallen short through being shot with insufficient force. "Please return within seven days if the effects on your imagination are not as expected?"

"It's not the effects on my imagination I care about," Fellows says, "although it was an interesting story," he admits.

"You disagree with your friend then? You have a place for fantasy?"

"When I was a writer," Fellows says, "that's what I wanted to write, you know? Stories set somewhere else but reflecting the real world back at... Oh I don't fucking know. That's all over anyway; it's all hogwash." He sighs. "Just tell me if it has worked."

"Yes," Boursier says simply. "Go back home and you'll see."

FELLOWS TRIES TO ENTER QUIETLY, wincing as the warped door sticks and he has to shove it closed. His heart is already beating too loudly for him to hear properly, and it is only at the last second that he hears the eager clatter of feet on the wooden stairs. Idiot, he thinks as Mogwai circles his heels, the ghost doesn't make a noise.

He has resolved to stick to his normal routine rather than go hunting for the ghost; it is not as if the wretched thing appears at a specific hour. As he goes about feeding the cat, making a simple meal for himself, settling in his favourite chair, he feels his actions ridiculous, like he is watching them from without. This self-consciousness means he can't focus on reading a book as he normally would, and it feels artificial when he gets up to stare out the window at the quarantined city. Night is falling and he realises that the soft, flickering gaslight he is so used to seeing has been largely replaced by brighter electric streetlights. The familiar view seems askew as a result, the angle of the shadows all wrong. But at least his unease cures any desire to go back outside that he might otherwise have succumbed to.

He pours himself a glass of port which looks almost black in the weak lights of his house; he pulls a book at random from the bookshelf and takes it upstairs to read. He props himself up in bed and Mogwai comes and settles on his lap and falls almost instantly asleep. Fellows starts to feel drowsy himself, feels his eyelids droop despite himself. And why not let himself go? The ghost is exorcised, crossed out like a poorly written sentence in one of Boursier's first drafts, and the footsteps he can hear as his heavy eyelids fall are just Mogwai for the ghost makes no sound and...

He starts awake, his body jerking as if thrown forward in a car that has braked too suddenly, and he realises Mogwai has gone from his lap. But the sounds he can hear aren't the cat for Mogwai is standing by the bedroom doorway, peering down the corridor at something Fellows cannot see. The cat's body is tensed, arched and fur on end to look bigger. What has he seen? Fellows thinks. There is no reason for *him* to tense, for the cat has never once reacted to the presence of the ghost. So what can it be? The noises continue—both a frantic scrabbling and simultaneously the slow dragging sound of something being pulled over the wooden floorboards. It's too loud for a rat surely; could another cat have got inside? An injured cat maybe, run over outside because it too is still unused to the new volume of traffic on the roads… And the sounds are not unlike something dragging its paralysed back half along by its front legs. But wouldn't it be mewing if it was a cat, and how could he have not noticed such a creature getting inside the house when he had opened the door?

Underneath the dragging and scratching sounds, he thinks he can hear laboured breathing. Fellows is choked with a sick fear; the images that the sound of the thing's approach conjure up are unbearable, but then so is the idea of moving from the bed to see what is coming for him.

He looks towards the window, towards the white flash of a gull's wing against the night, and thinks seriously about jumping so he won't have to see.

He looks back towards the doorway and sees a small hand black with bruises grip the side of the doorframe. One of the fingers is bent back at an angle that makes Fellows wince.

Fellows gags, feels the sweet sickly taste of champagne at the back of his throat. He gets quickly off the bed and vomits copiously onto the dusty floor. The room reeks of alcohol. But I only drank a sip, he thinks vaguely.

The hand on the doorframe tightens as well as it can with one finger immobile, and Fellows hears a shuffling, sliding sound, as something attempts to pull itself upright. The thing's breathing sounds like it is being dragged out of something broken.

Another hand grips the frame, and then a small face jerks into view.

Fellows can't help but cry out. In one sense it is the same ghostly face as before, with nothing but white in its eyes, but horridly more physical. More *individual*; a face so specific you might recognise it if you knew the boy in life. Fellows can see the boy's pouting lower lip and a run of freckles across his face that don't match the dark, curly hair; hair he can see is matted with dry blood. A broken nose. A bruised forehead, and a cheek so swollen it almost swallows one of the boy's empty, staring eyes.

The boy tries to pull himself further upright, leaving black fingerprints on the white paint of the doorframe. They don't fade.

Goddamnit, Boursier, what have you done? Fellows thinks. He is still spitting lengths of champagne-tasting drool from his mouth.

The boy tries to turn his head to face Fellows; it doesn't turn smoothly but in a series of jerks, each accompanied by the sound of something internal being dragged somewhere it shouldn't be. He doesn't know how pupil-less eyes can focus on him, but he is sure they do.

Fellows can hear the sounds of the street from downstairs, as if someone had left the front door open.

There is a shrieking noise, so full of hatred and fear Fellows thinks first the boy must be making it before he realises it is Mogwai. The cat hisses and yowls again as if it can't stand the sight of the child. Or as though it smelt funny, Fellows thinks. He sees the cat dart across the room and throw itself screeching at the boy; the boy makes a high yelping noise as if terrified as Mogwai's body hits him, causing his blood-wet grip to slide from the doorframe. The child crashes to the ground, limbs flailing like he is much younger, like a baby unable to right itself. Or like a bug overturned, Fellows thinks, waiting to be stamped on. Surely that would put an end to this haunting, and be kind to the crippled thing too. He imagines…

He shakes the thought from himself, horrified both at what he had almost contemplated doing and the hideous and baffling sense of deja-vu that accompanies the thought.

Mogwai flees from the fallen writhing child and he hears the cat clatter down the stairs and out the mysteriously open front door; there is the sound of car brakes and Fellows tenses... but there is no sound of collision. The car going past his house doesn't stop. He hopes Mogwai is okay; he wonders if he will ever see the cat again.

The boy is still kicking on his back; one of his legs is in some kind of black metal brace, Fellows realises, and that is why it is not as bent looking as the other. The boy is making wet gasping noises but there are no words, despite him looking of an age when he should be able to talk. He can smell the boy has pissed himself, maybe worse, and it is the *implication* of this—how physical it has all become—rather than the smell itself that makes him turn and gag again. There's a burning sensation at the back of his throat, and his eyes fill with tears that seem equally acidic.

When he blinks them away and the room refocuses, the boy is gone.

Fellows walks slowly over to the doorframe; he can still see the evidence of the boy's fingerprints on the paintwork, the blood so black it looks like ink. He can still faintly smell piss, underneath the alcoholic reek of his own vomit.

Everything is very quiet in his house and in the city outside. But quiet like something holding its breath, just like Fellows is. Wondering when the ghost will come back.

But, he supposes, he must stop calling it a ghost now. That bastard hack Boursier had been truthful on that score. The ghost has been exorcised, but in the process become something more real not less. Whatever the boy is, he is no longer silent or incorporeal... His blank white eyes can see

Fellows now, and presumably his crippled and stained hand could touch him...

The thought almost makes Fellows sick again.

Fucking bastard Boursier! he thinks.

FOR THE SECOND TIME THAT day he pounds on the door to the side of the liquor shop, yelling for Boursier until he is let in. His rage makes no impact on Boursier's calm, reaction-less demeanour, and Fellows shouts until he is hoarse.

"A ghost?" Boursier says finally. "But why would you think the boy a ghost?"

"Why? Because up until your meddling he was nearly see-through and...

"I mean, why did you think the child is dead?"

"What?"

"The boy's not dead." Boursier says.

"But of course he's..." Fellows says but trails off, unable to justify his certainty. And he *is* certain, despite Boursier's words.

Before Boursier can answer, there is a loud pounding on the door downstairs.

"Open up! Guardia!" a voice yells from outside.

PART FIVE

THE PANDA PRINCIPLE

"OPEN UP! GUARDIA!" A VOICE yells from outside Boursier's apartment.

"Quickly!" Fellows says, before Boursier can turn away. "What did you mean, the boy's not dead?" Fellows doesn't believe this, knows it to be untrue... but what if what he thinks he knows is yet another thing that can be changed?

Boursier isn't showing any sign of moving, he just stands with his head cocked to one side looking at Fellows quizzically. The infuriatingly placid look on his features hasn't faded. Fellows has to resist the urge to shake him; he imagines the author's head lolling if he did so, as insensible and hollow as a doll's.

The hammering at the door downstairs resumes, the angry shouting resumes.

"What did you *mean*? The boy was a ghost until you..."

"Guardia! Open up! We're armed!"

"Goddamnit!" Fellows shouts; Boursier still doesn't move. There is a warning shot fired outside.

"Go and let them in!" he says, then turns towards the stairs himself when Boursier still doesn't move. "For fuck's sake I'm coming!" he yells, hoping the Guardia can hear him, as he rushes down the steep wooden stairs.

He wonders how he can have got himself in this situation; has it really been only four days since he first read *The Smell Of Paprika* and all this started? Damn Boursier's stories! he thinks as he opens the door.

There are two Guardia outside, one of whom has his gun raised to sky to fire another warning shot; his piggish face can't hide his disappointment at Fellows's appearance. The other gestures for him to put his revolver away and pushes into Boursier's flat; the expression on her face already pissed off.

"Papers?" she says flatly to Fellows. "Look, go and search upstairs," she says irritably to her colleague who is fumbling his gun back into his holster.

"Boursier is up there," Fellows says as he hands her his identity papers. "He lives here, I imagine it's him you want so..."

"Can I see your hands please sir? Palms upward."

"My hands?" Fellows complies. He sees his hands are stained with ink; he sees the Guardia notices it too. He hears the muffled voice of the other Guardia quizzing Boursier upstairs; the writer's replies are too quiet to hear.

"Look, what is..." he starts.

"We've reason to believe you're producing subversive literature sir," the Guardia says. "Pamphlets protesting against our legitimate and beloved unity government, perhaps?"

"Me? No!"

The other Guardia comes back downstairs.

"Just the same idiot as last time," he says. "He doesn't know anything."

"You interrogated him thoroughly did you?" his colleague says. "No, never mind, I'm sure you did," she adds as he starts to protest.

"But it's *him* you want," Fellows says, his voice flustered. "Boursier?" he shouts. "Come down here!"

"He doesn't know anything," the male Guardia says again.

"*You're* in the home of a known protestor," the other says to Fellows, "albeit a low ranking one…"

"No, he's in charge," Fellows says.

She snorts. "That imbecile? C'mon. You've been seen multiple times over the last few days associating with the protestors, you've no job, you walk the streets at all hours…"

"And that's a crime is it? Are you actually arresting me?" Fellows says.

The Guardia smiles. "On that piss-poor evidence? Of course not. But you *are* coming with us."

Fellows calls again for Boursier to come and explain that he is no protestor, but the male Guardia grabs him from behind, twists his arms behind his back. The other opens the door and together they escort him out into the quarantined city. Faces scowl at them from the steps of the building opposite; the Guardia are not much liked in the old town. The various hustlers, dealers and street artists disperse, looking over their shoulders and muttering abuse, as much towards Fellows for getting caught as the Guardia themselves. They think him one of their own, just incompetent.

"Boursier! Goddamnit!" Fellows tries to twist to shout back towards the apartment, but the door has already swung shut behind him.

"Just get in the car, sir," the female Guardia says wearily, not looking at him.

Fellows turns to see one of the unity government automobiles parked at the side of the road (despite the fact Fellows remembers the roads of the old town being too narrow and uneven for automobiles to use). The car is a long sleek shape he finds almost sinister; with its tinted windows it would be almost completely black apart from a splash of gull shit on its bonnet. The female Guardia opens the rear door; the interior of the car seems as dark as its exterior, a black hole that the male Guardia starts to force him towards...

"No," says Fellows. "No, I'll come with you but I can't... can't we just walk?"

"Walk? Just because you tramp around this city all day it doesn't mean *we're* going to. Just get in." The Guardia gestures with her free hand towards the inside of the car.

"No!" Fellows shouts, stepping backwards and causing the other Guardia to stumble and loosen his grip. He pulls away and turns to flee; the Guardia kicks out, catching him in the leg and he falls to the dirty street. His head slams against the ground, causing his vision to fog and his gorge to rise with the stale and impossible taste of champagne... *Am I being lifted up?* he thinks groggily, words that seem to be from some other place entirely.

He gets to his feet again, hazy about his next move, and the Guardia behind fumbles at his gun holster with clumsy fingers...

"Fuck's *sake,"* the other says, grabbing Fellows roughly by the arm. In one motion, the physics of which he can't decipher, she smoothly and without apparent effort uses the momentum of his struggle to bundle him into the back of the car. He sprawls onto the worn leather backseat; hands grab his kicking legs and heave him fully in. He squirms to turn back towards the door.

"No, wait..."

The door shuts and the panicked part of Fellows knows even as he lurches towards the handle that it won't open from the inside. He still pulls at it, hands already shaking. The front of the car is separated from him by a partition, and this and the tinted windows give the impression that he is already in a cell.

He feels the engine shudder into life, and he starts to shudder himself.

There's a jolt as they pull away from the pavement, and then he feels the car accelerate. His hands scrabble against the smooth leather behind him, but there are no seat-belts in the back. He looks at the tinted glass separating him from the Guardia and the face he sees in it seems blank-eyed and lurching towards him... until he realises it is himself, jolted forward. The car takes a corner too fast, and as Fellows tumbles against the door he tenses himself for a squeal of brakes and the forward momentum of a skid...

In an effort to quell his panic Fellows looks out the window at the familiar streets of the quarantined city; they are the same as he remembers save for the darkness lent by the tinted glass. But how can the streets of the old town look the same while suddenly being wide enough for two lanes of traffic? He imagines the city laid out on the surface of a bubble that is slowly being inflated, stretched thin and translucent.

When the car pulls out of the old town and into stranger streets, it accelerates again. Too fast, too fast, Fellows thinks and he closes his eyes; but what he half-remembers in that blackness is no comfort. Lana's eyes the day she had left him, furious but also wet with a grief she had no right to, which was a hurt all in itself... Fellows opens his eyes quickly; sees as if hallucinating the park where he had first read one of Boursier's stories flash by, the prostitutes and gigolos gathered near the fountain posed as if in a painting. Fellows doesn't have time to figure out how they have ended up here so quickly before his stomach clenches.

He slams on the partition, shouts that he is going to be sick but either the Guardia don't hear him or they don't care. The car passes into the area of the city occupied by the offices of the unity government and civic officials; white stone buildings with an aggressive, angular architecture and flags fluttering from their rooftops. Fortunately the car slows, for there is more traffic here—more than Fellows has seen anywhere in the city before—and he manages to choke down his nausea. They are not going to crash, he tells himself, not at this speed. The car turns and descends a ramp, down beneath one of the imposing white buildings that seem alien to the city he knows. They stop at some kind of barrier and Fellows hears the two Guardia present their papers to a security guard, before the car continues its descent into a basement carpark lit by mercury lights so bright its empty space seems like an amphitheatre, its concrete a stage.

And that's when Fellows starts to slam his hands against the windows, starts to yell and then shrink back in his seat, as if to get away from something coming for him. Because for a split second the white light makes it seem like there is open sky overhead, and he imagines he sees a body laid out on the concrete.

THE GUARDIA LEAD FELLOWS THROUGH a long series of grey and windowless corridors, each so similar he soon gives up trying to memorise their route, although he is sure they must have crossed their own path. His legs are still shaking from the panic attack; the male Guardia is gloating under the mistaken impression Fellows had been scared of *him*. Nevertheless Fellows does feel a slight unease, in the heart of the unity government's machinery as he is. The corridors are windowless and lit only by flickering electric lights, so he suspects they are still underground. The few other people they pass are not Guardia but office workers who avoid making eye-contact.

At one point the three of them come to a demarcation that is nothing more than a strip of peeling coloured tape on the floor; nevertheless the Guardia pause before crossing as if it represents something more. Beyond the other side of the fading blue line they encounter no one else and the corridors echo with their footsteps.

Eventually, they come to a door which the female Guardia unlocks—it opens into a small room which the other Guardia shoves him forward into despite the fact that he would have gone willingly. The other makes a sucking noise with her teeth and follows, shutting the door behind her. Fellows had expected something akin to a police interrogation room or cell, but instead it seems more like an office meeting room: four chairs on wheels (like the one in The Echo Bookshop) around a wooden table smudged with old ink. Only the lack of windows, and the paint peeling from the walls to reveal breeze blocks behind spoil the illusion.

"Right then," the male Guardia says weakly; his hands flap as if he is itching to draw his revolver again. The other ignores him, gestures for Fellows to sit at the table and then does likewise, next to him rather than opposite. The male Guardia flaps his hands again and then abruptly leaves, seemingly in response to her continual indifference. Fellows hopes this is a good sign.

"So, some preliminaries," the Guardia says and double-checks with Fellows the information on his identity papers, before asking him about his movements over the last few days. Fellows doesn't mention Georgia, but otherwise tells the Guardia everywhere he has been, including the house in the Enclave—he doesn't want to mention that but because he was spotted by the patrol there he knows he has no choice.

"A known hangout for protestors," the Guardia says. "So what were *you* doing there?"

"I was looking for Boursier."

"Boursier?" she says questioningly.

"The guy whose apartment you found me at," Fellows says after a few seconds. "The writer."

"Oh, him,"—it's as if she had forgotten, and even now she sounds entirely uninterested.

"He's at the heart of all this you know," Fellows says animatedly. "The protestors and their weird theories and…" He stops before he says too much that is unbelievable, despite it being true. This building of grey concrete and solid walls is no place for ghosts or fracturing realities. "I'm not the person you think I am," he sighs.

She shrugs. "You'll do," she says.

"I'll *do*? What does that mean?" Fellows says.

"Look," the Guardia says, "you've not actually committed a crime. That I know of. You're free to leave if you want." She waits until Fellows makes the smallest possible movement to do so, then adds "but."

"But?"

"But, it *is* a crime for a civilian to be anywhere in the restricted zone unaccompanied." She points at the doorway, where Fellows sees another boundary of blue tape. "Leave this room before I say and you'll be arrested on the spot."

"But what do you mean, I'll do? You don't really think I'm guilty of anything do you?"

"I don't know," the Guardia shrugs again. "But you'll do. Bring in people who have been known to associate with the protestors, they said. I'm not going to bust a gut to bring in someone who might have broken the law when you're already here, am I? The quicker this gets done the quicker we can both go home." She stands, works at a crick in her neck, then picks up his identity papers and her forms. "I'll go and file all of these and see what they want to do with you—they always take an age to decide, with you idiot protestors. It won't do any *good* you know. They can't do anything to lift it, the unity government."

"I *know* that," Fellows says angrily. "I'm not…"

"That's why they hate you guys so much and want to frustrate you with bullshit like this. Because you might reveal how little they can actually do. So as I say, I'll be *hours*. You get to stay here. Lucky for you you bought your own entertainment, eh?"

"Huh?"

"Don't worry I checked it on the way here," she says, handing him a familiar looking bag. "Just a bunch of nonsense stories. No wonder you have some funny ideas." Fellows takes the bag of Boursier stories, holds them close to his chest although it is too late—she has already read them. "I should hand them in, *especially* that one called *The Quarantine*," the Guardia says. "But that's as much drivel as the rest of them. What the hell is a 'ring road'?"

Fellows shrugs hopelessly.

"Anyway. Whatever floats your boat. If reading them stops you getting distracted by thoughts of leaving this room while I'm gone, I'll turn a blind eye."

"I'm not reading those!" Fellows says, with more anger than he intends.

"Suit yourself. What do I care? Don't go anywhere," the Guardia says, leaving and shutting the door behind her. She doesn't even bother to lock it.

Fellows stares at the door, then sits back in his chair, idly spins in it a few times…

The anger and frustration he feels at his detention is gradually eroded by the boredom, and the absence of anything to look at in the room. There's no sound other than the hum of the electric light above, dull with dust and dead flies inside the casing. Fellows slaps his hands on the desk to make a noise (wondering just when he had got ink on them); he gets up and opens the door, stares at the blue tape border between him and the corridor, then shuts the door and goes and sits back down.

This is what you put Leianna through, he thinks, and she had the worry of her son waiting for her at home. Still, they let her out after a few hours, so obviously they will let you out as well. You just need to wait.

He glances at the bag of Boursier stories.

He remembers, back in his old-life, Lana mocking him for his habit of taking a book everywhere. "It's a ten minute tram journey," she'd say, "what's the point in taking a book?"

"What if it's delayed? What if it breaks down and I'm stuck?" he'd say. The thought of not having something to read in such situations filled him with an odd kind of unease. As though spending too much time just in the company of his own thoughts would be unhealthy; and he always wondered, glancing up from his book at the others on the tram who were staring vacantly out the window, just *what* they were thinking, just where their thoughts could be taking them. He didn't understand people who didn't read.

He picks up the bag, quickly puts it down again. Two left, he thinks, one called *The Quarantine* according to the Guardia, and one called... What is the other called?

The hum of the light seems to change pitch slightly, so that he becomes aware of it all over again. He drums his hands on the desk, self-consciously this time, putting on an act of a man who has no other choices.

Just looking at the *title* won't hurt surely? he thinks. Surely that can't change anything? He has no way of knowing that for sure, but Fellows knows he is going to do it anyway.

Give it another ten minutes to see if she returns, he thinks, but without his watch that so mysteriously vanished from his wrist he doesn't even know how long that is. He gets up, rummages through the stories to find the one he wants. Won't hurt, he thinks, but as he reads the title his eyes automatically slip to the sentence below:

The Panda Principle by Boursier

"This is the Boundary Stone," said Mr. Read—

FELLOWS WRENCHES HIS GAZE AWAY, blinking rapidly. Don't be stupid, he thinks, what will reading *this* change? But part of him, looking round the featureless room he is trapped in, and thinking about what awaits him back home, almost doesn't care.

The Panda Principle by Boursier

"This is the Boundary Stone," said Mr. Read, "where they washed coins in vinegar to try and get rid of the plague. In these holes, see?"

Stones, thought Amit, all those idiots had were stones. Vinegar to wash their stupid old money in, and stones to form a border round their stupid little village.

"Did it work, Sir?" Kay Dawson asked a little breathlessly.

"It was all they had," Mr. Read said, shrugging.

Amit sighed—he didn't see the point of having come on a school trip all the way from one boring English village to stand in a field on the outskirts of another. He looked around: all he could see were empty fields divided by drystone walls, and the low sky stooping to erase any individuality from them with grey fog. It was so deathly dull.

The details of the plague had interested him slightly, he had to admit; the buboes, the rats, the unbelievable number of deaths. But the whole story was just stupid—if he'd been in this village when they'd quarantined themselves because they'd known the plague had come, he'd have run like fuck.

"See, they didn't know about germs, about bacteria," Mr. Read was saying. "Sometimes what you have is hard to get rid of, despite the fact that there's potentially something better. The Panda Principle," he added and looked set to continue before he realised he'd lost his class entirely. The history teacher was known for his rambling, infuriating style. "Now Jenna," he said, changing tone, "don't step outside the boundary!" He was obviously joking but Jenna stepped away from the border stone quickly, as if she had done something wrong. Amit sighed loudly. These village kids were such pussies!

Amit had spent most of his twelve years growing up on an estate close to the centre of a Midlands city, in a grimy and graffitied block of flats with broken lifts and metal grilles over the windows of the first three floors. He'd loved it. The sense of urgency and excitement in the streets as they darkened, the illicit deals and trades going on that he pretended to his mother he didn't understand. The boys only a few years older prowling the streets as if they owned them; Amit had copied their cursing, their slouched walk, the sullen way they could imply violence with a shrug, a sneer. School had been a drag but none of the older kids had attended and Amit had begun skiving off himself.

But then...! His mother had won the lottery. Amit couldn't believe his bad luck. Not the big prize, obviously, but enough to buy the crappy big house in the country that had suddenly become her lifelong dream. She'd spent nearly all she'd won on the house; she still had to work and so she was now a cleaner for other people who lived in the crappy big houses but had the income to match. And the village was dull, dull, dull—so quiet Amit wanted to scream. There was literally nothing to do but school, and various after school clubs, eagerly attended by the posh kids. But despite its dullness, Amit was still slowly forgetting where he had come from, the feel and taste of his past—if he returned to those streets now would they still know him as one of them?

He'd thought the school trip might at least have been interesting, but they'd just come to a village equally as dead. Maybe the plague's still here, Amit thought, it's killed everyone. That would have explained why the villagers hadn't even looked at him as Mr. Read had led them from the carpark to the boundary of the village: they were ghosts. Amit looked dejectedly around the field; even his daydreams couldn't make it interesting. The mist seemed to be closing in, bringing the horizon closer.

"And now," Mr. Read said as if announcing a treat, "we're going to look at the church!" Oh for fuck's sake, Amit thought. "Not that they were allowed to bury the plague victims there," Mr. Read added. "They had to make do by..." He turned away towards the village and it was as if the mist swallowed up his words. The class lined up to follow him; Mr. Read looked back to give the group a quick count. Amit stood at the back of the line, wanting to growl in frustration. This trip was so boring there wasn't even any way to misbehave!

He took a step back, felt his heel bang into something. He looked and saw the boundary stone, its worn holes making it look like the face of a die. Fuck it, Amit thought, I'm getting out of this plague-y village! He turned and ran through the border and for a few feet into the fog, expecting Mr. Read's voice to summon him back any second...

But there was just silence, and when Amit turned round the fog had thickened so suddenly his class was no longer visible. Brilliant! he thought. Mr. Read will shit bricks when he realises he's lost me!

It was very quiet, he couldn't hear the sound of the other children even though they couldn't have gone very far. But then fog deadened sounds; Mr. Read had taught them that, Amit reflected.

He stood still, waiting for Mr. Read to emerge from the fog and for dull reality to reassert itself. But nothing happened; there was no sound and he could see forward only a few feet. Amit started to feel cold in the damp air. Sod this, he though, and started to walk back towards the invisible village. His plan was to find the carpark where the school coach was parked and wait there for his class to come back; Mr. Read would be frantic by then. As he walked he must have crossed the boundary although the fog was so thick he didn't see the stone.

When Amit finally found the carpark the coach wasn't there.

What the fuck? he thought, his mind's voice an imitation of the youths of his old estate. There were no coaches at all in the carpark, and those cars that were there looked old and sat on deflated tyres. On the streets behind the carpark he was aware of movement, the villagers hurrying head down through the fog glimpsed as briefly as birds in cloud. They seemed as unaware of Amit's presence as before.

The coach driver obviously just went somewhere more interesting, Amit thought, instead of waiting in this dump. Well, he'd had his fun; Mr. Read had probably already had a heart attack. He walked away from the carpark; occasionally as the mist swirled and shifted he caught sight of the squat church tower.

His class wasn't at the church either; no one was at the church. Amit stuck his head inside the doors, called out into the gloomy interior, but there was no response other than an echo. He stood indecisively in the graveyard, watching the fog make odd shapes as it moved between the stones. Was the whole village deserted? As if their response to the plague had not been to stay put but to scurry head down and away, leaving Amit stranded here.

Amit reached into his pocket; his mobile phone wasn't there. Fuck's sake, he thought, he must have dropped it. He imagined his old mates, laughing at him. He swore aloud to himself, but in the dead and still air it sounded pitiful rather than defiant.

A figure approached out of the mist, as if called into being by his curse. It was hard to see much about the person as they approached, but Amit was just glad someone had actually noticed him.

"Eh up, lad," the figure said, a deeper and more countrified version of the accent he and his mates had used to mock—fucking Derbyshire. He was even dressed like their caricature, in an old suit and flat-cap.

"Hi," Amit said awkwardly. Back home he'd have assumed the man wanted something, was a pervert perhaps, but since he and his mum had moved he'd learnt that people in the country just spoke to you, regardless of if they knew you or not.

"You were out near the stones?" the man said. Both his words and expression seemed flattened by the mist between them.

Amit shrugged. "I guess." Then weakening slightly: "I lost my class."

"I can help you," the man in the flat-cap said.

Later, after they'd looked round the village and its landmarks for Amit's class, and returned to the carpark where there was also no sign of them, the man said it again: "I can help you."

Amit looked round the deserted carpark; what if they'd left without him? Surely Mr. Read wasn't that shit a teacher. He wished he knew what time it was; he was sure the sky was darkening but the fog made it hard to tell. For some reason he didn't want to ask the stranger, who was peering at Amit from beneath his cap, as if trying to be certain of what he was seeing. Amit was almost sure the man was going to just walk away and leave him, and part of him hoped he would. But then the man gave a heavy sigh, and tugged at the tie around his neck with a meaty hand.

"C'mon lad," he said. "Let's get you inside where it's warm, get some food down you. Then we can see what's what."

Amit didn't see that he had any other choice.

The man, who introduced himself as Bob, lived in a squat cottage made of dull coloured stone. In the village where Amit now lived with his mum there were several 'cottages' which, when you stepped inside them, were expanded and renovated to look like any other house. But when entering the narrow doorway into Bob's house, the low ceiling and uneven floor really did make it feel like stepping back in time. He didn't notice the fusebox on the wall or the telephone cable pinned to the skirting board until his eyes adjusted to the dim light. Next to the phone on a wooden drawer was an incongruous digital photo frame, flicking between different pictures of Bob and his family. A small and rosy-cheeked woman presumably his wife, and a young boy about Amit's age constantly scowling as if affronted by the very act of having his picture taken. Amit supposed he was just squinting in the bright sunlight of wherever the photos had been taken, the light so strong it made the boy's pale face look ill-defined.

Amit started as he realised he had been staring at the photos as they flicked past, and that Bob had been watching him.

"Holidays?" Amit said, trying to hide his discomfort.

"Yep. Brittany. Lovely place," Bob said. "The boy's dead now," he added gruffly.

"Oh, I'm... I'm sorry man, I..." Amit said, feeling sick like he'd done something wrong.

"No need for that," Bob said. "Kid never felt like mine anyway."

Amit stared; if all fathers were such bastards he was glad he'd never known his own. Bob hung up his coat, started to undo his tie, his eyes not leaving Amit. Amit looked away, back to the photographs sliding past so quickly; in only one did the pale boy look happy, when he'd been caught in the act of licking something tasty from his fingers.

Amit's stomach rumbled.

There was the sound of footsteps coming towards them from some unseen part of the cottage.

"Don't tell the wife," Bob said. "The boy was mine, just didn't feel like it to me. Happens sometimes."

Before Amit could respond to this—not that he knew how to respond—the door to the hallway opened and an older and greyer haired version of the woman in the photographs burst in; for a second she looked at Amit as if he was unreal. And then she moved to engulf him in a hug, her voice a rush of concern. It made Amit feel uncomfortable (he wasn't used to such affection) and the heat of her flesh pressed against him, the faint smell of dry herbs or flowers, made him think fleetingly of the plague, of the posies the villagers thought might save them.

"Heather," Bob said, "the wife. Happened again," he added, speaking to Heather. "Found this one wandering near the church. Not sure though."

"Oh you poor dear," Heather said, as Amit pulled away from her embrace. "Are you cold? Have you eaten?"

"Look, uh," Amit said, "could you maybe call the police, yeah? I've lost my mobile," he added. He wished he knew his mum's number off by heart, but he'd never learnt it.

"Hmmmm," Bob said."Well we could try. Reckon Fletch is likely to have shut up shop by this time though." He spoke as if suggesting that, while Amit could be forgiven for having forgotten, what he said was obvious.

There was a silence. Amit glanced towards Heather and saw she was staring at the digital photo frame; the white boy licking his fingers slid from view.

"Um?" he said.

"Oh. Oh, yes," Heather said. "Bob you try and call Fletch and we'll get you nice and warm; what's your name, dearie?"

"Amit." He thought he saw the two of them glance at each other, but what the significance of his name to them could be he didn't know. Before he could decipher that Heather put her arm around his shoulder and led him though a low-beamed doorway into a small lounge. A real fire was the only source of light and it made everything around it seem as insubstantial as shadows.

Amit sat in a faded floral armchair, so comfortable it seemed to already know his contours as he sank into it. He felt tired, lulled into closing his eyes by the heat of the room and the dusty, lavender scent.

"Some food?" he heard Heather say. "Your favourite? Fish-fingers?" and he nodded, forcing his eyes open. His thoughts seemed as flickering and ill-defined as the flames of the fire. His favourite?

"No reply," Bob said, coming into the room, the floorboard creaking. Amit sat bolt upright, alert again. What had he just been thinking? Bob stared at him. "We'll try in the morning lad."

"The morning? But my mum will be..." He stopped, unsure how to finish. "Can't you call the police station back home, my home?" he said.

"Your parents will be doing that surely?" Bob said; the flickering light from the fire made the expression on his face shift, like those pictures that were two things a once. "Best wait."

"And when your mother knows you're safe she surely won't come until tomorrow?" Heather said, placing a plate in front of him: fish-fingers, oven chips and peas. "Your favourite," Heather said again. "So eat this up and then we'll get you ready for bed."

Amit's stomach gurgled hungrily.

His bedroom for the night had a sloped ceiling from being built into the eaves, and a small window that seemed to look out onto... nothing. Of course, Amit knew it was just because there weren't as many streetlights in the stupid countryside, but he still found it disconcerting and was glad when Heather drew the curtains. The curtains, and the bedspread, were decorated with faded patterns of superheroes; a poster of a Spitfire was peeling from the one straight wall. Amit wondered how long ago it had been when Heather and Bob's son had died.

He got under the covers of the bed and Heather put the nightlight on, and in the soft glow both Heather and Bob stood looking at him for an uncomfortable amount of time. Bob sighed, the fingers of his hands flexed and released.

"It will be better in the morning," Heather said and Amit nodded, even though she wasn't looking at him.

"Has he brushed his teeth?" Bob said abruptly, as if to change the subject.

"No, he's just..."

"C'mon lad," Bob said, ignoring his wife. "You know the routine," although Amit had never been made to brush his teeth. In the bathroom he had a sudden fear that Bob would make him use the dead son's toothbrush, but instead Bob took a brand new one still in its packet from a cabinet drawer. Amit noticed there were ten or twelve unopened children's toothbrushes in the drawer before Bob shut it.

"When... when did your son die?" he said all of a sudden, and he sensed the man freeze behind him. In the mirror, Amit's face looked overly pale as he waited to see if Bob would answer.

"Stephen?" Bob said slowly, as if the word were foreign to his tongue. "Ten years ago. A hit and run," he added gruffly. "Some drunken twat."

So they can't have kept it the same since he died, Amit thought as Bob ushered him back to the bedroom with a large hand on his shoulder. He didn't know much about the toys but the games console under the TV was only a few years old.

Maybe they had a nephew who came to stay?

The next morning it was as if he were jerked awake from a dream of bright lights on broken glass, his body tight with adrenaline as if he had just been thrown forward. He felt different to the day before, but also as if more than a day had passed; like he had crossed some kind of border in the night. He felt good.

He dressed with clothes from the chest of drawers—socks from the top, underwear the middle, white shirt the bottom—which all fit him perfectly, as did the trousers and school blazer from the wardrobe. He went downstairs; the kitchen seemed bigger with the sunlight streaming in from the windows and for a moment he didn't recognise the two pale faces that turned towards him...

Then his vision adjusted and he saw his mother and father.

"Morning!" his mum said, greeting him with a familiar hug. "What do you want for breakfast?"

"Fish fingers!" he said laughing.

"I know it's your favourite but you can't have fish fingers for breakfast!" Their morning joke.

"Second favourite!"—he continued the routine, while sitting at the table and pouring himself some milk. His pleasure was only dulled by the sense of disapproval from his father who was staring at him intently over the newspaper, and an itchiness to his vision, as if when he rubbed his eyes and reopened them things might look different.

"Put your tie on for school, lad," his father said, "you know the routine."

"Bob..." said his mother in a pleading tone of voice. As Amit left the room he heard her say, "Not again. I can't... Not *again*."

"Doesn't fit. Happens sometimes I guess."

"Sometimes!" he heard his mother shout as he ran up to his room. "Sometimes! How many bloody more times?" Their voices continued but he couldn't hear any more of the words.

Amit came downstairs a few minutes later, embarrassedly holding a tie limply in his hand.

"He can't tie a tie," his father said flatly to his mother, as if that clinched some dispute between them, and she turned away.

His father got up to help him, noosing the tie around his neck.

"You could *show* him how," his mother said, but his father ignored her. Amit felt flustered and unsure of himself as the man's rough hands moved so close to his neck. How could his father's calloused, pale hands seem at once so familiar and so alien?

He looked to his left, to where the digital photo-frame could be seen in the hall, flicking through the photos of their holiday to France. He had seen them so many times that even from this distance he could recognise each one—his memories rotating in strict order. But why did he look so sullen in each of them? Afraid even—of his parents? He looked like he didn't belong...

And for a moment it was like a whole set of other memories was about to overwhelm him, poised like a wave about to break over him. He saw as if through fog a tall blurred building, two figures casting about as if they couldn't see him, and an old and weather-worn vertical stone.

But then the picture in the frame switched and it was as if the one in his head did too. This was his favourite photo, where he had been caught slurping grease from his fingers; he had been eating paprika-flavoured potatoes his parents had bought him from the stall at the harbour. The taste had been one he had loved; his parents had teased him every time he'd asked for another taste of them back home in Derbyshire. But he'd had to make do with fish fingers. Sometimes what you had had to be good enough; surely?

But I don't even know what paprika tastes like, Amit thought. He blinked, slowly and deliberately, and then jerked away from the man with his hands around his neck.

The tie slid from Amit's collar to the stone floor.

Amit stared at the strange man in front of him, at the strange woman who had begun to cry.

The man sighed.

"Maybe next time round," he said to the woman, and then stepped towards Amit.

FELLOWS QUICKLY SHUTS THE LITERARY journal (it was called *QWERTY*) as if to pretend he hasn't just read the story. He feels the vague guilt he always feels whenever his willpower weakens, after drinking too much or masturbating, despite the fact that no one else knew or would care. Why has he read the whole damned thing? What has he *done*?

He gets up, looks around the room: the same desk and chairs, the same peeling paintwork and taped partition before the door. The hum of the light, at that same pitch. But the fact that everything between these four walls is the same proves nothing; in fact he would welcome some immediately visible alteration, for what would he care if some interrogation room in the depths of the unity government bureaucracy had changed?

What if all of the city outside has become something else, become Boursier's village voluntarily sealing itself off from the plague? Without any windows he is blind. Just a view of the fishing boats moored in the harbour, or the fish-topped spire of the Mariner's church or, if he was facing the other way, the houses of the Enclave on the hill above the park and old town would have reassured him. He flashes back to the other evening, to Georgia refusing to look at the darkness outside her apartment, fearful all had changed…

The door to the cell opens and the female Guardia reappears with a smile less vivid than the bags under her eyes. She gestures for him to sit down and then does so next to him. She opens a folder of paperwork and forms on the desk between them, like some collaboration they are working on together. When she meets his eyes she looks exhausted, as if they were both frustrated by the same thing, two travellers enduring the same delay.

"You're allowed to go," she says, "if you can satisfactorily explain the ink on your hands. I hope you can."

"The ink…?"

"Look, they want to arrest the writer behind the all these anti-quarantine pamphlets," she said. "So tell me why the ink doesn't make that you. Then we can both get home."

"I…" Fellows looks at his hands briefly and sure enough they are still smudged with ink. He remembers the scripted words on Leianna's palms, but any on his are illegible. It seemed a lot to have just come off a newspaper and he wonders whether the Guardia would believe him. "I'm a writer," he says instead. Same lie, different day.

"A writer?" the Guardia says. "Jesus…"

"Of stories," he adds quickly. "Not propaganda. That's why I was at Boursier's place, I'd gone because, uh, there's not many writers in the city because of the quarantine…"

"Careful," the Guardia says; she is writing down his words on one of the forms, although to Fellows her handwriting is indecipherable.

"And when I write, the ink from my pen… I write too fast and it's a cheap pen you see and…"

"Okay, okay," the Guardia says. "That will do; it's good enough even though it's crap. Just wash your hands the next time you print more of that rubbish, understand? Do the both of us a favour."

"No, it's true…" Fellows starts.

"Okay, sure, fine. You're a writer. Look, I'm writing it down. Hey you're right, I've got ink on my fingers too," she says sarcastically.

"Am I allowed to go?"

"Yeah, wait a second, I'll have to escort you back." Fellows watches impatiently as the Guardia continues to fill in her forms.

"Why were you so scared in the car?" she says suddenly.

"What? I thought you said I could go?"

"Just asking," she said. "It's not going in the report. But Jesus, I thought you were going to have a heart attack on us. Are you well? You should see someone."

"I'm fine." Fellows says stiffly. "Can I *please* go?"

The Guardia shrugs and gets up. She leads him from the room and through the maze of corridors. When they reach the demarcation of blue tape, she stops.

"Aren't you going to show me the way *out*?" Fellows says.

"Too much paperwork," she says. "You can find your own way from here surely? Just, if you get lost, don't cross any blue lines."

WHEN FELLOWS FINALLY EMERGES FROM the building, it is not the time of day he is expecting; the sun is seemingly in a different part of the sky than it should be. Maybe it is the tall, angular buildings that make the sun seem lower; there is a triumphant air to the architecture in this part of the city. The buildings are white as bone, picked clean.

Fellows is disorientated, not knowing which way to walk to head back home. He hopes he doesn't need to cross the road in front of him; the torrent of traffic flowing through it seems to have widened it, eroding the banks. He tries to picture the route the Guardia must have taken, but his memories of the drive are too shot through with panic to be of use. In the end he picks a direction to walk by looking up, and hoping the direction the gulls in the grey sky are moving in is seaward.

The pedestrians in this part of the city are presumably all unity government officials and they move with a haste and pushiness that Fellows isn't used to. His slow and uncertain progress serves to annoy them and they do little to hide that annoyance. There's a sense of aggression in the air, not helped by the fact that many of the people seem to be talking to themselves, or someone unseen, in a brisk and business-like manner Fellows can't decipher. No one else around seems to think it madness.

A man in an angular white suit, matching the buildings above him, stops in front of Fellows and sticks his hand out, yelling for a taxi.

Twat, Fellows thinks, doesn't he know that the petrol rationing... His thoughts stutter to a stop as he see a black cab pull up and the man get in. The taxi is the wrong colour and there's something almost futuristic about its appearance; maybe it is just because Fellows hasn't seen one for so long. He remembers, vaguely, a period in his life when he had caught taxis almost everyday; but why would that be when he used to drive? The memories are associated with his breakup with Lana, her voice hateful despite tears, and with the taste of stale alcohol and panic in his throat.

It doesn't seem like ten years, the bitterness seems closer than that. He deliberately forces away the painful memories of a city other than this one and watches the taxi pull away. The telephone number on its sides is too long for the quarantined city, he thinks, not enough people have telephones here to justify so many digits surely? He tries to memorise the number, thinking perhaps to call it from Georgia's place when she has forgiven him, but another of the crazed people talking to themselves bumps into him and he loses sight of it. Despite the fact Fellows was standing still the woman swears at him.

"Sorry about that," the woman says to whoever she thinks she is talking to, continuing on her way without giving Fellows another glance. "Just some tourist stood gawping at the cabs."

The streets of the old town are a relief when Fellows reaches them, the proportions of the buildings and roads not as daunting, the grubbiness and faint tang of open sewers more human. There are still crazy people here, but crazy in an understakable way; the dipsomaniacs and insomniacs scuttle past the beggars and buskers. Fellows isn't quite sure what route he took to get here—he had been walking with his head craned upwards to follow the white birds—but made it here he has.

He walks towards Georgia's apartment block, stands on the opposite side of the road and counts the windows up six storeys until he finds hers. It would have been quicker just looking for the one with the curtains still drawn. Against the chaos of the city, the changing city, he thinks; poor Georgia. He thinks what a shit friend he has been, so wrapped up in his own problems that he had failed to help her with her own. Just because her problems are all in her mind, unlike his vacant-eyed ghost and Boursier stories, it doesn't mean they are lesser than his.

Nevertheless, Georgia had been *furious* last he saw her, and after his day detained by the Guardia, Fellows is in no mood for further confrontation. He turns and walks away from Georgia's apartment block without entering.

At Boursier's house there is no answer when he knocks. He tries the liquor shop below, but they seem unclear about who he is asking after. He has never met anyone who makes so little impact on those around him than Boursier.

Fellows stands in the street, debating what to do. The sensible thing would surely be to go home; he is tired despite not being sure what time of day it is. But thinking of home just reminds him of the sound of now audible footsteps tottering towards him, the sound of drool being sucked back into a broken mouth.

"What do you mean the boy isn't dead?" Fellows says aloud—the question Boursier never answered. But where is Boursier now? Where else could such a recluse have gone?

Seller's instructions, a voice sneers in his memory.

AS FELLOWS APPROACHES THE ECHO Bookshop, he hears that voice from the open door, raised in exasperation. He is unsure if in the pause afterwards another, quieter voice replies or if it just the sound of the wind shaking the gutters. Fellows stands indecisive in the alley, wondering whether he should just walk away. Every time he has become more entangled in Boursier and his stories it has never gone to plan. Whatever power Boursier's stories have is fickle and can't be relied upon, and the man himself seems to pass through the quarantined city without any impact whatsoever. He has had a lucky escape: the fifth story doesn't seem to have changed anything. And what sort of crap title was *The Panda Principle* anyway? Fellows has heard the term but would never have used it for a title beyond the first draft. It referenced an evolutionary postulate, that once a given ecological niche was filled by a species it was hard for another to replace it even if the original species was not as well adapted to it as the second. Pandas were not very good at digesting bamboo; QWERTY keyboards were not the quickest to type on; vinegar was not the best way to sterilise. Sometimes what you have has to be enough, Fellows thinks.

So he should just walk away from here. He would get his things from his house, hopefully avoiding the damn ghost, and go and stay at Georgia's. She would forgive him, surely? He could stay with her while he tried to sort alternative lodgings. After all it was *houses* that were haunted, wasn't it? He's been ignoring the obvious solution with all his pointless walks across the city.

But what had Boursier *meant* when he said the boy wasn't dead?

Fellows looks up to the sky, seeking a world where he isn't about to go into The Echo Bookshop. The gulls above are turning in rigid circles, as if attached to the poles of a carousel. "Stop staring off into space!" he remembers Lana saying, with exasperated affection. Affection *then*, when his inattention had been to trifles. Later on, furious, she'd accused him of looking away from *her*, from their relationship. From the road.

"What game are you playing?" he hears the bookseller yell, in the tone of voice of a man who feels an argument should have ended in his favour many minutes ago. "You've *had* your money!" Fellows smiles—whatever else, the thought of seeing the cocksure and aggravating bookseller so annoyed appeals to him.

He walks up the alley towards the sound of voices; the bookseller's cries are as raucous as the city gulls, but as he gets nearer he can hear a milder voice attempting to reply. He had been right then; Boursier has come to collect his money.

Fellows steps into the shop, remembering with a smile his previous resolution never to return to the Echo. If anything it is even more unwelcoming and dilapidated than he remembers. The windows are grimier and let in less light; one of the shelves (*Fictions G*) has collapsed under the weight of old paperbacks, spilling its titles onto the volumes below. The layer of dust on every surface is thicker, so thick on the stone floor he thinks he can see the faint imprint of footprints heading down the aisle towards the hidden front-desk. I'm on your trail Boursier, he thinks, and there is no peeling boundary for me to cross here… Thinking of that makes him think of the Boundary Stone from *The Panda Principle* and how its description matched that of the stone he'd seen at the entrance to the house full of protestors in the Enclave. But how could that be, when he'd seen the stone *before* reading the story, before it could have changed anything?

As disquieting as that thought is, it is driven completely from Fellows's mind when he steps out from the aisles of bookshelves and sees Boursier and the bookseller in front of him.

Boursier is sitting placidly in the incongruous office-chair in front of the desk; the bookseller is on his feet, arms flung out in angry gesticulation. His face is pale and there is a cloud of dust faintly visible around him, as if the movements and pacings of his anger have stirred it up. For a brief second Fellows thinks that while one of the boy's misaligned eyes is glaring at Boursier the other is already focussed on *him*. But then the bookseller turns to look at Fellows directly; so does Boursier. The bookseller's face does something complicated as if trying to process contradictory inputs, before it finally settles into a wry smile.

"Well *this* explains a lot," he says, but Fellows is not looking at the bookseller but at the man who he feels he has never properly *looked* at before, never seen straight on.

Boursier has changed, or *been* changed, and now he looks exactly like Fellows.

Although not *exactly*, Fellows realises, looking closer despite his shock. Boursier's face is still unnaturally placid and settled; his eyes still lack any spark as if he were a poor copy, or a first draft. An illusion of being younger—Boursier looks like Fellows not as if the last ten years hadn't happened, but as if nothing had happened in them.

Fellows stares at Boursier, who doesn't get up out of his chair; doesn't even look surprised. Fellows is aware that the appropriate emotional reactions inside aren't occurring; aware that in their space he is filling up with an irrational *anger*. Why had Boursier written *The Panda Principle*? Why had he written any of it, chipping away at the foundations of his life here in the quarantined city…

"Well?" Fellows says to Boursier, flinging his arms wide. "Happy now?" He is aware the bookseller is speaking but he ignores him.

"Happy?" Boursier repeats placidly, as if he doesn't understand the question or what he has done.

"You fucking twat," Fellows says, and steps forward and punches Boursier in the face. The other man doesn't even try to avoid being hit and he feels Boursier's nose give under the blow; the chair Boursier had been sitting on rolls away on its wheels for a few feet before Boursier falls off in an ungainly sprawl.

The bookseller bursts into laughter at the sight, so suddenly and violently that Fellows finally turns to look at him. The boy looks like he is about to have a fit; his misaligned eye has rolled up into the socket while his other bulges. There's something repulsive about him and Fellows is still furious; he takes a step towards the boy and if it wasn't for the fact that the bookseller backed away in fear until he was against one of the bookshelves he would have punched him too.

"And what did *you* mean, that this explains a lot?" he yells at the boy.

"What did I... *This*, this explains a lot," the bookseller says, gesturing at Fellows and Boursier, who is struggling up off the dusty floor. "Are you twins? But then how come you didn't know who wrote those weird stories? Is it a pen-name, Boursier, does it mean anything?"

"What are you talking about?"

"Well *I* thought you were the same person didn't I? Each time one of you came in."

"But you can't have!" Fellows slams his fist into the rickety bookshelf behind the boy, causing it to shudder and some of its stories fall. "It's only just happened! He's only just been changed!" The boy looks at him google-eyed, as if he is mad.

Boursier stands up, brushes dust from his linen jacket.

"That's not strictly speaking true," he says.

Fellows rounds on him, his body tensed as if he had been insulted, as if this were nothing more than a brawl in one of the bars near the harbour. Maybe that is what he would prefer, for when his anger fades Fellows does not know where he will be stranded. Boursier does not react to the threat in Fellows's pose, which infuriates him the more. If Boursier were to fade from his vision like the ghost Fellows wouldn't be surprised, the writer seems so little a part of the world around him.

"What you're seeing," Boursier says, "aren't changes as such. They seem like changes to you, but they've always been there. A different waveform. The quantum city." He gives a brief laugh, a teacher laughing at a joke his class doesn't understand.

"What," Fellows says, "the fuck are you talking about?"

"Before, what you were seeing was good enough, it made sense to you so nothing could dislodge it. But now…"

"Now, because of your fucking stories?"

"If you like. You always thought the stories changed things didn't you? Typical writer; so arrogant! Stories can't change things. Stories can only change how you *see* things."

If this *were* some bar brawl, Fellows feels as though he has just taken a punch to the gut, for he is sick and breathless at Boursier's words, and can't instantly respond.

"But some people, like our friend here," Boursier says, nodding at the bookseller, "are able to see the other side, especially if they have imagination. Imagination is just seeing what the world would look like if it were different, after all."

"I'm with him," the bookseller says, "what the fuck are you talking about? What is this hippie shit?"

"But *why*," Fellows says, "why do you want me to see the world differently? Why write the stories; isn't what I could see good enough? Why am I now seeing you looking like me?"

"What makes you think it's *me* you're seeing differently?"

Fellows's head rings as if struck. He feels weary and wonders why he ever came here. He should have gone to find Georgia, apologised… His thoughts crumble before he can even finish building them in his head. Would Georgia even recognise him? Or want to talk to him if she did?

He imagines bending down to offer his hand for Mogwai to sniff, and the cat reacting by arching its back and snarling, as if his very odour was wrong.

"If you want to know *why*…" Boursier begins.

"Oh I know, I know," Fellows cuts him off. For once Boursier looks surprised, and Fellows feels a weary satisfaction as he goes to the chair, rights it, and sits gratefully down.

"I mean it's a bit bloody obvious isn't it?" he says. "I'm sure you think you've been clever, with your little games behind the scenes, but you've given too much away now."

"Yep, obvious," the bookseller says. Fellows glances at him, shrugs. A truce then. He gestures at the bookseller to speak.

"I assume this idiot has read all but one of the stories he bought," the bookseller says snidely, causing Fellows to dislike him all over again. "And he's going to ask more gormless questions and you're going to answer with your bloody Buddha-on-the-mountain act that fools no one. And eventually you're going to tell him to read the final story, whatever that one is called…"

"*The Quarantine*," Fellows says, glaring at the bookseller, who just laughs.

"Too bloody predictable," he says. "But yeah, you'll do your 'all will be revealed' spiel to get Mister Gullible here to read it and…"

"I don't want him to read it," Boursier says.

"You don't?" Fellows says. He had agreed with everything the bookseller had said, despite the bastard's goading.

"No," Boursier says, with a shrug. "I want you to finish writing it."

There is a silence, broken only by the sudden panic of gulls taking off from the roof above their heads, as if reacting to a loud and monstrous noise only they can hear. Outside, the city seems to darken perceptibly, like time-lapsed photographs of the night falling.

"Wait," the bookseller says, "you've tricked me into selling stories that aren't even bloody finished?"

Fellows isn't listening; his head feels muffled, and the gloom outside is replaced by a bright light pouring in from the windows, a flash as if of great violence. He takes the bag of stories he has been carrying around and puts it on the bookseller's dusty desk. He finds the story headed *The Quarantine* and flicks through it; sure enough it is full of crossed-out words, false starts, marginalia. A first draft, Fellows thinks. The bookseller sits on the opposite side of the desk and attempts to read the story upside down. Fellows finds the act oddly intrusive; he rolls up the story and places it in the inner pocket of his jacket.

As he does so he glances at his hands; they are stained with ink.

He remembers, ten years ago, on days when he'd been struggling to write with a cheap biro as fast as the inspiration came to him, how he'd used to stain his fingers ink-black and how Lana had never let him touch her until he'd scrubbed his hands. Remembers it as if it were yesterday.

He stands up; he feels a strange kind of calm, as if his feelings were being held at bay, or being felt by another. He wonders if this is how Boursier feels, and in doing so he looks over at the writer: he sees Boursier's pale hands, familiar and equally as ink-stained as his own. Because of course they are the same.

So much so that…

He is looking at his own hands.

When he looks up Boursier is gone.

He is sitting at the desk in front of the bookseller, who is looking at him uninterestedly, as if they have never met before. He has just placed a bag with five stories on the desk between them. He feels different to just a minute before, but also as if more than a minute has passed; he feels good. For a moment it is like a whole other set of memories is about to break over him, overwhelm him, but some instinct guides him. When he speaks, it is just as if he is following a script written in ink on his palms.

"Morning," he says to the bookseller. "I was wondering if you'd be interested in selling these stories for me? On commission."

The bookseller peers at the first story suspiciously; it is in a literary journal called *Other Rooms, Other Cities* and is entitled *The Smell Of Paprika*.

The light of a summer heat-wave that has lasted three months is streaming through the Echo's windows; the quarantined city outside has the quiet air that has lasted ever since the unity government imposed petrol rationing.

He can still remember the events leading up to this point, even if the bookseller can't: his purchase of the Boursier stories, the strange changes to the city, the house in the Enclave and that idiot Jaques, his argument with Georgia and his time in the Guardia's offices. And he knows these things are still not without effect. But he also knows what he must say next. Like he has said it before.

"Fifty percent," he says and sees the bookseller's interest although the boy tries to hide it. "Although there are some special instructions I'd want you to follow…"

The bookseller sneers. "How many stories?"

Maybe this time round, Boursier's voice says in his head, and Fellows changes his mind about what to say next. Ad libs.

"Five."

When Fellows leaves The Echo Bookshop after the inevitable fractious conversation with the bookseller, the pages of the first draft of *The Quarantine* make a rustling sound in his jacket.

I want you to finish writing it, he thinks.

JAMES EVERINGTON

PART SIX

THE QUARANTINE

Fellows steps out the alleyway that leads to The Echo Bookshop, and into the marketplace. The scene in front of him seems static for a second, a photo taken in the soft light of sunset, before it blurs with movement. The market is busy, noisy with the sound of people chattering and gossiping over the scarlet peppers, stuffed olives, and bunches of radishes bigger than Fellows's fist. In the other direction he can see flat fish laid out on ice, alongside slowly struggling crabs, trussed up and out of their element.

Fellows lifts his face, closes his eyes, and feels the sun's heat on his face.

There is a sudden commotion; from a stall selling bootleg spirits and cassis he sees a small jerky figure dart away into the dappled sunlight and shadow beneath the canvas. For a moment it seems like… but no, it is not the crippled child impossibly loose from his house, but a flesh and blood thief, trying to run with a bottle clutched to his pigeon-chest. The stall-holder's cries have alerted the Guardia, and a pair of them come pushing through the crowd after the kid. The thief runs with a limp, there is no way they won't catch him.

"Look," he remembers Lana saying, on a holiday together before things had gone bad between them, "that Guardia is well pissed off with her colleague." They had just emerged from a Cathedral Lana had lit a candle in, and in the sunlight he saw two figures striding across the square bickering; as a foreigner Fellows had been uncomfortably aware of the firearms strapped to their hips.

"Is that right?" he had said. "Is 'Guardia' singular or plural?"

"Fuck it," Lana said with a grin, "one Guardia, two Guardia, three Guardia, four—hopefully we won't need to know, we're only here a week." It had been their private joke for the rest of the holiday: 'the Guardia'.

Fellows blinks and comes back to the quarantined city. The lame boy is more agile than he looks, and he eludes the clutches of the Guardia by changing direction in the last second; Fellows finds himself rooting for the kid. As if reading his thoughts, the boy dodges again and starts running directly towards Fellows.

As he passes, Fellows takes the boy by surprise and grabs him, lifting his kicking legs from the ground.

"I can help you," he says as the boy yells and curses; the Guardia approach, the male one visibly out of breath.

"You want to check out that bookshop down the alley," he says before either of them can speak. "Trading with pre-quarantine money. Subversive literature."

The male Guardia isn't listening and starts to reach for the still struggling boy, before his colleague puts a hand on his shoulder. Although he has never seen these two before, Fellows feels the doubling sensation of deja-vu when he looks at them.

"Subversive literature?" the female Guardia says suspiciously; Fellows meets her gaze so she doesn't look down and see his ink-stained fingers.

"Definitely," he says. "Have a look at a story called *The Smell Of Paprika* he's selling. It's not on the shelves, he keeps them behind the desk."

"Paprika?" the male says. "That doesn't sound very…"

"Shut up," the other says wearily.

"And I'll make sure this criminal mastermind returns what he stole," Fellows says. There is a cry and the boy kicks him in the shins.

After checking both their papers to prove their residency in the city when the quarantine began, the two Guardia leave them be. Fellows watches them disappear into the gloom of the alleyway towards The Echo Bookshop. This time I really can't go back, he thinks. He escorts the boy back to the stall (the bootleg nature of it seemingly hadn't concerned the Guardia; kickbacks he assumes) where he pays for the bottle of red wine the boy had pilfered.

"What's your name?" Fellows says to the kid, who is clutching the bottle to his chest as if still afraid someone will take it from him.

"Amit," the boy says after a pause.

"You know Georgia, don't you?"

"Huh? Who?"

"The lady in the apartment, who buys this stuff from you."

"Oh yeah. Her. Crazy woman."

"Give that bottle to her from me; tell her she can't open it until I come round. Tell her the twat says he's sorry."

With a shrug the boy, who Fellows guesses isn't called Amit but has just plucked the first false name he can think of from the air of the quarantined city, turns away.

"Wait, wait," Fellows says. "What's your mother do?"

"Her? A waitress. Some boring café. Hey don't tell her will you? She thinks I hang around all day waiting for her to come back from work. Nah."

"Tell her sorry too," Fellows says.

"Crazy," the boy says under his breath as he walks away.

HIS HOUSE IS EMPTY WHEN he returns, both from any hint of the supernatural and of the more mundane presence of the cat. He calls for Mogwai for a few times before he shuts the door, but there is no sign of him. He is sure the cat will turn up; they can go a long way from home, he reflects, and still somehow return.

Fellows goes to pour himself a drink before sitting down to write. As if noticing for the first time, he realises how spartan his abode is: a writing desk, a dining table with one chair, a bed, and piles and piles of books. Like an echo.

I want you to finish it—he fishes out the story from the inner pocket of his jacket, rolls it as flat as he can. He reads it through; the story is confused with two seemingly contradictory plot-lines, but what did he expect from a first draft? Fellows finds a cheap biro and starts to mark where changes are needed.

The first thing he does is cross out the name at the top of the first page. After all, this is his story now.

The Quarantine by Fellows

> "Couldn't you have picked a better pen name?" Lana said. She was looking out the window at the lights of the ring road, with the city beyond. It was late, there were no other cars around and Fellows just wanted to get home; he increased speed ever so slightly. "I felt so embarrassed

everyone calling you that poncey foreign name. I kept forgetting they meant *you.*"

"But it fits, don't you see?" said Fellows, who was having doubts himself. "If you look it up..."

"Yes, yes," Lana said, waving a hand in his general direction; she was drunker than he was. Fuck it, he thought, it was a celebration even if I didn't win. I was on the short list, my story was on the short list. Like somewhere he had been aiming for all his life had finally come onto the horizon, a city of shimmering lights.

"Want me to call you it tonight?" Lana said giggling. "When we get back and I give you your prize. Boursier, Boursier..." she said in a slurred and geographically uncertain accent, which still turned Fellows on. He turned to grin at her but had to quickly look back at the road.

They were approaching their turn-off, but as Fellows slowed something didn't look right to him; it was as if the road layout had been changed overnight. There was no exit where there should be, no sign of road-works or other temporary obstructions; no sign of it at all. What the hell, he thought, what have the local government done now? Annoyed, he sped up again.

"Fellows what are you doing?" Lana said sleepily. "That was our..."

"It wasn't there," he said.

"What do you mean?"

"I mean it wasn't there, didn't you see?" He looked at Lana, then back to the road quickly. The streetlights seemed harsher than he remembered, illuminating the deserted stretch of road. There were no turnings ahead; a thick white line was painted horizontally across the road, but it made no sense to him even as they crossed it. He didn't recognise where they were, and he was unsure if the fuzziness in his head was tiredness or if he had drunk more champagne than he'd realised.

"Of course it was there," Lana said. "Why are you driving so fast? I just want to go home." She sounded like a petulant child.

"Well, if I don't drive fast we won't get..."

"Jesus, Fellows are you on the right side of the road?" Lana shouted, jerking up in her seat. Fellows jumped, turned to her.

"What are you talking about, of course I'm..."

Lara wasn't looking at him but ahead; he saw her scream and throw her hands up in front of her face. His foot was already slamming on the brake as he turned to look forward...

He just had time to register that the overly bright mercury lights made the child's eyes look pure white before there was the sickening sound of collision and the boy vanished from view. Fellows shut his eyes; when he reopened them the car had stopped and in the road ahead he saw the crumpled and unmoving body of a child. As if it had just been lying there all along and he had only just seen it.

This isn't happening, he thought, this isn't happening. The taste of champagne in his mouth had gone stale and he gagged.

Lana was crying in the seat next to him; she had her hands placed on her flat belly as if protecting something already gone. Even in his fear and apprehension the sight angered Fellows—always bringing their problems into everything; always *that* problem even though they'd made the decision together.

"Don't be hysterical," he snapped at her, although she wasn't. "Call an ambulance." He got out the car onto the oddly-lit road. It was completely silent, with no hum of traffic even in the distance. He shut the car door, not wanting to hear Lana's spluttering conversation with the emergency services, and walked slowly towards the body.

The lights and silence combined to make the scene seem unreal, as did the still unmoving body of the boy, which had landed flat on its back, pale arms stretched out like white, featherless wings. This isn't happening, Fellows thought again; there is a rushing noise in his head like the absent traffic. A part of him distantly wondered how he would describe the scene if it were in a story.

He knelt by the body of the boy, and 'body' seemed the appropriate word for he could see no movement, not even the rise and fall of the chest. He guessed the boy was about seven or eight, although he was not good with kids' ages. The blank light from above had washed the boy's face of identifying features other than the bruises, the blood on his scalp. The boy's eyes were completely white, just like he had hallucinated in the split second before impact. He supposed when he had hit the child the eyes had somehow rolled up in the sockets. He wondered whether he should attempt CPR—Fellows wasn't sure how, and he told himself this was the reason he didn't, and not the resurgent nausea he felt at the thought of touching the boy's skin in the strange blank light.

The silence was finally broken by the noise of a siren, threatening to bring the enormity of what he has done home to Fellows. He shut his eyes again but the bright mercury lights still cut through...

Something touched Fellows's hand.

His eyes snapped open as he instinctively pulled away, sprawling backwards. He saw the boy's arm outstretched, broken fingers reaching for him. The rest of the body seemed as immobile as before, although the boy's head had turned towards Fellows and despite the colourless eyes they seemed to focus on him. Fellows's body felt like he had touched an exposed wire or something numbing. He tried to right himself and was distantly surprised when he couldn't. His heart seemed to be beating twice as fast but half as effectually; his lungs seemed unable to draw any oxygen from the pallid white air. The boy reached his hand for Fellows again, and Fellows kicked away whimpering. The whiteness began to fill his vision, from the centre outwards.

He was vaguely aware of the ambulance screeching to a stop, of Lana crying out, and a faint white noise in his head that sounded almost like a distant sea. He felt a far off, fading sense of surprise when the foggy figures of the paramedics came to *him* first, and not the boy he had hit. They knelt beside him, turned him so he was face up to the pale light overhead.

So bright, he thought, and he wondered if the light and noise were getting closer; if they were falling upon him or if he were rising...

Am I being lifted up? he thought.

And then the whiteness cleared like a blindness healed, and he was somewhere else entirely, with sunlight on his face, and white birds circling above him. He smelt spicy food from somewhere and heard the sounds of rigging in the breeze and men calling from the sea...

Then a dreadful, wrenching pain in his chest, a yanking back, and he was gasping for air in the back of the ambulance he had been lifted into, Lana weeping, and the paramedics looming over him like some sci-fi vision of the future, ready to give him another shock.

FELLOWS IS DISTRACTED BY MOGWAI, nudging the pen in his hand. Everyone's a critic, Fellows thinks. He doesn't even remember letting the animal into the house; maybe he found an open window or gap in the crumbling exterior; cats can often find their way in anywhere, he thinks.

After feeding the cat he looks again at the words of the story, a mixture of him and Boursier. The boy's not dead, he remembers Boursier saying, but when he writes the tight feeling of an old dread in his chest says different.

It's just a story, he thinks, you can change how it goes. That's the *point*. It's a first draft; you can make it good.

He flexes his cramped hands like a magician about to perform a trick, to make something disappear.

They are stained with ink.

The tips of Fellow's fingers were stained with ink; why had they needed to take his fingerprints, he had asked them, for a traffic accident? Standard procedure for suspicious deaths, they had said, and left him to stew in a room no one had called a cell—he wasn't under arrest and the door wasn't even locked—but which no one had not called a cell, either.

"Why do you think it was suspicious?" he asked when the two officers came back. "The kid ran out in the middle of the road! I didn't have a hope of stopping."

"And then you had a convenient lapse of consciousness and had to be brought back to life," said the female officer. "Rushed off before we even arrived. So no breath test. No one even called us until you were gone. And here you are, the next day, fit as a fiddle."

"I know that's... odd, but..." (Fellows thought of white wings) "... but what does this have to do with the accident? He ran out in front of me!"

"Ran out in front of you. At 2 AM. On the ring road," the officer said flatly.

"Blame his parents, not me."

"We haven't been able to trace his parents," the male police-officer cut in; Fellows thought the other hadn't wanted that revealed yet from the look she gave him.

"We haven't got a clue who the kid is. Was."

And they still hadn't hours later. They let Fellows go, as the evidence from the scene and the child's body hadn't contradicted his story, nor had Lana's testimony. He had been driving slightly too fast, but not enough to have made a difference and so not enough for them to prosecute—but just enough, apparently, for Lana to avoid him, for the sound of her crying in the spare room to be as perpetual as the sea. Fellows angrily refused to let her make him feel guilty. But...

Had he been over the limit? It was as if he could still taste the champagne at the back of his throat. How much had he drunk?

The sound of a storm blowing in outside had given no answer; Fellows had watched the rain splattering through the open window of their kitchen but could not summon the energy to shut it. He pictured the same rain lashing the road where the accident happened, erasing the black skid marks and dried blood. It's over, he thought. But the next second the image of the rain and the road washed clean seemed ridiculous; he pictured empty road beyond where he should have turned off, isolated and under separate weather, the evidence of what had really happened preserved in that bubble of bright and silent light.

He looked at his hands again; no matter how much he had scrubbed at them he hadn't been able to get the traces of black ink from them. Just then the sound of the storm seemed to increase, as if the front door to their townhouse had opened.

"Lana?" he called uncertainly. "George?" Had the cat been caught out in the rain and somehow made his way inside?

He walked out from the kitchen; something brushed against his leg and he looked down to see the cat, just emerged from the lounge where he had no doubt been sleeping. Not George then. The cat walked to the top of the stairs then paused, as if staring down at something below. When Fellows went to look, there was no one in sight, but the front door was wide open.

Confused, he went downstairs to shut it; the light spilling in from outside seemed too bright, out of synch with the roar of rain persistent as traffic. Fellows noticed the floor was damp with rainwater when he was still a few metres away from the door. He looked out before he shut it, but there was no one.

Behind him, George shrieked.

As he turned he was reminded of the accident, for it had the same sense of inevitability about it. He saw the blank, white-eyed face of the boy he had killed, moving towards him too quickly to take in its features. He threw his hands up, and then something translucent was upon him in a blurred and fading rush...

He felt the briefest touch of something against his face, insubstantial as a draught in the air. Nevertheless he was pushed backwards, he felt his gravity go and the world darken as if tiny hands had just clamped over his eyes...

Fellows blinked, and he was sitting at a table in a café he had never seen before, but which nonetheless looked familiar. An attractive curly-haired waitress was placing a cup of coffee and black and white newspaper in front of him. The walls were mirrored and he struggled to understand that his reflection was him. He heard the cry of gulls as he reached for his coffee, and noticed his hands were stained with...

Then he awoke spluttering, to see Lana's face above him, crying and shrieking. Her hands on his chest felt as much like they were beating him as trying to bring him back to life.

It kept happening.

He kept seeing it.

Kept going *there*.

The hospital tests revealed no physical sign of disease, no infection or brain tumour pressing against some vital nerve. Psychosomatic, they said. They talked of what had happened to Fellow's body—the blackouts, the collapse—and not his experience of a foreign sun on his face, the sound of waves against unknown harbours...

In their house, Fellows had once set up a digital photo frame that flicked through the best photos of the best holidays he and Lana had taken together: old medieval towns with narrow cobbled roads, seafood stalls right on the quay in France, the imposing white buildings of Mussolini's Rome, the salmon-topped church in Cork. Each picture encapsulated a weekend or a fortnight, small and private worlds in Fellows's mind as he watched them flick past. There was no guilt or responsibility in those worlds, he thought. He found himself staring at them often.

"What the fuck are you doing?" Lana shook him. "It's like you're in a trance, like you've quarantined yourself off! Come back to reality Fellows, you killed a goddamn child and you have to take..."

"Killed..?" Fellows said vaguely, thinking of the boy's face, translucent and depersonalised every time he saw it. "The boy's not dead..."

"Of course he's dead! And we're paying for the funeral you shit!" Lana said. The boy's family had still not been traced, his identity was still unknown as if unwritten. (Fellows had written nothing since the accident.)

Walking away from Lana without saying anything, Fellows called a taxi to take him into town. He had panic attacks behind the wheel now but if he closed his eyes and concentrated on the wave-like rhythm of his pulse he could survive a short taxi ride. Once there he went into the first bar he could find, drank Belgian beer, Italian wine, French cassis (anything but champagne). Drunk so much he didn't feel the native chill as he walked back, and so the blurred and doubling city in his vision seemed a new place entirely.

HE IS CROSSING THROUGH ALMOST everything Boursier has written now, for none of it rings true to him. The boy's not dead—and without that through-line, Boursier's *Quarantine* descends into a structureless mess: scenes of alcoholism, arguments, being slapped in the face by the boy's mother, legal and medical bills for a child who unrealistically survived the accident. And no proper ending; Fellows works hard to put some plot back into *The Quarantine*. The boy must die and it all needs to lead to the inevitable climax: the night Lana leaves. But not Boursier's fictitious version of that scene which Fellows has been carrying around in his head; not the lawyer's phone call where he'd been offered the chance to avoid paying for the crippled boy for the rest of his life... where had *that* come from? It hadn't happened like that, or at least that isn't what he writes down.

It has been worse than that.

> The downpour during the walk home wasn't enough to sober Fellows, despite the length of time it took him to navigate the strange and mutable streets. In his drunkenness he had not been able to visualise the straight route to his house, and so he'd approached it in an elaborate series of zig-zags and loops via the landmarks he *could* remember. Several taxi cabs slowed upon seeing him trudging through the rain, but his panic attacks had grown too strong for him even to be able to ride in the backseat anymore. And at least the walk gave him time to think.
>
> Think about getting back together with Lana.
>
> They'd not officially split but Lana had done little but shriek at him or ignore him since the accident. His anger at her attempts to make him feel guilty when he'd done nothing wrong (even though he felt guilty himself) had given him the confidence to try and chat up both a waitress and a woman obviously with a female partner that night; the confidence but not the ability. As he walked back, the rain washing his face, he had decided it was Lana he really wanted. His plan was pure drunken stupidity. He'd go back and suggest a holiday, a tour round all their favourite places from previous trips. Like in the photo frame. It was so simple, so obviously *right* that in his head they'd practically made up before he'd got home.
>
> The front door to their house stuck again and Fellows had to force it, stumbling inside in a more clumsy manner than he'd intended. He went from room to room calling Lana, becoming more and more aware as he did so of the sodden weight of his clothes, of the damp footsteps he was leaving on the polished wooden floors.
>
> Lana was in the kitchen, and as he entered she turned to look at him with unreadable eyes. The cat was circling

around her ankles mewing, wanting food or just her touch, but she ignored it.

"Hey," Fellows said. "Hi baby... Listen. I've got it all, all figured out."

"Got what figured out? How to bring a dead child back to life?"

He knew she could be talking about more than just the boy he'd hit.

"The... The boy's not dead, not really, he's inside the *house*, Lana, this house, so that's why we should go, go somewhere..."

"Go somewhere?"

"A *holiday*. Holiday to all the places... All the... Where we've *been*."

"You're drunk. You're *a* drunk. Look at yourself, sopping wet and stinking. You killed a child because you were drunk and now you want a fucking *holiday*?"

Lana was staring at him hatefully but underneath he knew there was a pain she wanted to hide, and he felt a childish need to make it all okay.

"C'mon baby," he said, a drunken reversion to the cliches he'd used when they'd first got together. He felt cold and anxious, and he couldn't bring himself to say exactly what he meant: "C'mon, let's make... Baby, *please*."

Her face darkened, as if he had said something worse.

"Don't come near me you stinking drunk," Lana said, stepping backwards. "Jesus Christ fuck off, are you *horny?* You're never fucking touching me again."

"C'mon, we need a, a getaway..." He was aware he was whining, like a kid denied a treat; he realised he *was* horny now she had mentioned it. He moved towards Lana, wanting to touch her—just a touch was all, a hand on his to tether him...

With a cry, Lana punched him in the face and he fell. It was not like his painless swoon by the roadside, with its accompanying visions, but an ungainly collapse, smashing his head against a drawer handle on the way down. Am I being..., he thought, but that thought cut off when Lana bent down to him.

"The next time you have one of your drunken falls and babble about ghosts, I won't be here to bring you back. Go to Hell, Fellows."

He passed out.

When Fellows came back to consciousness it was still night, but enough time had passed for Lana to have packed and gone. She'd taken George with her, he noticed, stumbling from room to room, feeling a sense of loss even though she'd barely taken anything. His head had stopped bleeding, although it still felt like it had split in two.

He went to the front door and opened it as if he might catch a glimpse of a retreating taxi, but the street was deserted. No traffic at all. At least it had finally stopped raining; the night air was almost warm. Still feeling woozy, Fellows left the door open as he walked away from it.

Sod her, he thought, in ten years' time you won't care so why care now? In ten years' time you'll be a successful writer living in a city *she'll* only be able to visit by budget airlines. Ten years—he could almost taste it.

He heard a noise upstairs, like something scrabbling across the wooden floors. Had she left the cat after all? Maybe she had wanted to take George but he'd hidden out of sight; he'd often done so at the sight of a suitcase, fearing another stay at the cattery while they went away.

Fellows walked up the stairs, calling the cat's name. George didn't come at his call and he wondered if he was stuck in one of the bedrooms; the cat was constantly turning up someplace unexpected. He reached the top of the stairs; the sounds were coming from the bedroom. He now noticed the oddity of them. It didn't sound like a cat at all, but like something slow and clumsy with pain. Wondering if the cat might be injured somehow, Fellows went into the room, and bent to peer under the bed.

And saw the white mercury-lit eyes of the ghost peering back at him.

But no, not quite the *ghost*, for even as he lurched backwards and almost fell he realised it was no longer some nebulous and already fading phantom, but something of flesh and blood, something that smelt of dried sweat and rain damp cloth. One hand reached for Fellows from under the bed, stained black and with one finger bent almost ninety degrees at the knuckle. Fellows turned and ran.

He heard the clumsy sounds of the thing struggling out from under the bed. He didn't dare look back in case he stumbled, but from the dragging, scrabbling sounds of its movement he knew the thing hadn't righted itself, but was coming for him on all fours. Maybe the boy *can't* walk, he thought.

As he turned and started down the stairs he began to get the better of his panic. He was quicker than the ghost or whatever the fuck it now was. He could easily outpace it to the front door, which he had even left open earlier as if anticipating his need to flee. And surely the boy can't follow me away from here? he thought. What else do ghosts haunt but haunted houses?

He reached the bottom of the stairs before the boy was even halfway to the top, and he felt a giddy sense of relief as he sprinted towards the door, as if in escaping from the crippled ghost he was escaping from his past, from all his fuck ups. The front door blew open in the breeze, eager to aid him in his flight...

There was a figure standing in the doorway, blocking his escape route. Fellows stumbled to a halt, blinking. The lights were off and the hall was dark, and the person was impossible to make out properly in the shadows.

"Hello? Lana?" Fellows said uncertainly. The figure didn't react. "Who are you?" The panic was rising in him again as he heard behind him the sound of the crippled boy falling down the stairs in its frantic pursuit of him. He couldn't help but wince and he almost expected the thing to have dashed itself unconscious or worse in its fall. But after a silence of a few seconds, he heard its hands scrambling at the wooden floor again, dragging the weight of is body behind. Its wet gasping breaths sounded like they were coming from something broken, for all their eagerness.

You need to get away, he thought, and how else but by the door? Whoever this person was didn't matter—Fellows started forward, meaning to force the stranger aside if he had to.

As he got nearer, he was unsure if it was the shadows lifting or somehow the figure changed, but Fellows stopped and stared. He felt a terror, colder than his hot panic at the ghost behind him. He felt like if he touched the stranger they might both vanish, matter and antimatter cancelled out. For the stranger looked exactly like him.

Although not *exactly*; the stranger in the doorway looked like Fellows maybe ten years hence.

"This isn't how it happens," the figure said. Or had he said 'happened'?

"Please," Fellows said, unable to force himself towards this doppelgänger but knowing the boy was still closing in behind him. He risked a look over his shoulder and saw the thing had paused in its pursuit to pull itself upright, leaving black handprints on the walls. It tottered forwards, one hand on the wall for support like a much younger child, the other held out and grasping. "*Please,*" said Fellows again; he had to get away.

"This isn't right," the man said, blank and with no emotion, "What you are seeing isn't right. He's not a vampire, a leech. It's like in a dream; the things you are frightened of in a dream are not those which..."

"What the fuck are you talking about!" Fellows yelled. He couldn't focus on what the man was saying; it was like the words were inside his own head the voice was such a match to his own. The skin of his back itched anticipating the boy's deadening touch.

"Let me past!" But the man just continued his smooth, lunatic babble about waveforms and invisible cities and even pandas. It was like a voice of madness in his head, and Fellows couldn't help but step backwards away from it, even as he heard the mewing of the ghost become more eager as he did so...

He didn't dare turn to face it.

The hand that touched his was tentative, as if tender with pain and almost as repulsed by the contact as Fellows. He felt small fingers clutch at his, pull as if to lead him somewhere. Then another touch to the small of his back, and despite their weakness the boy's hands felt like they were casting him down into the darkness away from...

No, Fellows thought, *no.* He remembered... He remembered what he had felt and seen before the paramedics brought him back to that deserted ring road. Remembered warmth and the faint sounds of a tide, the feeling of being somewhere safe and self-contained as the womb. Am I being lifted up? he thought.

And opened his eyes, ten years later, to the sight of pastries, a monochrome newspaper being placed in front of him, and the smell of fresh coffee.

Quarantine Declared! the headline of the paper read. *Unity government to be formed.*

So they finally did it, Fellows thought, finally some sense. It had been an odd morning; since getting up and starting towards The Carousel he'd had a faint but distinct feeling of panic in his chest. Like he was experiencing secondhand the emotions of some poor sod elsewhere. But the feeling was fading now. He pulled out some change for a tip; everyone said the old coins would be worthless soon, but what else could he give? Sometimes what you had had to be good enough. He doesn't want the waitress with the black, curly hair to think him ungenerous. Sipping his coffee, watching the gulls circle, he wonders if he will ever find out her name or that of the surly chap who runs the place...

FOR A FEW DAYS AFTER writing the story, Fellows feels empty, purged. He doesn't try to rewrite or improve *The Quarantine*, despite its flaws. Indeed he feels little urge to do anything; his life in the quarantined city is quiet again. If the ghost is still in his house, he doesn't see it. Fellows tries to let things slip back into their previous routine, and largely succeeds.

There is one oddity though, as if *his* stories can change things too: his cat has disappeared. He calls its name each morning, but to no avail. He supposes it will turn up; cats often do.

The new café he has found for his early morning coffee is further away from his house, but Fellows doesn't mind walking. The Swallow Café is named as such because of the birds nesting in its high, crumbling eaves. Over a coffee Fellows watches them each morning, circling and swooping, as they must do every year—nature itself resetting just as it seemed the city had after his confrontation with Boursier. Not everything is back as it was though: when he had tried to go back to The Carousel one look from Leianna had been enough for him to know his apology via Amit had not been accepted. The things he has done cannot be so easily undone or evaded.

It is for this reason he doesn't dare call to see Georgia, much as he longs to.

One day the waitress hands him the newspaper; she is a softly-spoken blonde, but where has he ever got with brunettes anyway? As he turns the pages made of cheap paper which feels damp, the ink smudging his fingertips, a headline catches his eye, for he has read it before.

Reclusive writer rumoured to be living in city.

It is the headline of the first article he had read about Boursier, the one which had sparked his interest all those months ago under a sun as bright as this. But this time, Fellows knows where Boursier is. He stands up, places a tip for the waitress on the table (there is no tip jar at The Swallow), but as her fingers fumble picking up the thin quarantine coins she doesn't even look at him.

Fellows shields his eyes from the sun as he walks; his shirt is damp and sticks to his skin like he has been caught in a rainstorm. The streets are deserted; people are keeping inside as the heat of the day nears its peak. Fortunately, since he last saw Boursier he has ceased to suffer the gaps in his mental map of his adopted home; he knows the city again, it fits into the palm of his hand.

As he walks, he thinks he hears the faint sound of an automobile's exhaust backfiring, somewhere in the quiet streets.

When he reaches his house he calls again for this missing cat, trying both 'Mogwai' and 'George', but again there is no sign of him. Sighing, Fellows goes briefly inside to collect the manuscript of his version of *The Quarantine*, and then he heads towards the narrow streets of the old town, to the familiar flat above the liquor shop.

He climbs the stairs, and Boursier's front door swings open at his touch.

Fellows pauses before entering, as if he is about to cross some mental boundary. His reasons for being here are opaque even to him. As he steps inside he wonders if he is doing the right thing.

Boursier's apartment is not as he remembers it.

He remembers a space as lacking in personality as Boursier himself, a room so sparse it looked like it was still waiting for someone to move in. He can still see the outline of this beneath the filth and clutter that now confronts him. The apartment looks like someone has lived in it for years, decades, and never cleaned up. The curtains are tightly drawn making the air seem murky; the dust motes illuminated in the light from the moth-eaten fabric floating like undersea creatures. There is a coat of dust over everything: the sagging sofa, the empty cat food bowls, the broken backed books lying face down. Only the floor itself seems to have been given a half-hearted sweep to clear it of grime, and that only because someone has stuck semi-circles of fading blue tape on the floor. Fellows stares at the patterns for a few seconds before he proceeds. Has Boursier gone mad?

As Fellows's vision adjusts he sees something moving at the far end of the room; he hears a faint scribbling sound. As he steps forward he sees the back of a man in a white linen suit (at least, it must once have been white) bent over a desk that faces the window. Boursier, Fellows thinks. How has he let himself go so quickly?

Boursier doesn't react as Fellows approaches, he is intent on whatever he is writing. You could walk away and he'd never even know you were here, Fellows thinks; why *are* you here? Tentatively, he lays a hand on the other man's shoulder.

Boursier shrieks, spins around in his chair. He flinches from Fellows, blinks like he can't quite see him, holds up his ink stained hands to ward off a blow. Fellows steps back in surprise. Boursier still looks the same as he, but thinner in the face, gaunt and with thinning hair. Older.

"Fuck's sake," Boursier says, lowering his arms. "I thought you were *him*." His eyes glance over Fellows's shoulder as he says this, fear obvious beneath his annoyance. Both emotions seem to Fellows as distant as the open sea, beyond the quarantine.

"What do you mean?" he says blandly.

"What the hell have you been writing?" Boursier asks in return. "The damned thing is *here* now, inside my house!"

"You told me to rewrite it."

"I told you to *finish* it, not to... Christ, how many times must we go round this? Alternating back and forth like Schrodinger's fucking cat! It's a trap, Fellows, don't you understand? The city, the quarantine, is a trap, it wants you stuck here nothing changing..."

But Fellows isn't really listening (and why would he believe Boursier's claims anyway?) but looking over the other man's shoulder at the cheap uncapped biro atop a writing pad, which is covered with handwriting he recognises:

The Quarantine by Boursier

*"Couldn't you have picked a better pen name?" Lana said.
She was looking out the window at the lights of the city...*

FELLOWS'S CALM SUDDENLY FEELS SOMETHING secondhand and ill-fitting. It slides from him and he feels the familiar sense of unease and disorientation.

"You're writing it again?" he says, feeling sick.

Boursier doesn't answer, he is looking behind Fellows again, towards the top of the stairs. There is a creaking sound and then a thud, and then again and again, sounding like something dragging itself up the stairs one laborious step at a time.

"You left the front door open," Boursier says, but calmly. The panic rising is Fellows's own. Boursier sighs, turns back to his writing desk as if weary of the whole scene. "And so here we go again. The boy creeping closer, blah blah."

Fellows looks around Boursier's apartment; there are no other exits.

"What the fuck are you doing?" he says to Boursier, noticing with a touch of hysteria that the other man has started writing again. Boursier replies in a familiar placid tone; familiar from Fellows's own mouth these last few days. But things seem to be flipping back. Fellows looks around; everything—

the dragging sound of something hauling itself closer, the doorway where he knows it will appear, the sudden thunder of his heart and the backdrop of the rain (and when had it started raining?) is shot through with a deja-vu both dreamlike and uncanny.

But the cat, Fellows thinks, there should be a cat shrieking at the top of the stairs. The significance of his thoughts is obscure even to him. But why the difference?

There is the familiar sight of a small hand, with one finger bent back, gripping the doorframe, so the boy can pull himself up, heave his smudged face into view... It is impossible to tell from the boy's dead, pupil-less gaze whether he is looking towards Fellows or Boursier. Fellows's breath is shallow, a struggle against the murky air, as he watches the boy let go of the doorframe and totter forward like a child just learning to walk. Re-learning, Fellows thinks, seeing the old-fashioned metal brace clamped around one of the boy's legs. He feels a whimper catch and die in his throat.

"Boursier what do we do?" he manages to say, but Boursier doesn't react or look up from what he is writing. The child is still a distance away, arms outstretched and mouth hung open, drooling, but Fellows backs up so that his hip is against the back of Boursier's chair. "What the fuck do we do?" he repeats, and is again ignored. The scribbling sound of Boursier's pen seems too loud, and despite himself Fellows looks behind to see what the other man, with the same handwriting as he, is writing:

> "Fellows what are you doing?" Lana said sleepily. "That was where we were supposed to..."
> "I know, I know, I missed the turning," he said. "We'll take the next one." He shook his head, to bring his vision into focus and rid his mouth of the taste of champagne.

FELLOWS LOOKS UP FROM THE page; the boy is approaching the odd lines of blue tape on the floor, and from this perspective Fellows suddenly realises what the semi-circles represent; they are a *border* around the writing desk. What the hell? he thinks. He looks back to the boy, whose every wrenching, painful (can ghosts feel pain?) step evidences its eagerness to reach him. But the boy's face darkens and is obscured somehow from sight; the small tottering shadow stretches out towards Fellows as if behind the boy were...

> The ring road lights seemed harsher than normal, maybe because his heavy eyelids just wanted to close. He thought about pulling over but they were so close to home, and he didn't want to prolong the drive and risk getting caught by the police. Tonight of all nights! he thought.
>
> "Why are you driving so fast?" Lana said, her voice seemingly divided from him by something fuzzy that muffled her concern. He felt his eyes start to droop again and when he forced them open it felt like time had passed, although surely...

... BEHIND THE BOY IS A bright, artificial light. It grows brighter as if something were rushing closer, although given the dimensions of Boursier's apartment nothing can be. The boy pauses, slowly starts to turn his head...

Boursier is still writing.

"Jesus Fellows you're on the wrong side of the road!"

A MERCURY LIGHT OBLITERATES FELLOWS'S view of Boursier's flat; all he can see is silhouettes that don't make sense and deformed shadows straining to reach him. This isn't happening, this isn't happening, he thinks, blinking rapidly to try to see clearly:

In time to see the boy knocked off his feet by something vast but invisible in the light; the boy sprawls ungainly across the blue tape border on the floor.

Fellows sees in the fading light a vision of tall electric lamps and an empty road that seems impossibly wide... and then the vision vanishes, and the boy with it.

> When Fellows reopened his eyes the car had stopped and in the road ahead he saw the crumpled and unmoving body of a child. As if it had just been lying there all along and he had only just seen it.

"WHAT THE FUCK JUST HAPPENED?" Fellows says; Boursier turns to him and shrugs with that maddening passiveness of his.

"Borders only exist when you let yourself see them," he says. Your bloody Buddha-on-the-mountain act, Fellows thinks, remembering the sneering tones of the bookseller. Boursier has already turned back to his writing desk.

Fellows leaves, nervous thoughts pursuing him all the way down he staircase. He keeps checking over his shoulder to make sure the boy isn't about to reach out and touch him, but Boursier's house seems empty of the ghost. But now he has seen that it is not confined to his own house, he wonders if the boy could appear anywhere in the city. He imagines walking the streets, the boy pursuing him, a race he should win but for the fact the city's layout is so malleable... He could turn a corner, and get caught in a dead-end that shouldn't exist, the sound of traffic on the other side of the wall, the boy limping towards him in the rain. The city is a trap...

He rushes out the door to the street, with a desire not just to be away from Boursier's house but from the whole city, quarantine be damned. The impulse is so strong that he doesn't ask wherever his change of heart is his own, or something he is seeing through Boursier's eyes.

Outside in the old town, people are standing about in the street; pushers and card sharps and drunks and even Guardia stood together. There is a sense of expectation, as if something were about to happen, but also nervousness as if no one knows quite what.

"What's going on?" he says to a knot of people in front of the window of the closed liquor shop.

"Haven't you heard?" one of them, an ex-sailor staring at the dusty stock inside, says. "They say the quarantine is finally going to be lifted!" He looks around himself as if the quarantine were something visible; he looks to the sky and Fellows looks too and sees the gulls moving in concentric circles like a carousel, like the shapes taped to the floor of Boursier's apartment. "After all this time!" the man says. "After all this... time," he repeats, less confidently.

"Six months," Fellows says, and the man looks at him oddly, before offering him a slug from a hip flask. Fellows wipes the rim on his sleeve then takes a swig: a vile tasting but familiar spirit which he remembers sharing with Lana one time in a foreign bar, daring and double-daring each other to have another shot.

"Don't worry, be able to get the real stuff again soon!" the sailor says, and as he steps forward to reclaim his flask Fellows sees the man has a limp; he looks down and sees a metal brace on the man's left leg. Feeling uneasy, he nods at the man and walks away.

As he does so he looks back; it is getting dark now and he sees a bright light spilling from Boursier's window. He can almost hear the scratching sound of Boursier's pen, rewriting *The Quarantine* yet again...

> "One chance." Lana said, "you've got one more chance if you ever want to see me again, and it means you have to come with me right now. You can either sit around here like you're in fucking quarantine or something or you can come with me, now."
>
> Fellows looked away from her, back to the bottle of imported, tasteless beer he was drinking, which he had got from the new immigrant shop at the end of the street. He didn't venture any further from home anymore, a shallow-breathed panic took him if he did so, for the city, the *world,* seemed something so vast and borderless it could only be inimical to him. He remembered when he had been a kid, reading fantasy books with a map of some imaginary realm at the front—a whole world in black and white which you could take in at a glance...
>
> "Fellows? Are you *coming?*" Lana said in frustration, interrupting his thoughts.
>
> He looked fuzzily at the beer in his hand (not his first), convinced something about it looked different to before... The peeling label with the seagull on the front had no words he recognised other than one, tiny and at the bottom: 'Georgia'. Was he drinking beer all the way from Georgia? It made no sense but then nothing did; how could a world where a child could just *appear* in your headlights make sense?
>
> "*Fellows!*"
>
> He took a swig from the flat, lifeless beer, looked at Lana unsteadily, then took another. Go with her? He wasn't sure himself what his decision was going to be.

"*FELLOWS!*"

"Georgia," he says uncomfortably.

"Fuck Fellows, where have you been? And are you *sober?* C'mon in, have a drink..." She gestures for him to come inside as if to a lost child stubbornly refusing to come in out of the dark. Her eyes look at his face and then quickly away, over his shoulder. Faintly audible are the sounds of the crowd outside; the muffled hum of the world.

"Quick, quick," Georgia says, her red-rimmed eyes focussed on the corridor behind him. Something about her expression he recognises from himself: she is looking to see if anything has *changed*. He can't help but look himself; he wonders if he remains in the city whether in a few months he'd be looking at a featureless and peeling magnolia wall with such trepidation too.

He goes inside, and Georgia closes the door quickly. There is an awkwardness between them not normally present and he doesn't know what to say. He almost turns and leaves.

"What are those twats doing out there?" Georgia says; her flat is haunted by the sporadic jeers and catcalls of outside.

"The quarantine," Fellows says. "They think it will be lifted soon. Today. I don't know how they know. But good news for you eh?" he adds in a forced tone of voice.

Georgia raises an eyebrow at his words, laughs without humour. Without saying anything, she places two glasses on the table in front of them. The bottle she pours from is familiar but Fellows doesn't say anything. The red wine is black as ink in the gloomy room, for the curtains are all tightly drawn.

"Sit down," Georgia says, "don't stand on ceremony."

"Georgia, I..." Fellows says. "When I was last here..."

"Oh, come on," Georgia says. "Are we really going to do this? The whole 'sorry' conversation?"

"But I..." Fellows does want to say sorry, he supposes, to take some responsibility for his actions. But it is a weak urge (after all, what did *he* do wrong?) and he is unsure how long it will last.

"Fellows," Georgia says, taking his free hand. "You're my only friend in this city, okay? Which basically means, in the entire world. So just hush and sit down and have a bloody drink with me, okay?"

And Fellows does sit, sinking into the comfortable, sagging sofa as easily as he acquiesces into not mentioning their argument. It is easier. The wine is faintly musty and has more sediment in the bottle than it should have; nevertheless he drinks it gratefully, keeps pace with Georgia. The silence between them becomes companionable, the relaxed and empty silence of not doing anything, like a blank page.

A thought nags at him, jerks him from his slump. He sits up, puts down his glass on the table (which is stained with interlocking circles from the bottom of countless wine glasses before, like the patterns of the tape on Boursier's floor or the flight of gulls). Fellows reaches into his jacket, takes out his version of *The Quarantine* from his inner pocket.

He attempts to flatten the pages of the rolled up manuscript on the coffee table. Georgia had been sitting almost dozing with her head on his shoulder and her legs tucked beneath her; now she straightens.

"Well, you always said you wanted to read one of my stories," Fellows says; Georgia gives him a baffled look.

All the pages are blank except for the first which just shows the title and a single sentence. *Am I being lifted up?*

Fellows drains the wine from his glass.

"I don't think I'll be writing anymore," he says. "This town aint big enough for the both of us."

> Fellows drained the beer to the last dregs (Boursier writes). He didn't want it to end, for then he'd have to make a decision. He thought again of those fantasy books he'd read as a child; some had let you control the action:

turn to page 37 to go with Lana, turn to page 269 to continue drinking. He peered at the empty bottle before putting it down. Either his vision was blurred or it no longer said 'Georgia' or anything else he recognised on the label. The creature on the front might not have been a seagull but something else; his muddled and drunken sight made the task of looking as problematic as those pictures that could be a duck or old woman one moment, a rabbit or young girl the next.

But even in his doubling and underwater vision, the sight of Lana making to turn away, hand raised to hide her tears, was in focus. Fellows made an effort to stand up.

"I'll come with you," he said, surprising himself; seeing himself differently. "I'll try and come with you."

"WHAT ARE YOU GOING TO do," he says to Georgia, "if they do lift the quarantine? Where will you go?" Although she has never said it, he has always assumed Georgia is like him, not a native of the city but another wanderer who somehow got stuck here. He wonders why Georgia left where she came from.

Georgia doesn't reply straight away but picks up the wine bottle to refill their glasses; he goes to put a hand over his but she angrily bats it away. When she pours, he sees her hands are trembling, and drops of wine stain the table.

"Fellows I can't even leave my sodding apartment," she says, not looking at him. She takes a big gulp of wine, licks her lips. "What does it matter to me whether those unity government lunatics impose an official quarantine or not?"

"I can help you," Fellows says. "Baby-steps, I'll go with you outside, just to the corner the first time, then next time down to…"

"Baby steps, *Jesus*," Georgia snaps. "Do I look like I need saving? Don't answer that." Her hand is still shaking as she lifts her glass again; when she looks at him her lips are stained red. "But there is a way you can help me; it would help us both I think."

"How?" Fellows says, wanting to tell her to wipe her mouth. He jumps at the surprise touch of her hand on his.

"Stay here. *Live* here, with me. There's room. It will be *fun*," she continues, seeing his reaction. "We can drink, you can write and go and screw your waitress friend, do whatever you want but come back to me here at night…"

"Georgia, I don't think…"

"*Please*, Fellows."

"I…"

"I know you've always wanted me, Fellows," Georgia says in a rush as if daring herself. She has leant so close to him he can smell the wine on her breath. "Get me pissed and in the same bed on a cold night and who knows…"

He stands up to interrupt her, to stop the story she is telling from seeming real, to either of them. But her words have made him ache and he is honestly not sure what his decision will be. *Georgia*. When he looks at her his vision blurs and for a moment she seems like a woman old before her time, head bent downwards, and not the twenty-something girl looking at him direct. He blinks the doubling away, forces a smile.

"You don't even *like* cock, Georgia," he says.

> Fellows walked unsteadily towards the car; he'd not been outside in daylight for days and it felt unnatural, the emptiness of the sky vast with hidden threat. Only Lana's hand on his back stopped him from bolting back inside.
>
> When she'd come outside she'd looked left and right, called something softly that she didn't want him to hear. The name of their missing cat. The cat he'd been against getting; Lana had seen it as a distraction from their problems, from what they didn't have, but at first he'd only seen it as a reminder. And he'd never told her he'd actually

grown affectionate towards George, and so she called his name softly now he had gone missing. *How did things get so shitty between us?* Fellows thinks.

Lana unlocked the car on the drive, and his tension increased, felt like all that he was. Shaking and sweaty he closed his eyes so as not to see, and got in the back seat of the car. Like a child. He fumbled the seat-belt on, winced as Lana slammed shut the door.

"Where are we going?" He didn't know if he'd said it aloud or not, but there was no reply.

When Lana started the car it backfired, and Fellows screamed.

GEORGIA DOESN'T REACT TO HIS attempt at a joke.

"I think I'm going to go now," Fellows says; from the look on Georgia's face he knows she realises he means more than from her flat. Her eyes scan his face in the same twitchy, paranoid way they had scanned the corridor outside her door...

"Fellows," she says, questioningly.

"It's bigger than me, the city," he says suddenly—the memory of her peering nervously outside has made him think of something; the memory of Georgia lost amid the changing streets of her neighbourhood. *Georgia.*

"Well of course it's bigger, it's a *city*"—the opportunity to take the piss allows her to regain some composure.

"No I mean all of this. It's always been about more than me, than my stupid story. It's a whole city, full of people, real people. And *you* could see it changing too, Georgia. You and that bookseller and maybe even Jaques and... How did you *get* here?" he adds.

"Huh?"

"How did you get to the city? You're not a native, so how..."

Georgia goes very still and seems to shrink into herself; her eyes are far away. For a minute she doesn't speak, then:

"She hit me Fellows."

"Huh?"

"No, not hit. Just touched, really. Just a touch but she could hurt so much..."

"Georgia, who...?"

She suddenly snaps herself upright, stands from the sofa and comes over to him. Fellows only now realises she is taller than him. She grins, a smile full of old pain, and throws out her arms.

"Who? Someone who isn't *here*, Fellows. Don't you see? She isn't fucking *here*."

Fellows looks her in the eyes for a few seconds, nods, and touches her hand briefly.

"You're my only friend here too," he says to her, and knows that the doubling in his vision is this time just the natural result of his tears. He goes to the door and opens it as quickly as he can, cursing as it sticks in the frame. Georgia follows behind almost on tip-toe; she stands at such an angle that she can't see outside. As he meets her gaze, he knows what her final words to him will be.

"You're a twat yourself, Georgia," he says back to her, then quickly steps outside and shuts the door.

As he hurries to the escalator his weeping is as rhythmic as the sea.

HE COMPOSES HIMSELF BEFORE HE leaves the apartment block; outside night is starting to fall but there are even more people out in the street, drinking and laughing. On the steps of the apartments opposite a group of men are playing music with accordions and guitars, and the crowd sways slightly in time with their off-key rhythm. But there is an edge to the convivial atmosphere, and the eyes that turn to look at Fellows as he descends the steps to the street are by turns expectant then disappointed. *As if I can lift the quarantine*, Fellows thought.

Someone steps from the crowd arms out and Fellows sees the ghost reaching for him with its deadening touch; he blinks and it is just a woman offering him a jug of hooch that is being passed around. She looks offended by his reaction and he mumbles an apology. Not that he hallucinated as such, just saw things differently in that second. The whole city is haunted, he realises. Not by ghosts, but by how things could be other than they are, flickering images of entangled realities, glimpses of other stories that you could almost slip between. The boy's not dead, he thinks, but the boy is dead, too, here in this city and still reaching for him. Boursier was right, this has gone on long enough—but how long is that? How many dead-end combinations of this game have he and Boursier played out? The sense of repetition, of having done all this before, feels like another ghost dogging his footsteps as he pushes through the crowd of the old town, not looking back at Georgia's apartment.

So he should try and leave the city; how hard can escape be? Fellows walks down towards the harbour, from which he can walk along the sea wall towards the west bay. And then just keep walking? He has never, in all his perambulations around this city reached its edge—what will the border of the quarantine look like? Loops of barbed wire, searchlights, men with dogs and automatic weapons—really? There have been rumours—there are always rumours in the city, and as rumours are *stories* he supposes he should take them seriously—but how could the unity government keep such a massive undertaking secret? But if not that, what? A ring of weather beaten stones?

Fireworks start to explode above the city like the start of a war. Where have people got *those* from? he thinks. The flashes of colour seem to freeze the buildings and streets into place a second at a time, but in the blackness between Fellows can't be sure things don't shift. The effect is like being drunk, or maybe he already is drunk, on all that wine at Georgia's, for his pulsing vision accompanies a rough and painful beat in his head. His mouth feels gritty with the sediment of the cheap red wine and realising this causes him to gag. He leans against a tree at the edge of a normally deserted square, now thronged with people; he watches groggily as a woman hands over every last note she has of the new money to a street gigolo as if it were worthless. As they walk to a nearby alley they both turn their heads in unison to look at him; an explosion above means both sets of eyes are the dead white colour of mercury lamps.

Fellows is suddenly and messily sick onto the gravel in front of him; I need to get out of here, he thinks. The woman and her paid-for companion have stopped to stare at him, and even though there is a temporary lull in the fireworks their eyes still seem the wrong colour. Fellows edges around the square in the opposite direction to them, and darts down a street which he hopes will take him towards the sea. If only he could travel straight as the crow flies rather than through the city's twisting streets. As the *gull* flies even, he thinks, looking up at the white shapes high above him, seemingly unafraid of the fireworks. He has never known gulls to be nocturnal, but then he has never known them to fly in such concentric patterns either, like a bull's-eye overhead.

He puts his head down, keeps walking. He can't be sure, but he thinks people are following him. Each time he glances over his shoulder they look different, but what does that prove? Whoever they are, they don't close the gap with him, and he can't tell in his fleeting glimpses if that is because they are limping.

He leaves the old town behind him but the docks are as busy, full of raucous sailors as drunk as if they are celebrating the first night of shore leave rather than having been marooned here for months. A fire has been lit on the quay next to a pile of abandoned lobster pots, and the shapes of people dancing flicker around it; he hears the sounds of singing, a smashed bottle, someone crying out.

Fellows walks past the harbour, past the street that curves up to the salmon-topped Mariners' Church, past the civic park and into the broader, tree-lined streets of the Enclave...

No, he thinks, this isn't right. The Enclave should be behind him. He stops and looks around the streets as if doubting their existence, but it is true—as if he has lapped himself he is somehow only a few houses down from the one the protestors had squatted in. He remembers all the times he has become disorientated walking the city streets, remembers all the times he has found himself somewhere unexpected or back where he started... How *has* he wandered the streets of the quarantined city for six months, often aimlessly, and never once reached a boundary?

At a loss, Fellows stands in the centre of the street, perhaps even the centre of the city. If its geometry even allows a centre...

There's no way out, he thinks, it never ends. You're as stuck here as Georgia is in her flat. Because despite the sun, the drink and the spicy food, despite Leianna and Gregor, despite the many secondhand books and despite his house that he has no idea how he pays for, the quarantined city is a trap.

> Fellows sat in the back of the car. The sudden silence after Lana had killed the engine felt oppressive, as if the noise that would break it was bound to be violent. He had shut his eyes to ward off the panic and the memories while Lana

had driven round the ring road, and he still hadn't opened them. She had not told him where they were going, or if she had he hadn't heard her. His mouth tasted of stale beer and bad breath; a hangover had begun a rough and painful beat in his head.

Lana had put the child locks on, not trusting him. As she opened the door and let in the outside, visions of the accident, of the child in the road, assailed him. Beneath the empty sky he felt even more vulnerable, exposed to whatever might be hidden in its patterns. And yet he was in a perfectly normal street, and all he saw in front of him was a terraced house, with a small front lawn that needed cutting and a path of uneven slabs leading up to a peeling blue door. Number 6.

He asked Lana again where she had brought him, and this time she answered him.

"I can't go in there," he said.

FELLOWS FEELS THE DESIRE TO leave even more strongly, now he knows he can't. But he knows the feeling won't last; if he can't escape the city soon he'll have choice but to go back to his house. And tomorrow morning he will visit The Swallow Café, try to catch the eye of the blonde waitress and feel his age if he doesn't, feel it doubly so if he does. Will he start to forget, is that what happened before? In a few months' time will he be searching the quarantined city for a reclusive writer who he thinks he has never met?

People are looking at him, for the crowd has not dispersed, although as he predicted their mood has soured. Most of them are moving normally, although here and there a few stand as still as Fellows. When he moves, they do too, lurching shapes in the uneven gas light. In the corners of his vision they seem too small, reaching out as they stumble, but when he looks them face-on they're just normal people, oblivious to him.

I need to get out of here, Fellows thinks, walking hastily away. But how?

Borders only exist when you let yourself see them, Boursier had said.

Fellows pictures a rain-lashed perimeter fence with searchlights and guard-towers circling the city... But that picture fades for it is too ridiculous. And instead he sees peeling blue tape on dusty floors, a worn vertical stone in a foggy field.

And sees his own front door, and remembers how it always seems to stick when he tries to open it.

> Lana led Fellows up the path towards the door to Number 6; she had her hand on his back as if he were an invalid and that was how he felt, his breath fluttering through him too quickly to grasp in his panic, his whole body tensed as if for collision. The path up to the house was curved rather than straight, and Lana insisted on leading them round it rather than cutting across the unruly grass. They moved from slab to slab, Lana careful not to let either of them step on the cracks between. Step on a crack, break your mother's back, he remembered from childhood, playing in the streets. It had been different then—fewer cars.
>
> He shook his head to rid it of such pointless distraction and Lana guided him the last few steps to the door. It was just a normal wooden frontier, at one point painted blue, the '6' not quite straight. To one side was a full length pane of frosted glass and on the other, newly fitted, a bar at waist height for disabled access.
>
> His life felt like a trap that had led him this point with no chance of escape; he was suddenly and messily sick onto the paving slabs.
>
> "Fuck's sake Fellows!" Lana yelled, but before either of them could say more they saw a confused shape materialise in the panel of frosted glass. It reached out a distorted arm. When the door opened Fellows flinched,

anticipating hatred and even violence, but in front of him was only a middle-aged woman wearing a blank expression of terrible, terrible tiredness. She looked at the two of them, and at the vomit on her pathway, with no surprise.

The woman gestured for them to come inside.

It had just started to rain.

FELLOWS STANDS BEFORE HIS FRONT door, studying its peeling paintwork. Sea blue. Has it always been blue? He struggles to remember. He presses his ear to its wood; is the boy on the other side, a nebulous phantom or white-eyed child waiting to touch him with broken hands?

Fellows starts as something does touch him, looks down and feels a moment's happiness. Mogwai! "Where have you been?" he murmurs as he bends down to pet the cat. Mogwai circles his legs, impatiently mewing to be let in for food.

A knot of figures has appeared at the top of Fellows's street; the same people he had been convinced were following him earlier. The sun is rising, although it is surely only a few hours into the night, and in the bright low light their shadows seem to waver, as if they were shifting in size.

Fellows glances in the other direction, down the tree-lined street which leads to the Carousel. It *is* real this place, he thinks, and you might not see it again. Might never eat paprika-flavoured potatoes down by the salt-smelling quay again, listening to the squabble of gulls... The day is already promising to be very hot in the quarantined city, hot under a blank open sky. You *could* stay..., he thinks.

Before he can doubt himself further, he tries to open his front door, which has always stuck in the heat. Never more so than now. Heart beating loudly, he puts his shoulder to it, and all at once it seems to give and he stumbles inside before he can stop himself. The cat slips through before the door slams shut behind them. Fellows looks up.

It is not his house. He turns.

Behind him, he sees the chaotic shapes of rain against frosted glass.

> Lana gestured Fellows to cross the threshold first, and the enormity of what she was asking him to do paralysed him for a second. The anger he felt towards her was misplaced— *she* hadn't been driving that night—but vivid nonetheless. He had avoided thinking of the accident since it had happened: by drinking, by raging, by dreaming up alternative and soothing versions of what might have happened instead. But now, sober and trembling, he was being asked to see the reality of it: inside the house was his responsibility. The boy whose life he had ruined. Although he should stop thinking of him as 'the boy'; his name was Lawrence.
>
> The tired-eyed woman didn't wait to see if they would follow, but turned into the gloom inside. Reluctantly, Fellows stepped inside and followed her into the lounge. The thick patterned carpet seemed to catch at his sluggish feet; the misaligned wallpaper drew his eye like a glitch in reality. On a coffee table a single mug steamed; the woman picked it up but didn't drink from it. Her husband, she said, was out, just out and Fellows read between the lines: he was too angry to be here. He imagined the man walking the streets in the rain, stopping for drinks as he does so, eventually finding himself blurry eyed and so far from home he can't remember how to get back…
>
> "Fellows!" Lana hissed at him, bringing him back to reality. The woman was speaking to him and he'd missed what she'd said. She was now apologetically explaining they'd had to convert a back room to a new bedroom for Lawrence and it wasn't finished yet, as if everything were her fault. She gestured towards a door at the back of the lounge.

Fellows realised she meant for him to go into the room alone.

The voice in his head urging flight seemed loud with echoes, as if he had been here many times before. But Lana and the woman were both standing directly behind him, and he could still hold it together enough not to turn and barge through them. It will be his eyes, he thought, when you see the boy's eyes is when you'll run, for who knew what they might hold?

FELLOWS LOOKS IN CONFUSION AT the room in front of him. It is a living room that seems at once thrillingly futuristic—it has electric lighting and an impossibly slim TV (and when had he last even thought about television?)—and old-fashioned, with misaligned flock wallpaper and a faded, swirling carpet. No books. A coffee table in the centre of the room has a single mug on it, still steaming.

"Hello?" he calls out; the only reply is from the rain outside.

Something brushes past his leg; Mogwai mews up at him, still hungry. For some reason the fact of the cat being here seems more mysterious than his own presence. Was this house in the place of Fellows's own where the cat has been while missing? Mogwai walks towards an open doorway at the far end of the room, which presumably leads to the kitchen. The cat pauses, looks back and mews again at Fellows, expecting him to follow and feed him. The cat *knows* this place, Fellows thinks.

Looking around the strange new room he sees an uncapped biro on the coffee table, and he instinctively looks to his own hands to see if they are ink-stained. Is Boursier still out there in the quarantined city, he thinks, writing about someone with my name...?

Fellows took a deep, ragged breath, and pushed open the door.

For some reason he expected it to stick and he opened it with too much force, causing it to…

THERE IS A CLOSED WOODEN door at the end of the lounge; much to the cat's disappointment Fellows walks towards it and not the kitchen. He pushes the door open, accidentally causing it to bang against the wall.

It feels like he is stepping across another boundary for the room is so bright with light streaming in from twin patio doors. Wasn't it raining here five minutes ago? he thinks. There is an overwhelming smell of new paint and disinfectant. The light makes him blink repeatedly and as he walks in he stumbles against a small walking frame which is propped up against a single bed. Outside, a bird clatters away on heavy wings which slice the light with shadow.

As such, he is taken by surprise when the boy lurches out of the light to touch him.

It misses, but not because Fellows was quick enough to dodge away. Instead, something seemed to have restrained it, causing it to fall back. As his eyes adjust he can see the hateful thing is lying on the bed, not strapped in but under sheets and blankets tucked so tightly over its slim body it can't fully rise. Its arms are free and it had reached for him, but it hadn't been able to lean far enough forward. Thank god, Fellows thinks.

His relief soon gives way to despair, a bitter anger. Here? Here, *again*, in this mysterious and futuristic house, is the fucking crippled ghost boy? What is he to do to escape it; what does the fucking thing *want* from him? It is propped up against some pillows stuffed behind its back, like someone cared about its comfort; he can hear the curious wet sound of its breathing. Why does the fucking thing need to drag air in and out of its dead lungs? he thinks with something like hatred. Incapacitated like it is, it is the first time he has been able to study its bruised and stained form properly. He can't think it human. He doesn't get too close, it is still lunging for him. Its hands dirty with motor oil and blood wave a few inches from his face as it mews and slobbers in excitement before slumping back. Its white eyes never blink, never look away from him.

Its efforts have dislodged one of the pillows that was propping it up, and it falls near Fellows's feet. He picks it up, noticing the brown stain where the back of its head had been pressed against it.

"What do you want from me?" he yells at the ghost in frustration. "How many times? How does this fucking end?" Boursier likes his endings ambiguous, he thinks, but maybe he could do something more definite.

He hears the ragged but urgent sound of breath from the thing that shouldn't be breathing, and he looks at the pillow while turning it over in his hands.

> ...to bang against the wall.
> The light in the room was very bright, coming from a set of patio doors which had obviously been used to access the garden before the room had been converted. A bird clattered away outside; its wings looked pure white. Wasn't it raining five minutes ago? Fellows thought.
> He stepped inside, smelling new paint and disinfectant. His vision adjusted and he saw the bed and the boy within—Lawrence, he reminded himself. The boy's head had been completely shaved, and his thin arms which clutched the sheets up to his face were still bruised. The boy had the sheet pulled up over his nose and his eyes stared at Fellows from above it. They were blank and without expression, without reprieve. Fellows couldn't meet them.

His throat was dry with desperation for a drink. Any words he thought he might say died every time he looked at the boy. The silence felt accusatory; he knew Lana and the boy's mother were just behind, waiting for him to speak.

He noticed that one of the pillows from the boy's bed had become dislodged and fallen to the floor; eagerly he bent to pick it up. Turning it over to the clean side in his hands, he moved closer to the bed meaning to urge Lawrence to lean forward so he could add the pillow to those behind him; do him that small kindness.

But when he approached the boy's eyes went wide; he lurched away from Fellows, straining against the confining bedding, crying out—wordless cries like from a child years younger. He thrashed against the covers and drew the sheet over his eyes. Fellows wordlessly dropped the pillow and stepped back, shaking.

The panic that rose in him was almost comforting because it felt like an excuse to flee.

The boy lowered the sheet and stared at him with eyes that seemed even emptier than before; he remembered the blank white look those eyes had had under the ring road lights.

He knows who I am, Fellows thought, he knows what I've done.

Wanting to muffle his own thoughts, he clamped both hands to his ears; the sound he heard was that of the sea in a shell.

Where the hell was the boy's mother, when he reacted like that? he thought. Why hadn't she rushed in? Emboldened by the idea that the responsibility for the boy's panic attack was not his, he turned to look behind him at the open doorway back to the lounge...

FELLOWS PLUMPS THE PILLOW IN his hand again and steps forwards. It's not alive, he thinks. This thing that looks like a boy isn't *alive*. Doesn't the very fact it appears in impossible places and vanishes as impossibly prove that? Plus the very wrongness of it: the wordless cries, the frantic clumsiness, the dreadful mercury eyes. *The boy's not dead*, Boursier had said, but in his gut Fellows has never believed him.

But it certainly is breathing, with its torn, imitation breaths, and so its breathing can surely be stopped. Maybe it will even be a blessing for a being that seems to exist in such torment? The fact such thoughts contradict those of just a few seconds before doesn't bother Fellows; if there's one thing Boursier has taught him it's to be able to see two things as true at once.

Fuck whatever story Boursier thinks he is writing; *he* can bring this charade to an end here and now. If he is careful, the thing won't be able to touch him as he does it. Quickly, before his nerve runs out, he walks to the bed, holding the pillow in both hands before him.

> Fellows gasped in surprise.
> On the other side of the doorway was not the lounge he had come in through, but somewhere else entirely. The room beyond might still have been intended as a living room, but it had bare wooden floorboards, mismatched and old-fashioned furniture, and what looked like gas lamps on the walls. The light that came in from the small windows illuminated swirling motes of dust. Even in his surprise Fellows noticed there were well thumbed paperbacks on almost every available surface.
> There was no sign of Lana or Lawrence's mother.
> He looked around him, but sure enough the room he was in was still the same; the boy's gaze was still as pitiless as before.
> He took a few steps towards the other room; something about the dusky light from its windows suggested the warmth of foreign climes. And then he realised that, even though he had taken his hands away from his ears, he could still hear the sea-shell sound of waves…

Could I just walk through? he thought. He has never seen such a room before, but something about its very emptiness appealed.

What also appealed was not just what he might be walking into, but what he might be walking away *from* The panic, the guilt, the sick despair to be someone else. Even, he realised painfully, Lana. How can he ever escape from all the shit he feels when she is so desperate to rub his face in it?

Quickly, before his nerve ran out, he took a step towards the mysterious room. The boy watched him as he did so.

BEFORE FELLOWS CAN REACH THE boy, a dark shape races past him and jumps up onto the bed. He had completely forgotten about Mogwai. The cat lands on the boy's chest and hisses and bares its fangs; it raises a paw with its claws extended but doesn't strike. The suddenness of the creature's appearance causes Fellows to drop the pillow in surprise.

The boy bucks and shrieks in the confines of his bed; the tucked-in sheets and heavy blanket make it impossible for him to dislodge Mogwai from his chest. His arms flail, waving in jerky motions like an upturned fly's legs, but never making contact. He shakes his head from side to side, spittle flying, and it should be impossible for his blank white eyes to widen any further but they seem to.

It will fade away, Fellows thinks, surely the damned thing will just fade away now and I can get out of this crazy house and back to…

The cat hisses and shrieks again, its fur on end and the claws of three paws digging in to help it cling on to the bucking form of the dead boy. With the other, it swipes at the boy's face. The scratches the cat's paw leaves don't bleed, and the flesh inside seems as pale and dead as that outside, albeit whiter for not being so stained. Nevertheless the thing's shrieks intensify, as does its bucking efforts to escape. There is the sudden smell of urine, and before Fellows knows what he is doing, he is running forward yelling, and chasing the cat off from the boy's chest.

Mogwai bounds off, streaks towards the door. Fellows turns to watch him go...

And just like that the cat is no longer visible; or at least Fellows can no longer see him. In passing through the doorway, Mogwai has vanished from the strange house.

> Before Fellows could reach the doorway, a dark shape raced past him from that strange other room and jumped up onto the bed. He stopped in surprise. Something was standing on the boy's chest, padding the soft blanket: a cat. And not just any cat, Fellows saw but:
> "George?" he said. Their missing cat? The animal looked up from pawing at the boy briefly and Fellows was sure it recognised him. Finally settled, it sat itself contentedly on the boy's chest. Confused, Fellows walked back to the bed; he reached out and stroked the animal, heard it start purring. He noticed there was a tag on its collar where there had been none before. He turned it round so he could read it.
> *Mogwai*
> He stopped stroking in surprise, but the cat still kept purring; he realised Lawrence was petting the animal too. The boy's hand was a few inches from his. Fellows looked up to the boy's eyes again. He felt like he was being given the chance to see them afresh.
> How did I ever think them blank? he thought, for the boy's gaze was deep with emotion and pain, although these were sealed off from Fellows, on the other side of the barriers the boy had erected to protect himself.
> It's your fault, he thought. The barriers you'd have to cross to reach this kid are ones you created yourself. He was too dry-eyed to cry, and as such his vision remained

clear as he stared at the boy's hand, just inches from his own and impossibly far away. What right did he have to take it, to seek comfort from the guilt of his own actions in the forgiveness of the one he'd hurt? For some reason, he felt nauseous with the taste of champagne although he hadn't drunk any since the night of the accident.

He looked up, wanting Lana to be there to guide him, even to yell at him to do the right thing, but all he saw was the hazy warm light of the room on the other side of the doorway. There was a chair to sit in, he saw, and on the table next to it was a book open face down as if he were already halfway through reading it, and next to it a bottle-opener…

George was still purring, and he feels rather than hears the very tentative beginnings of laughter in the boy's chest. But still, the distance to reach out to touch the boy's hand where it stroked the cat's black fur seemed impossible to cross, compared to the three quick strides with which he could be out the room and somewhere else…

He wasn't sure what his decision was going to be.

AFTER THE CAT HAS FLED the room, Fellows feels drained of emotion; when he turns back to the boy he is so weary he almost falls into his embrace. Instead, warily, he sits at the foot of the bed—the boy is so short there is room—out of reach of its straining arms.

"The cat's called Mogwai," he says, "he was just a little scared of you." As if in reality this is a real boy curious about an animal Fellows has brought to see him, a distraction for an ill child. "He's run off now but he'll come back; cat's can get in anywhere. We could stroke him together." The words come to him as if from memory; not words he has said, but words he should have said, once, but didn't dare to. Meanwhile the dead child slobbers brown drool down its chest, makes periodic attempts to lurch forward to grasp at Fellows. Was it in hatred,

Fellows thought, was its touch so deadening? If he ignored the oil stains like bruises, ignored the blank white eyes—didn't see them—then when it opened its arms it would look almost like a child seeking comfort,

If it wasn't for the cat being here you would have killed it already, he thought, this would be over. He knows he won't be able to muster up the strength to do it again; the way the boy had struggled in terror against the cat would have been how it would have struggled beneath a pillow pressed to his face, and how could he face that? It wouldn't be like the movies, he knows, twenty seconds of muffled sobs. He'd have to press down hard against the thing's screams for three or four long minutes, as it kicked and shit itself.

He looks up; the doorway out of the child's bedroom now leads back to his house in the quarantined city. In thirty seconds you could be out on those streets, he thinks, heading towards The Carousel for a coffee or Georgia's apartment for a drink. Or even, and this idea appeals the most right now, down to the harbour to sit watching the sea and eat paprika potatoes. Forget all this, for now, before it starts again. Or he could stay in this room and... what?

He looks back at the boy, at his reaching hands. The boy who he has done so much wrong to, in another time, in another city, but who is still reaching for him. His eyes are the white of bird wings, he thinks obscurely.

He raises a hand, holds his fingers outstretched so they are just inches beyond the reach of the boy, who seeing the proximity redoubles his efforts, his eager breath the only part of him seeming fully alive.

Is what he needs to do to escape the quarantine, Fellows wonders, merely to stretch out and bridge the scant inches between his hand and the boys own? Would Boursier write an ending so simple and sentimental?

Yet still, that distance to reach out to touch the boy's hand where it wavers in the air seems impossible to cross, compared to the three quick strides with which he could be out and into another room, another city entirely...

He isn't sure himself what his decision is going to be.

BOURSIER SETS DOWN THE PEN from his cramped, ink-stained hands. The last line, he knows is not up to him, it will be dictated by whatever Fellows does out there. He was always shit at endings. The cat nudges at his arm, impatient for food. Where had it been? he wondered vaguely. Its sudden reappearance had taken him by surprise, but he hadn't let it interrupt his writing, merely incorporated it into the text.

The crowd is still outside, waiting for the quarantine to be lifted but growing more and more frustrated that it won't be. There'll be riots if not, Boursier knows...

When a ragged sound erupts from the crowd, almost like a single broken breath, he isn't sure at first if it is a cheer or the start of the violence, and of all this beginning again.

Boursier's vision blurs; doubles.

Am I being..., he thinks.

BUT WAIT, FELLOWS THINKS AT the last moment. The city is a trap, Boursier had said, but what if *this* was the trap, a double bluff and he has been right all along?

Something touches his hand.

And then there is a wrenching sensation, a tightness across his ribs like he is being squeezed, the taste of champagne in his mouth, spice, and the brightness of mercury lights fluttering like wings in his crazed vision.

Am I being lifted up? he thinks.

MORE FROM INFINITY PLUS

Falling Over
by James Everington
www.infinityplus.co.uk/book.php?book=jevfo

Sometimes when you fall over you don't get up again. And sometimes, you get up to find everything has changed:

An ordinary man who sees his face in a tabloid newspaper. A soldier haunted by the images of those he has killed from afar. Two petty criminals on the run from a punishment more implacable than either of them can imagine. Doppelgängers both real and imaginary. A tranquil English village where those who don't fit in really aren't welcome, and a strange hotel where second chances are allowed… at a price.

Ten stories of unease, fear and the weird from James Everington.

"An excellent collection, well-crafted, imaginative and chilling." —*Amazing Stories*

"Good writing gives off fumes, the sort that induce dark visions, and Everington's elegant, sophisticated prose is a potent brew. Imbibe at your own risk." —Robert Dunbar, author of *The Pines* and *Martyrs & Monsters*

"There are times when you read a new author's work and you simply sit back and admire. This is one of those times… without a doubt an author to watch, a burgeoning talent we are likely to be talking about in years to come." —Phil Sloman, *British Fantasy Society reviews*

**For full details of infinity plus books
see www.infinityplus.co.uk/books**

One Of Us
by Iain Rowan
www.infinityplus.co.uk/book.php?book=irooou

Anna is one of the invisible people. She fled her own country when the police murdered her brother and her father, and now she serves your food, cleans your table, changes your bed, and keeps the secrets of her past well hidden.

When she used her medical school experience to treat a man with a gunshot wound, Anna thought it would be a way to a better life. Instead, it leads to a world of people trafficking, prostitution, murder and the biggest decision of Anna's life: how much is she prepared to give up to be one of us?

Shortlisted for the UK Crime Writers' Association Debut Dagger award, *One of Us* is a novel by award-winning writer Iain Rowan.

Praise for Iain Rowan's *Nowhere To Go*:

"Fine examples of modern crime stories, gripping and perceptive, probing the dark secrets of the human soul, just like an old Alfred Hitchcock movie... Crime enthusiasts must not miss the book: this is noir at its very best." —*SF Site* featured review

"A short story writer of the highest calibre." —Allan Guthrie, winner of Theakston's Crime Novel of the Year

"Every story in this collection is a gem... classy and clever Brit Grit at its best." —Paul D Brazill at *Death By Killing*

**For full details of infinity plus books
see www.infinityplus.co.uk/books**

Genetopia
by Keith Brooke
www.infinityplus.co.uk/book.php?book=kbrgen

Searching for his missing sister, Flint encounters a world where illness is to be feared, where genes mutate and migrate between species through plague and fever. This is the story of the struggles between those who want to defend their heritage and those who choose to embrace the new.

"A minor masterpiece that should usher Brooke at last into the recognized front ranks of SF writers" —*Locus*

"I am so here! *Genetopia* is a meditation on identity – what it means to be human and what it means to be you – and the necessity of change. It's also one heck of an adventure story. Snatch it up!" —Michael Swanwick, Hugo award-winning author of *Bones of the Earth*

"Keith Brooke's *Genetopia* is a biotech fever dream. In mood it recalls Brian Aldis's *Hothouse*, but is a projection of twenty-first century fears and longings into an exotic far future where the meaning of humanity is overwhelmed by change. Masterfully written, this is a parable of difference that demands to be read, and read again." —Stephen Baxter, Philip K Dick award-winning author of *Evolution* and *Transcendent*

**For full details of infinity plus books
see www.infinityplus.co.uk/books**

The Fabulous Beast
by Garry Kilworth
www.infinityplus.co.uk/book.php?book=gktfb

A set of beautifully crafted tales of the imagination by a writer who was smitten by the magic of the speculative short story at the age of twelve and has remained under its spell ever since.

These few stories cover three closely related sub-genres: science fiction, fantasy and horror. In the White Garden murders are taking place nightly, but who is leaving the deep foot-prints in the flower beds? Twelve men are locked in the jury room, but thirteen emerge after their deliberations are over. In a call centre serving several worlds, the staff are less than helpful when things go wrong with a body-change holiday.

Three of the stories form a set piece under the sub-sub-genre title of 'Anglo-Saxon Tales'. This trilogy takes the reader back to a time when strange gods ruled the lives of men and elves were invisible creatures who caused mayhem among mortals.

Garry Kilworth has created a set of stories that lift readers out of their ordinary lives and place them in situations of nightmare and wonder, or out among far distant suns. Come inside and meet vampires, dragons, ghosts, aliens, weremen, people who walk on water, clones, ghouls and marvellous wolves with the secret of life written beneath their eyelids.

"Kilworth's stories are delightfully nuanced and carefully wrought.' —*Publishers Weekly*

"A bony-handed clutch of short stories, addictive and hallucinatory." —*The Times*

**For full details of infinity plus books
see www.infinityplus.co.uk/books**

Printed in Great Britain
by Amazon